GW01403309

Forbidden Flames

Irish Honor, Volume 2

Amara Holt

Published by Amara Holt, 2024.

Prologue

Taisiya

Russia

Past

H eat.

I can feel the heat of the flames and the scorching on my skin.

My body is feverish, and I don't have the strength to open my eyes, but I hear their screams *and* my heart shatters into a thousand pieces because I can't help them.

Daddy. Mommy.

Help, someone has to save them...

I hear footsteps, and then arms surround me, lifting me off the bed.

They are saving me, but I don't want to leave without my family.

"Please, my parents need to get out too," I say to the stranger carrying me. "They are still there."

"Quiet! Don't say a word or I'll leave you here to burn. You should be grateful. After the betrayal you and your bitch of a sister orchestrated, it would be fitting, but luckily for you, I have other plans."

His words make ice run through my veins, and only then do I realize I'm not being saved. The person carrying me wants to harm me.

I try to break free from his arms, desperate, and finally open my eyes. When I see who's holding me, I scream as loud as I can.

He puts me on the ground and grabs me by the hair. He's hurting me, but he doesn't seem to care. Then, he places a cloth over my mouth and nose. I know I'm going to lose consciousness, but I still remember what he said about my sister.

Someone needs to warn her. Anastacia is in danger.

I fight against the numbness. I want to escape, but I can't breathe anymore, and a deep sleep engulfs me.

Chapter 1

Lorcan

About Three Years Later

"Don't come in. I'm almost there," my cousin Odhran says on the phone, his voice sounding annoyed because we both know I'm coming in.

I look around the perimeter, where the sons of bitches who stole from us are probably counting our money right now, believing they've gotten away with it.

"Meet me at the north exit in fifteen minutes," I say. "If I'm not there, send in the cavalry."

"You crazy motherfucker!"

"No, that's you. I'm just the guy who never backs down."

"You're a fucking lunatic. Cillian will rip your head off when he finds out you risked yourself like some ordinary soldier. We're his trusted men, Lorcan. The elite."

"I'm elite until someone tries to screw me over. Because after that, I become a goddamn beast out for blood, and today, cousin, it will be spilled."

"What can I say to make you wait for me? I'll be there in ten minutes."

"Nothing. I don't need a babysitter. Cillian has known me since I was born. He knows how I act. You calm down. Just come in if I'm not outside in fifteen minutes. If we don't see each other again, have a beer at my funeral."

"Stubborn bastard!" I hear him shout before ending the call, but by then, I'm completely disconnected from him, my mind focused on punishing the enemy.

Some would say I'm an uncompromising guy.

I disagree. I consider myself a simple guy. In my world, there are no gray areas or any nuance of a fucked-up rainbow. Everything is two-dimensional; the color palette, limited.

Either you're on my side or against me. Either you're loyal or disloyal. Either you're a friend or an enemy. And for the latter, there's only one fate: death.

I take a deep breath, not because I'm nervous, but because I know that in a few seconds, the adrenaline will explode in my body just like a parachute jump.

It's not just a job; it's the thrill of the risk. The uncertainty of the outcome.

Rubbing my boot against the opposite ankle, I check if the knife is where it should be. Although I prefer firearms, in the midst of a war, we have to be ready for anything.

I glance quickly at my watch, wondering how long it will take to eliminate everyone. I have a date with a redhead. I told her to wait for me at home tonight because every time I return to the field, which has been happening less and less as Cillian seems worried about my safety, I get wound up and need to fuck. I usually don't sleep on these nights. The urge to drain the energy from my body is stronger than the need to rest.

"How many are there?" I ask Keiron, one of my most loyal soldiers, who is positioned next to me.

"No more than ten. We have three times as many men with us."

"We could have half. No one will leave there alive."

He nods in agreement.

"What do we do with Driscoll?" he asks, referring to the bastard who organized the diversion of money and weapons.

"What we do with thieves. I want his hands to take to Cillian."

"Do we give him the usual treatment?" he continues, referring to dismemberment.

"Yes, and make sure all the younger soldiers know what happened."

"And the rest of the men inside?"

"A quick death. I have an appointment. Recover what they stole from us, money and weapons. Is there a report of the amounts and quantities?"

"Yes. Kellan gave it to me before we came."

"Ready?"

"Always, boss."

"Then let's get this show on the road."

Every time I kill, it feels like a bit of the poison I carry inside my body and heart is diluted. It's a break for my mind. It's when I can breathe. The sensation doesn't last, but still, it's like being numb for a few hours. My drug of forgetfulness.

In the quiet of early evening, the only sound is our boots hitting the ground, a mix of stones and brush.

Today's action needs to be exemplary. It's not as if we don't already have enough shit to deal with—endless turf wars with other organizations, buying off corrupt federals and cops, and trying to keep our path clear of the honest—and now, we'll have to fight thieves within our own ranks.

Sons of bitches we call brothers, who should honor the Syndicate, have sold out to the enemies.

"Driscoll is mine," I announce just seconds before we storm in. "I've changed my mind. Don't shoot him. I'll use the knife."

The moment they are surrounded on all sides, doors and windows exploding, they can't react.

I should be satisfied; after all, it was easier than I imagined, but instead, it brings out the worst in me. They didn't just steal from us; they lived, even if for a few fucked-up days, under the illusion that we wouldn't catch them.

I know all my men are following the orders I gave, neutralizing the enemies present. I don't see that, though. All I can see is Driscoll, the bastard who once sat at Aunt Orla's table, ate her food, was welcomed like a son, and then, like the trash he is, betrayed Cillian.

He rises as fast as a fucking bullet, but the surprise paralyzes him, giving me the advantage. In a split second, I have my weapon aimed between his eyes.

"Lorcan."

I shake my head.

"You don't speak, motherfucker."

The sound of gunfire echoes through the warehouse, and I watch him shrink back, waiting for his own end.

I almost smile. He should have known it wouldn't be that simple.

I signal for one of my men to search him for weapons.

When he confirms there are none left, I drop my own weapon to the floor and advance.

I rarely let my darkness come out through my fists, except in the ring. For me, killing is a job. Just that. However, killing the enemy brings out the primitive side of me.

The first punch tells me I've broken his nose because he screams like a coward. It doesn't even hurt that much. I've had mine broken half a dozen times in fights.

"Let me talk to Cillian... I can..."

The second blow hits below the belt, around the liver, and he doubles over in pain.

"You've lost the right to say his name. He's not one of us. He's trash."

I couldn't say how long I beat him, hitting the right places so he doesn't pass out.

Everyone around us, who betrayed us with him, is dead. Only my soldiers remain, who I know are aligned behind me, watching.

"Lorcan..."

"You betrayed us for money, Driscoll. Not only did you steal from us, but you almost led our Boss straight into a trap. We would die for you and yet, you traded his life for gain."

"I didn't..."

He doesn't finish because Keiron comes to my side and hands me a sickle. The blow I deliver is so fast that by the time the traitor realizes, he has lost one of his hands.

He screams in despair. I take the other one.

He's still awake, despite the pain.

"There's a special place in hell waiting for you. I made the reservations myself. Say hi to Satan for me."

"You think you're better than me? You're a killer too."

"I am. And of the worst kind, because I know no remorse. But I have one quality: I'm not a traitor. I'd die for any of you."

"Forgive me, fuck!"

I don't think he even knows who I am anymore or what he's saying. He's about to lose consciousness.

I bring the knife to his throat.

"Forgiveness is for God. I doubt you'll meet him where I'm sending you."

Chapter 2

Lorcan

Boston

"I t's never going to work, Grandpa. Cillian won't agree to this," I say to Ruslan.

If he weren't who he is, I'd ask if he'd been using drugs.

A union between the Russian and Irish mafias? Not even in dreams.

I knew, when he said he needed to see me, that it had to be serious since we rarely meet in person, but I had no idea it was such a huge mess.

"He needs to understand. You're my only grandchild with contacts in both the FBI and Interpol. You can navigate both sides of the law."

"The FBI doesn't love me anymore," I scoff. "In fact, they'd love to lock me up in a federal prison and throw away the key. Too bad for them they can't prove anything against me."

I joined the federal agency for a couple of years in the past to satisfy a crazy request from Ruslan, who said he'd consider it a sort of family baptism, even though I'm not part of the Brotherhood but rather the Syndicate. In reality, what he wanted were details only someone inside the FBI could obtain.

There are many agents on the payroll, both from the Russian organization and ours, but Ruslan doesn't trust corrupt feds and never gives them exactly what he's looking for.

When we got what we needed, I left—information about whether they were close to issuing arrest warrants for the members of the Russian Brotherhood, or if it was just rumors.

Along the way, I helped Lara, the wife of the Russian mafia consigliere, who is also my cousin, escape from an agent obsessed with her. But it wasn't something I did for Grigori's wife in particular. We share the same blood, but I don't feel like I owe him anything. However, I don't like cowardly acts against women in general.

That incident was the only concession Cillian made because I'm Ruslan's grandchild. Beyond that, I need to stay away from the Russians.

He doesn't take it personally that I have contact with the former Pakhan. He knows that blood ties are indissoluble, but he doesn't want me mingling with the current head of the Organization, my cousin Yerik.

Ruslan spread his seed all over the world and wouldn't be surprised if there were grandsons in the Italian mafia, maybe even in the Chinese.

With that, he created a fucked-up family quilt where we all love him but not each other.

I shake my head, thinking about the mess it would be if we discovered cousins among the Chinese, considering they're at war with almost every other organization at the moment.

"What are you thinking about?"

"I don't blame you for being my grandfather, Ruslan, nor for being Russian, but our relationship is a hell of a mess. It only gets worse when you think I could go looking for Maxim's missing wife's sister, who happens to be one of Yerik's trusted men."

"Ana isn't just Maxim's wife; she's my girl. A beloved goddaughter, and she's suffering from the loss of her family. If I can at least tell her that we have a body buried for her to visit when she feels nostalgic, maybe it will help her move on."

"And what makes you think that where you failed to find her, I will succeed?"

"We've turned Russia inside out and haven't found any results so far."

"And are you sure she's still alive?"

"No. In fact, from what I know about what we humans are capable of, I'd bet the opposite, but I owe Anastacia an answer."

"And you haven't discovered anything? We need at least a starting point, Ruslan."

"We don't have one; we only know they didn't find a body. Whoever did this took a risk. Their father, Timofey, held an important position within the Organization, which means the bastard who orchestrated this massacre hated them, or wouldn't have put his own neck on the line."

"'Hated them,' in the plural? You think the target wasn't just the father?"

"In our world, we can never be sure. What you need to know is that Taisiya, the missing girl, was going to a convent. She wanted to become a nun. Ana, on the other hand, was promised to one of the Organization's men. The two of them planned to have Anastacia spend some years in the convent too, temporarily ruining the plans of her future husband, who wanted to marry her immediately. Maybe there's something related."

"If that's the case, it's very simple. We go after the fucked-up abandoned fiancé."

"I've already been. He married someone else. Apparently, he moved on. There's no evidence, not even a hint, that he was the one who took Taisiya, but I don't trust human nature. There are basically three things that drive people to do fucked-up shit: money, power, and lust. Even if there's nothing related to him, it's the only lead we have."

"Years have passed. The chance of finding her is slim. Maybe we can punish the culprit, but rescuing her is almost impossible. If she survived, she might even have become a victim of human trafficking."

"Possible, but unlikely. There are many more viable candidates. She would be too high a bet. Rich, a well-known face in the Russian elite and far beyond: my goddaughter's sister. Not just any man would have the balls to mess with someone close to me."

"Yes, it would be risky. On the other hand, she would be worth a fortune to sex slave buyers. If she was practically a child when taken, she must have been a virgin. Beautiful? Well-educated? They could make a lot of money from her."

"If that's what happened, I'll kill them one by one. Their families, too, even if it means breaking my own rules about not involving relatives. No descendant of those motherfuckers will be left on Earth."

I know why the issue affects him so deeply. Yerik's younger sister, the current Russian Pakhan, was killed in a similar situation. Kidnapped "on order."

"For now, it's all just speculation. I'll try to contact some of my old partners from the agencies. I can't promise anything, but maybe we'll get an answer and won't even need to try forging this unlikely alliance between Cillian and Yerik."

"It's not an alliance. It would be a temporary arrangement."

"That's not how things work in the Syndicate, Grandpa. Everything is business. Even if there's a slim chance that Cillian agrees to let me work, even indirectly, with the Organization, he'll want something in return."

"I'll come up with a proposal then. Besides, I have other interests involving the Syndicate, and I'm sure we'll reach an agreement."

"Forget Anastacia and answer me. Do you have any hope that the girl, Taisiya, is still alive?"

"Not much, but at least I want to avenge those who destroyed Ana's family. If Taisiya was kidnapped and we find the body, we'll also have the trail of the bastard. When that happens, I'll rip his eyes out with my own hands."

I nod in agreement. I wouldn't do anything different.

"Tell me about her."

"If she's still breathing, she's seventeen now, since Ana will turn nineteen in a few months. I don't know much more about my goddaughter's sister except that she wanted to be a nun. She was a good girl. A mafia princess trained to obey, despite the crazy plan they came up with to try to outmaneuver Anastacia's marriage."

"Do you have a photograph of her?"

"I do," he says, pulling something from his blazer. "When can you give me an answer?"

"In a few days, after doing a preliminary check."

Chapter 3

Lorcan

Weeks Later

The idea of meeting with any Russian who isn't my grandfather doesn't sit well with me, but I can't avoid a meeting with Maxim because after a preliminary search, I'm still completely in the dark about the whereabouts of his sister-in-law.

We've only met once before today, when I saved Lara's life and I was still an FBI agent. It was a hell of a surprise for everyone when they found out that I, a federal agent, was Ruslan's grandson—and a kind of ally among enemies. To protect me, my grandfather kept me hidden from the entire world. God knows I have my own enemies, and there are plenty. I don't need dozens more Russians chasing after me.

The decision to hold the meeting at my grandfather's apartment was made because it's neutral ground and also out of respect for our leaders, Cillian and Yerik.

Cillian agreed to let me help Ruslan much more readily than I thought he would. He'll never admit it, but I think it's the fact that they took Taisiya when she was still a little girl that bothers him. Despite what he does, my cousin has the concept of family—and especially the safety of our homes—as something sacred.

"So, what's your opinion: do you think the target was Taisiya or not?" the man trusted by Yerik asks.

"I don't know, but if that's the case, if she was the one the bastard wanted, it's unlikely the attack came from within the Organization. It's probably the work of a pedophile."

"Unlikely and not impossible?"

"Nothing is impossible. There are perverts everywhere, even among us. However, killing an entire family just to get a sex slave, no matter how valuable she might become, is an extreme act."

Yes, certainly, the girl would be valuable.

Taisiya is not only beautiful; even at fourteen, the age she was in the photo Ruslan gave me, she already showed signs of becoming stunning when she grew up, despite her youthful appearance.

With very fair skin, eyes in a mix of blue and green, and nearly black hair, she looked like a model in the making.

"But there are girls more accessible for the sex trade, right? That's what you're talking about?" Maxim asks.

"Exactly. Girls from broken families, poor girls who dream of a better life and would easily be deceived by fake boyfriends who would soon turn into pimps. Unless it's a specific request for a type, they rarely risk taking a rich little girl, especially one who's a mafia princess."

"So where should we start looking for her?" he asks, while I catch Ruslan pouring himself a shot of whiskey. "I mean, not the obvious places, because I've already done that."

"I assume that once you suspected she was alive, you started your own investigation, right?" I ask just to confirm, because I needed only two minutes with Maxim to realize that he is extremely methodical.

I know that initially it was only my grandfather searching for her, but after Yerik's man married Anastacia, he took on the task himself.

"Yes, there's no sign of her. I had brothels all over Europe searched, even the most secretive ones that cater only to billionaires.

We have people everywhere. The girl, if she's alive, has vanished into thin air."

His voice is monotone, almost as if the subject doesn't concern him, but I was trained as an FBI agent and know how to read facial expressions. There's a slight clenching in his jaw that tells me that not being in control right now, with no idea where his sister-in-law is, is driving him crazy.

"I worked with a profiling expert. Actually, the best around," I say, "but I need more details about the girl to create a profile of the person who supposedly took her. Ask her sister. Anastacia is your wife, isn't she?"

He immediately tenses up and I almost roll my eyes.

Damned suspicious Russians. Just like us Irish.

"How do you know that?"

"It's not just you who watches us. We always return the favor, friend. Anyway, in this case, it was my grandfather who told me when he came to me about Taisiya. Have your lady list details about the sister as quickly as possible. Basic things like: movies she liked, places she enjoyed going."

"I don't think we'll have much success in that area," Ruslan interrupts. "As I told you, the girl wanted to be a nun."

I nod.

"Yes, I know, but did she study for that?"

"I don't think so, but she went to church regularly, as far as I know," my grandfather explains again.

"Did she attend a specific church?"

"That I can find out from Anastacia," Ruslan says.

"Ask whatever you can about the girl's religious routine. Maybe we'll get a lead there."

"What are you thinking?" Maxim asks.

"There are many crazies inside churches. There are extremists in any religion. You told me that the girl only went out for religious functions, Ruslan. Probably there, the family didn't worry about leaving her alone. And what if someone became obsessed with the teenager?"

"It's a possibility. Insane, but still, a possibility," he says.

All three of us stand up.

"Setting fire to a house to kidnap a girl seems extreme," I say, "but desiring a fourteen-year-old girl isn't normal either, so I think we agree that if this is true and only Taisiya was the target, the man who took her has long crossed the line of madness."

"If you're right, we need to find her as soon as possible," my grandfather says.

I don't say what I know we're all thinking: if Taisiya was taken by a pedophile, the chance that she can ever return to what she was before is very slim, no matter how fast we act now.

"I'll start investigating more deeply, but I need those details that only the sister can provide, as soon as possible."

A FEW HOURS LATER, a messenger from Ruslan delivers what I asked for.

After just half an hour of examining the documents, which are nothing more than questions answered by Anastacia about her sister, I get up from the table incredibly frustrated.

There's nothing there that sheds any light on the situation.

I run my hands over my face, exasperated, and decide to do what I didn't want to: contact a profiling expert who, even knowing I'm now on the *other side*, is still a good friend.

I send a quick message.

I hope he gives me some answers so that I at least know what kind of bastard I'm looking for.

Chapter 4

Lorcan

Two Weeks Later

"My grandfather is in Boston," I say to Cillian when I meet him in the hallway of our aunt Orla's house during one of the Sunday lunches.

"And why should that concern me?"

I've just caught him with Juno, the girl he's cared for his whole life, but now that she's back in the United States, it seems she won't just be Cillian's protégée but his wife. The tension between them during lunch was palpable.

"He wants to negotiate mutual protection for the routes in the central part of the country."

"Why?" he asks.

"The Mexicans are causing trouble."

"Tell me something new."

"No. This time it's serious. *Los Morales* are out of control. They're completely suicidal. If a war against the Russians starts, we'll have to pick a side."

"And you're suggesting I ally with Yerik? No way."

"This isn't about him being my cousin, Cillian, but because if the FBI starts a witch hunt, all organizations will be dragged into it."

"We can take care of our own asses, Lorcan. I don't want any kind of deal with the Russians."

"At least hear what my grandfather has to say. He wants to make a proposal."

He runs his hands over his face, looking incredibly pissed off.

"When?"

"Tomorrow."

"As long as it's somewhere we won't be seen together."

"I'll arrange it at my apartment. Neutral enough for you?"

"I'll give half an hour of my time out of respect for the fact that he's your grandfather, Lorcan, and not because he's an ex-Pakhan. Fuck the Russian hierarchy."

"It doesn't matter the reason, as long as we can take out those damned *Morales*."

"If shit hits the fan, you'll have to choose a side, cousin. You can't light a candle to both God and the Devil."

I smile.

"In this case, it would be lighting a candle to the Devil and another to Satan. You know there's no choice to be made, though, Cillian. I'm your blood. I'll die for you."

"Then why the hell should I meet with Ruslan?"

"Because he's my grandfather. My blood too."

"Does Yerik know about this?"

"If I had to guess, not yet, but he will eventually."

THROUGH THE WINDOW, I see Cillian getting out of the car on my street.

Wary, he looks around even after all the bodyguards have swept the perimeter for an ambush.

He didn't get where he is without reason. Distrust is in his DNA. Seconds later, I call him.

"My grandfather is already here," I say.

"I know. There's at least half a dozen Russians thinking they're being discreet, hiding in cars on your street."

Before long, he arrives at my floor. I'm already outside, waiting for him. For the *Boss*, it's a big concession to agree to meet with a Russian, and although I'm sure he secretly admires my grandfather, I don't want to push the situation more than necessary.

"What he has to say is much worse than I thought."

"You're looking incredibly agitated. What's wrong? Is it just the Mexican problem that's getting to you?"

"There could be an unprecedented war if the FBI decides to crack down on all the organizations. My grandfather is already thinking two steps ahead."

He shakes his head, giving a wry smile.

"I go crazy when I hear you call the ex-Russian Pakhan 'grandfather.' Fuck me, I like Ruslan, but not to the point of having a common family member."

"Being a grandfather and father to so many people is part of the good times when I used to run around the world spreading love, my boy," the old man says, coming into the hallway.

My cousin smiles because we know Ruslan's sexual appetite is legendary.

"How are you, sir?" he greets him.

"Getting by. Old age is a bitch. But aren't you going to come in? As secure as this building is, what we're going to discuss requires privacy."

He drapes his arm over my shoulder and together, we enter the apartment like a fucking happy family.

I wonder what the Italian mafia would think if they saw us talking. They'd probably go crazy, thinking we're teaming up to fuck them over, which, for now, is far from the truth.

The three of us sit in the living room. We're drinking beer because Ruslan's Russian grandsons' wives torment him, regulating his diet and alcohol, and when he has the chance, he escapes the strict diet.

He nods to Cillian, offering him one, but he declines.

"There's no comparison to how much better this beer you Irish make is," Ruslan says, gesturing to a bottle of *Guinness Draught Stout.* "American beer tastes like piss."

"I'm a whiskey man," Cillian says.

"The best, I suppose? From that Scottish kid's distillery, Duke MacQuoid?" Ruslan asks.

"Yes. The man bottles liquid gold," my cousin agrees. "This week we even received three cases of an excellent batch from his distillery."

"A few years ago, I was invited to an auction for the MacQuoid distillery," Ruslan continues. "Rare vintage, bids starting at seven hundred thousand dollars. I won a case for a million."

"Fuck me!" I shake my head and the old man laughs.

What the hell could be in a whiskey case to cost a million dollars?

Then I remember my motorcycles, which are fucking expensive too, and conclude that everyone has their own poison.

I notice that, gradually, my grandfather, with his unique way, is managing to make Cillian relax.

"I think we can now address those Mexican fuckers, right?" Ruslan asks.

"I'm listening," the *Boss* responds with a neutral tone.

The three of us know that, regardless of the respect at this meeting, there can never be friendship between my grandfather and my cousin.

"Lorcan told you about *Los Morales*, right?"

"Yes, but I've been keeping track of their expansion from afar. They're ambitious, even invading other cartels' territories."

"And they're at open war with us," Ruslan says.

Cillian remains silent because it's not his problem, but Yerik's.

"I know what you're thinking, son. There's no reason to get involved in a war that's not yours, but I also know you're starting in the arms business."

"Which makes us your competitors," Cillian retorts.

"Not necessarily. We can negotiate routes. We've done it in the past with other organizations."

"In exchange for what? Mutual protection?"

Ruslan takes a sip of his beer.

"No. We'd need protection if we wanted to keep them alive, which is not the case."

"They want to wipe out the entire cartel," I explain.

"They're weeds. They follow no rules," my grandfather concludes.

Cillian understands what he's saying. There's a greater risk for all organizations if one leaves traces. If the FBI picks up the scent, they'll come with their *dogs* after us, resulting in a bloodbath, numerous arrests, and worst of all, delays in delivering our goods.

"I suppose your *Pakhan* doesn't know about this proposal you're making to me," the *Boss* says.

"No, not yet, but I still have autonomy within the Brotherhood to forge alliances," he replies.

"Even with me?"

It's no secret how much he and Yerik despise each other. Since they took power as heads of their respective organizations, this is the longest period without a bloody dispute, and that's because they discovered they have me in common as a relative. Although the Russian makes a point of pretending not to know me as a cousin, he doesn't want to upset our grandfather.

"Even with you," Ruslan finally responds. "My grandson is as stubborn as I am, but he never lets emotions override the greater good, which is the safety of the Brotherhood."

"How long would this truce last? Until *Los Morales* are wiped out?" he asks.

"We don't even need to go that far. Just until they start to retreat. This war isn't yours, but ours. Just make sure that when you encounter them along the way, you clean them up."

"And what does the *Syndicate* gain in return?"

"As a gesture of good neighborliness, we'll open up two routes for your weapons."

Cillian knows he's not telling the whole truth.

"It's not just that. You've been at war before. There's never been a need for a pact with us," he says.

"Besides the common interest of getting the FBI off our backs and ensuring that goods move through your routes without external interference, what made me propose an agreement was because, like us, you understand the concept of family. The Mexicans don't. I have great-grandchildren now. Kids who have nothing to do with our business. *Los Morales* don't care about that. To them, there's no distinction between women and children. If something happens to one of Yerik's children, the country will explode. My grandson won't leave a stone unturned. Everyone loses in the end, but my loss can never be recovered."

My cousin stands up, signaling the end of the meeting.

"Talk to your *Pakhan*. If I get into this with you, I don't want just two routes; I want six. And with the guarantee that we won't incur any losses during the truce. If a single case of weapons is lost, the deal is off."

"I'm heading to Atlanta today. We'll have an answer tomorrow."

He nods and I open the door, but before he leaves, I follow him.

Chapter 5

Lorcan

"**W**hat the hell was that?" my cousin asks as soon as we get outside my apartment, just so I can hear.

I shrug.

"A proposal. It's beneficial for both organizations."

He looks at me silently for a few moments because we both know I'm right. Even though we dislike this deal with the Russians, right now, securing new routes for weapons would be advantageous.

"But to do that, we'll have to go to war with those Morales assholes."

"If you haven't noticed yet, they're already at war with everyone."

"I don't like this proximity to Yerik. First, I authorize you to go after the kidnapped girl, and now this fucked-up partnership."

"It's not a *partnership*. It's business."

"Something's happened. Ruslan talks about Yerik starting an unprecedented war, but it wouldn't be the first time the Russians blow up the country. Just like we do in the Syndicate, they need to fight fire with fire because the respect other brotherhoods have for us depends on it."

"These aren't empty threats they're facing, but real ones. My grandfather told me they tried to kill Anastacia, Maxim's wife. Traitors within the Russian Organization, on the orders of the *Morales*.

"Fuck me, so why couldn't he just be honest about why he wanted a pact?"

"Would you be, in his place?"

"No. I don't like spreading the word, handing out Syndicate secrets."

"Then you have your answer."

"Let's do this shit. I want to expand the arms trade, but let it be clear that once you find the girl, alive or dead, and after we neutralize those Mexican motherfuckers, the conversation is over. I don't want any proximity with anyone connected to Yerik. We're not a family. Do you understand that, Lorcan?"

I nod because he's right. On the other hand, I can't deny help to my grandfather. Ruslan is my only paternal reference. Even though he's kept me hidden my entire life and only Cillian and his brothers—besides the tight-knit group around Yerik—know of my existence, blood has tied me to Ruslan and it will remain so until the day we take our last breath on Earth.

"We can't talk on the phone and I can't go to Boston right now.

"I can't wait. Tell me whatever you can," I ask Remo Pellosi, who is currently considered the world's top criminal profiler. He knows everything about forensic science; he finds what no one else can.

"*You know very little about the girl, but let's start with the obvious: a man, between thirty-five and sixty years old...*"

"That's a huge window."

"*Yes, but what you need to consider is that this is someone who has the patience and resources to organize something as grand as setting fire to a house in the dead of night and leaving with a girl in his arms, assuming she's still alive. Someone under thirty would choose to wait for her to come outside. They wouldn't take such risks, they'd find her at a party, at church, something like that. Instead, he dared to invade her home. I'd say it's a meticulous man with a bit of a god complex.*

"Pedophile?"

"*It's too early to say, but if the target was the girl, then yes, probably.*

"And if it was the sister?"

I told him, without naming names, about the marriage agreement Anastacia ran from, and how she and Taisiya planned to delay the commitment, spending some time in the convent. I also informed him that a nun was murdered in the convent where Anastacia was, as Ruslan revealed to me.

"*If that's the case, and it seems to be since they pursued the elder one at the convent, then our man is seeking revenge. He wants the other one, the firstborn, his betrothed. In that scenario, there's a chance the younger one is still alive.*

Few things can evoke emotion from me, but imagining a girl so young, for three years, at the mercy of a perverted bastard makes me question what the hell is wrong with the world.

"He married someone else."

"*Could be a disguise.*"

"But he was investigated too."

"*Look for the unlikely, not what's on the surface. I'd start with isolated properties that could belong to that bastard.*"

"If you remember anything else, let me know."

"Yes, I will. I'm working from home these days. A complicated murder case."

"Murders are simple," I scoff.

"Not when someone is accused of a crime they didn't commit. Especially when that someone is so young and has no family to support them."

If you need any help..."

For the first time since our conversation began, he laughs.

"I don't need your kind of help, friend. Take care."

After we hang up, I take another look at the photograph Ruslan gave me of Taisiya.

The girl's eyes are so expressive it's as if they're focused directly on me.

"If she's still alive, hang in there, and I'll find you. Then, I'll punish whoever hurt you. You have my word. It may not be what you want to hear because you dreamed of being a nun, and as far as I know, religious people preach forgiveness. I don't understand that concept. I never forgive. I will avenge you."

Chapter 6

Taisiya

Somewhere in Siberia

"Grandpa, will I ever be able to remember my past?" I ask, frustrated, after taking a sip from my mug of milk.

He sighs.

"The only way to find out who you are is if we go to the police, Ela. We've had this conversation before."

"*Ela...* I've gotten used to you calling me that. It's better than being 'the nameless one.' As for going to the police, I don't want to. I'm afraid. I feel safe here with you."

"But you can't live isolated forever. I'm never leaving here, daughter. You're still young, with a whole life ahead of you. Maybe there's a family out there looking for you."

I feel my eyes welling up with tears.

"There isn't."

"What? You remembered them?"

"No, I wish I did, but my heart tells me I am alone. Except for..."

"Except for... what?"

"I dreamt again last night."

He closes his eyes for a moment, a look of pity overtaking his face.

"I know. I heard the screams. Did you manage to remember anything this time?"

I shake my head from side to side, indicating no.

"It was the same old dream, with the smiling girl with golden blonde hair. Could she be some relative of mine?"

"Do you look like her?"

"Not much, I think," I reply, lowering my head. "I don't remember what I look like."

"Because you don't want to look in the mirror," he says.

"The person staring back at me is a stranger, Grandpa, and I don't know if I like her."

"You don't like yourself?"

"No. I think I'm stupid for not remembering the past."

"My daughter, I'm an old lost soul, but even for me it's clear that you need help that I can't provide. Medical help, I mean. You're hiding. It's not just that you don't remember. You *don't want* to remember."

"I'm not ready yet. I'm afraid of everything."

"Afraid of what? Do you remember the day I brought you here?" He looks tense.

"No. It's like living inside a dream. I remember waking up here, as if my life started from that day."

"Three years ago..." he says, running his hands over his head. "Ela, I care for you as if you were my own blood. I would love to have your company for the rest of my days on Earth, but it doesn't seem right for you to be trapped here with me. You're a young woman. You should be living, and yet you dress like a boy, in my old clothes that you've adjusted for yourself."

"I'm fine, Grandpa Abramov. If we go to the police, you'll be in trouble, right?"

"Probably."

"Because of me? For staying with me?"

"I don't think so. From what I told you: I take things that aren't mine to survive. Everything I have is from theft. That's how I found you."

Once, I asked him for details about the day he brought me here, but he looked at me in silence for so long that I was afraid to hear the truth. After that, I never asked again. I know my back was hurt and that he took care of me, but nothing more than that.

"But you have so little! You've always taken only what you needed to survive, right?"

"Yes, only the essentials, but it's still not right."

"Don't you miss the world?" I ask, changing the subject, since I've noticed that talking about his sins makes him sad. "Living closer to society?"

"No. I don't like it there."

"What is *it* like there?"

"I wouldn't be able to tell you, Ela, it's been a long time since I isolated myself."

"I don't remember anything. I mean, I look at a mug and know it's a mug, but if I don't see the actual object, I don't remember its existence."

"Like when I showed you my bicycle?"

I smile.

"Yes. I was surprised when I saw it and even more so when I realized I could ride it. It's strange to only recognize something when it's in front of me. It's like my imagination has ceased to exist. It only happens in the presence of the object. I can't think about the past."

"And the future?"

"I don't know. I don't feel like leaving."

"Because you're afraid to face everything."

"Yes. I don't even know how old I am, Grandpa."

"When I brought you here, you seemed to be around fourteen, fifteen, so you must be of legal age now or very close to it." He looks thoughtful. "You can't hide here forever, my daughter. At some point, you'll have to go out."

I feel my throat tighten.

"Are you telling me to leave?"

"No, I'm saying that you can't pretend the world doesn't exist. The real world, not a cabin isolated in the depths of Siberia."

"Then why don't you tell me about the day you found me?"

"Because I researched it on the town library's computer. In cases like yours, with amnesia, it's better if the person remembers on their own."

"That's not all."

"What?"

"Do you think I'll suffer when I remember?"

He remains silent for a few seconds, but I can see from his face that I'm right.

He exhales a deep breath before saying:

"Yes, I think you'll suffer when you remember everything."

I stand up, take my nearly untouched mug to the sink, and wash it.

I'm trembling, but I do my best to hide the fear that he might be right. When I face him again, it's with a fake smile.

"You're right, I'm not ready to remember yet. Now, I'll enjoy the beautiful sunny day and go for a walk."

"Don't go too far and take the rifle."

Grandpa taught me how to shoot and says I'm very good at it.

"I don't like guns."

"It's not a matter of liking, it's that you might encounter a wild animal. It's for your protection only, not an act of gratuitous violence. Now, make this old man happy, take a warm coat and the rifle, my angel."

"I will, but only because I love you, Grandpa Abramov."

Chapter 7

Lorcan

Boston

Days Later

"Do you think it's a promising lead, then?" Maxim asks me. "I know it is."

We had to meet again at Ruslan's apartment. It's not safe for our organizations to be seen together, even though both Yerik and Cillian know about our deal.

This time, my grandfather isn't present, which makes everything even more surreal.

"How many men will you need?"

"None. I'll bring my own. You'll have to trust me, Maxim. I don't even know if she's alive, and if she is, in what condition she's in. As I said before, it's just a lead. The best thing is not to give your wife hope right now."

He looks at me as if trying to find arguments to refute, but there aren't any, and we both know that. Two groups that have never worked together going on a possible rescue greatly increases the chance of it going wrong.

"I want to be informed as soon as you're sure it's her."

"Believe it or not, I'm not your enemy right now, despite our organizations being rivals. My interest is to help my grandfather and bring his sister-in-law home."

33

"Why are you doing this, Lorcan?"

"Maybe because there's still a living part of my soul. I don't like thinking about a little girl at the mercy of a sicko."

"Have you ever worked on rescues?"

"Yes, I know it's not easy for you to trust us, but I would never break the word I gave to Ruslan. If the girl is alive, I'll bring her back. Until then, she'll be safe with me."

He still doesn't seem satisfied when he leaves, but I'm not willing to back down. If there's a mistake in the rescue due to operational differences between two teams, it could cost her life.

On Remo's advice, I went to research properties owned by Ayrtom Stepanchikov and found nothing except for the publicly known ones, but I'm used to digging beneath the surface and finally discovered one that, theoretically, belonged to Ayrtom's driver, as it was registered in his name.

It's literally in the middle of nowhere in Siberia, and when I sent one of my men there, what he discovered gave me clues that the son of a bitch Stepanchikov wasn't using the house just for vacation trips. The basement was practically a torture chamber.

I still haven't talked to my grandfather about it. Ruslan can have an even more explosive temper than mine, and I don't want to take any rash action that might put the girl's life at risk.

I know that if he found out what I discovered—the property of Ayrtom—his first move would be to go after the Russian. The problem is that Taisiya wasn't at that house anymore, and if we kill him, we might never find out what happened to her.

"You seem to be fucking anxious," Kellan, Cillian's other brother, says when he walks into my office hours later.

"It's not anxiety, it's adrenaline. I enjoy the hunt."

"Are you talking about your girl?"

"She's not mine, it's just a favor I'm doing for Ruslan."

"A *nice* favor?" he mocks.

"Fuck, do you only think about sex?"

"No. I think about killing too. Both give me pleasure," he says, and not for the first time, I wonder if it's just me who notices my cousin's sociopathic personality.

None of us are exactly angels, of course, but I firmly believe that he enjoys torturing.

"I'm going to Russia in a few days."

"There's a fight scheduled in a month," he says, referring to the underground fight circuit that the Syndicate owns, which would be comparable to the WCC if it were legalized.

"Yes, I know. And I'll be ready by then."

"Fucking arrogant."

I shrug.

"I've never lost. I don't plan to start now."

A Week Later

"*What's going on, Lorcan?*" Maxim asks over the phone. "*I don't want an answer only when you have results.*"

"I'll be visiting our friend in a few days. Everything is ready. I'll update you at any moment."

"*Visiting? News about what? Is it her? Is Taisiya alive?*"

"Yes, I'm going to Russia," I reveal as little as possible. "As for the rest, I only work with facts, Maxim. I'll confirm if it's really Taisiya soon."

He hangs up with a growl, and in a way, I understand the frustration, but I can't tell him more than that at the moment. Even if the girl I believe is hiding in Siberia is identical to Anastacia's sister, we'll only be sure through a DNA test.

I pick up the phone again, this time to talk to my grandfather.

"I'm arriving in the area tomorrow," I notify as soon as he answers.

"*Why the delay in getting her back?*"

"Because we still don't know who's there with her or even if it's her."

"*There, where?*"

"In the middle of fucking nowhere. Until I'm sure I can break into the house without the girl getting hurt, I'd rather do things my way, grandfather."

"*Sometimes, you still act like a damned federal agent. Meticulous to the point of being annoying.*"

"Some of what I learned from them is still in me. In this specific case, however, it's about her safety. I've been looking for Taisiya for a while. I'm not going to risk her being killed now that we're so close."

"*Just tell me who you think did this.*"

"Not for now. Trust me, Ruslan. If it's indeed your goddaughter's sister, I'll bring her back to you."

"*What support do you need?*"

"Nothing. I have everything arranged. The place is not easily accessible."

"*I'll trust that you know what you're doing, my son, but I want to know everything as soon as you find her.*"

Chapter 8

Taisiya

Smoke.

The smell is so strong it feels like I'm in the middle of a bonfire.

In my nightmares, I always feel this way. Sometimes, even after waking, I could swear that the smell of burning has seeped into my nose.

There's also the heat, as if my skin is on fire from the inside out.

Something in my heart tells me that my memory loss has to do with a fire, but I'm too cowardly to check it out further.

I have some strange clues about my past. The other day, for example, I picked up Grandpa Abramov's book written in English and was able to read it from cover to cover, as easily as I do in Russian.

I thought about it and it can only mean that I had a good education and that maybe my family has money, but a part of me, deep down in my soul, insists that I stay in the present and not try to remember what happened.

The fear I feel when I try to force the memories is so intense it makes me nauseous.

I look at the clock on the bedside table, certain that I won't be able to sleep again, so I decide to get up and have a glass of warm milk. Maybe that will help me relax a bit?

I get out of bed on tiptoe to avoid waking Grandpa. He's been sleeping poorly, even though he denies it when I ask. His hands are getting worse.

He has a condition he told me is called arthritis, which causes him tremendous pain in his joints.

I light a candle and open the bedroom door carefully, trying not to make noise, but the floor starts to creak.

Damn, I don't want to wake him, but it's hard to be quiet with this wooden floor. I hope Bolinha, his cat, isn't awake too, or he'll make a fuss wanting to play.

He told me he found Bolinha during a walk when he was still hunting.

He taught me how to hunt, as well as self-defense, though I think in his current physical condition, the techniques would be of little use to him.

Grandpa said I need to know how to protect myself from an attacker in case something happens to him and I'm left alone.

I don't like to think about it. We work well together. We're a family, and the idea that someone could hurt him makes me sick.

I hear Bolinha meowing and silently plead for the pampered cat to behave so he doesn't wake Grandpa.

A second later, I smile as I remember he says it's my fault the cat is so demanding.

I can't be any different with my "brother." From the first time I saw him, I instantly fell in love.

I'm already at the end of the hall when I hear voices in the kitchen.

My heart races because I know something is wrong. We never have visitors. To protect us from outside curiosity, Grandpa Abramov doesn't even allow food delivery people to enter here.

I take a deep breath and try to calm myself before continuing, and when I finally reach the kitchen, where the noise seems to be coming from, there are at least five men there, in addition to Grandpa.

"Get up slowly," one of them instructs. "One wrong move and I'll blow your head off."

"You're not Russian," Grandpa responds.

"What I am doesn't matter, you fucker. Do what I'm telling you."

"I can save you some trouble. You came for her, right?"

Without thinking about what I'm doing, I run and step in front of him, protecting him and facing one of the intruders, the biggest of them all. A gigantic, strong blonde.

Thor!

It's the name that comes to mind when I look at him, and at the same time, the image of a movie with a blonde character holding a hammer flashes back into my memory.

Where in the sky did that come from?

He looks at me too, and incredibly, given his size and apparent strength, I don't feel afraid.

His hair is blonde and long, his eyes as blue as a turquoise stone.

A ring.

Another inconvenient memory returns.

I once had a ring with that stone, a gift from the smiling girl in my dreams.

The memory fades as quickly as it came, and I force myself back to reality.

"Don't hurt my grandfather. He saved me," I say, desperately, in English, because that was the language the blonde man used with Grandpa.

I'm so nervous that I didn't even stop to think that if the man asks me "*saved you from what?*" I won't have the slightest idea of what to answer.

His face changes. It becomes as still as a statue, watching me as if he's seeing a ghost.

Does he know me?

However, he recovers quickly.

"Get out of his way, Taisiya."

Taisiya?

Who is this man?

"The girl doesn't remember her own name," Grandpa says. "She doesn't remember anything."

"And how about the flame?"

"*She.*"

He looks at me more closely, as if he's doing a mental study of my face, of me as a whole.

I'm terrified, but I try to act like I'm not.

"*She,*" the blonde man tests my name. "Get out of the way, I need to talk to your grandfather."

"Don't hurt him, sir. I beg you. Grandpa is all I have in the world."

At this point, I've already thrown my dignity out the window. Nothing is more important than protecting my savior.

"Go inside," he says to me, and ice runs through each of his words. I can't control my shivering. "Escort her," he continues, ordering one of the other men. "Don't let her out of the room."

I want to protest, but I'm afraid they'll hurt my grandfather if I do.

I look back, seeking permission from the man who has taken care of me for the past three years.

"Do what he says, daughter. I'll be alright."

I finally give in, obeying him, but inside, my heart is tight.

Chapter 9

Lorcan

Moments Before

Only a lantern light illuminates the cabin in the remote corner of Siberia.

Even though I've been here for a week, I haven't told Ruslan exactly where we were coming, because I thought he might send the cavalry and I want to work with the space I need.

I also didn't tell Maxim. I only explained that our plans would be delayed by a few days because I needed to be careful.

When I first spoke to him about the clues, I was certain that the culprit behind his sister-in-law's kidnapping was Ayrtom Stepanchikov. But although his property is near here and everything points to him being involved, Taisiya is not with him at the moment.

If it really is you, how the hell did you end up in this place, girl?

I mean, I have an idea of how she ended up in the house that belonged to that bastard Ayrtom Stepanchikov, but his residence is on the other side of the forest.

And that's not the only difference. While the Organization member's house is very luxurious, this one is nothing more than a shack.

How did I find her? By following clues that normal people usually ignore. When I confirmed that the girl was no longer on Ayrtom's property, I began investigating the neighborhood within a five-kilometer radius until I noticed that in this particular house, the residents hardly ever leave.

Then, early this morning, after we had surrounded the property for a few days, I saw a girl who seemed completely out of place in such a remote location, leaving with a cat in tow.

She didn't seem injured or scared, but that doesn't mean much. I've worked with kidnapping victims who came to consider the bastard keeping them captive as a "friend."

I signal for my men to follow me quietly, feeling the adrenaline spread through my body.

Working with the FBI didn't give me any excitement. They are too straight-laced and follow too many rules.

I enjoy battles against the Syndicate's enemies.

Now, however, as Cillian's right-hand man, my ass is too valuable for me to be exposing myself out there. My cousin is adamant on this point.

So, aside from it being a personal favor to Ruslan, to whom I would never say no, the thrill of being back on the front lines makes my blood pump fiercely through my body.

I think of the man I consider a father, but who I also disappointed in the past by refusing to join the Russians.

Soon after I left the FBI, he told me I could join the Organization, even though I was Irish, because as his grandson, I would hold a prominent place there.

I said no, of course.

That will never happen. My loyalty is with the Syndicate, Ruslan being the only exception regarding the Russians.

Anyway, these days, my life giving orders and commanding operations only from behind the scenes isn't as fun as when I was on the battlefield.

"There are only two people inside, but only one is moving at the moment," one of my men informs.

"The place is too remote. Is the sick person some kind of Unabomber?" I ask.

"I don't think so. From what we've checked, he just doesn't go out much."

"Let's go. I want to wrap this up quickly. If the girl is inside, we eliminate the bastard and take her," I say.

"And how can we be sure it's her? It could be a legitimate relative of the guy," another of my men argues.

"The girl will tell us the truth. Anyway, we brought a DNA kit. We'll stay here until the results come back. We'll get the answer in less than twenty-four hours."

"Alright. We'll wait if necessary," I say.

"Could there be a bomb on the property?"

"I don't think so. It might just be an old pervert with a prey."

My stomach churns, now aware for the first time that we are about to rescue a potential victim, almost a child, who has been in the hands of a lunatic with perverted desires for years.

"At my signal," I say, and everyone takes their positions.

The entire action doesn't take a minute, but when we finally breach the cabin, nothing we find is what I expected.

The first thing I notice is a lit fireplace and blankets scattered on the armchairs.

The small house is tidy and clean.

There's a cat in the room, completely indifferent to our entrance, but I stay on alert when I hear movement in the kitchen.

When I get there, gun in hand, ready to shoot if necessary, my men are already aiming theirs at the head of an elderly man, who must be around my grandfather's age, sitting calmly with a mug in front of him.

"I was wondering why you took so long to come in, considering you've been circling my property for more than a week."

I study him, recalling what the profiler told me.

Nothing fits. He doesn't seem scared, which should be the case if he were doing something wrong.

Or maybe he's just a miserable bastard without a conscience.

More of my men come in, but he doesn't even blink.

"Get up slowly," I instruct. "One wrong move and I'll blow your head off."

"You're not Russian."

"What I am doesn't matter, you bastard. Do what I'm telling you."

"I can save you some trouble. They came after her, right?"

Before anyone can respond, the girl we saw earlier rushes into the kitchen and places herself between me and the man.

"Don't hurt my grandfather. He saved me," she says in English, perhaps because she overheard our conversation.

I'm in shock. I don't need a DNA test, though I'll do it anyway.

I know that in front of me is who we were looking for. We found Anastacia's sister.

Despite this, I don't care what she said. She might be defending him out of fear or even suffering from Stockholm syndrome.

"Get out of the way, Taisiya."

She looks at me confused and doesn't move.

"The girl doesn't remember her own name," the supposed grandfather clarifies. "She doesn't remember anything."

"And what does she go by?"

"She."

I observe her carefully. She looks at me like a frightened deer. In the photos I received, she seemed more robust; now she has a slim body and is tall.

According to the report, she is seventeen.

"She," I test carefully. "Step aside, I need to talk to your grandfather."

"Don't hurt him, sir. I beg you. Grandpa is all I have in the world."

Something tightens in my chest.

She doesn't show fear, but I know she's feeling it—and from me. Still, she stands up to defend the old man.

"Go inside," I say seriously, determined not to be swayed by her beautiful face. I notice she shudders. "Escort her," I tell one of my men. "Don't let her leave the room."

The girl looks back, as if asking for consent from the man.

"Do what he's saying, daughter. I'll be fine."

Her shoulders slump, and she finally gives in.

When she leaves, I pull up a chair, the gun resting on my lap.

"Now you're going to tell me this story about saving her. You'd better be a good storyteller because patience isn't my strong suit. If I think for one second that you're lying, you're dead."

He smiles.

"Are you going to kill me? You can't kill a dead man."

"Death isn't what I have in mind, though after a few hours, you'll beg for it."

Chapter 10

Lorcan

"**A**re you telling me you found her in a mansion, chained and injured?" I ask the man, who I now know is named Abramov, after he tells me a story worthy of a horror movie, but very consistent with what I've discovered so far.

It's been about half an hour since Taisiya left the kitchen, and by now, one of my men has already collected a saliva sample from her so we can do a DNA test to confirm her identity.

According to Abramov, he entered Ayrtom Stepanchikov's property to steal, as that's how he lives, without the slightest idea of who owned the place. It seems the house had been sold recently.

I doubt that if he had known the owner was an important figure within Yerik's Organization, feared in Russia and beyond, he would have dared to act so boldly.

"Yes, but please, can you speak quietly? The girl doesn't remember anything. I researched amnesia cases. Doctors say they must recover their memory on their own."

I look at the man in front of me and can't deny that he seems to care about Taisiya. I've dealt with liars all my life. Someone who was pretending wouldn't be calmly sitting here, talking with a dozen armed men, in the middle of the night, inside his own house.

The elderly man doesn't match any of the characteristics given in Remo's profile, and besides that, he isn't sweating; his voice was steady while recounting the events, and his hands aren't trembling.

Abramov is telling the truth.

"Can I ask you a question?"

"Do you think you have the right to? You kept a missing girl without notifying the authorities for about three years. How do I know you're not the one who captured her?"

"If I were guilty, I'd be dead by now."

He's right, of course, but I need to find out how much he knows about her kidnapping.

Instead of swearing his innocence, he shows me his hands.

"It took me almost two days to bring her here on a sled. I have arthritis and feel a lot of pain. I could never have kidnapped a teenager."

"And how did you manage to rescue her? How did they not come after you?"

"The owner of that house wasn't familiar with the region, if I can guess. Besides, it snowed heavily in the days following her rescue, which erased any tracks."

Lucky bastard. I have no doubt that if Ayrtom had known the direction Taisiya had taken, the story would probably end with both of them dead.

"Ask your question," I say.

"Who is looking for her? The family?"

"Ruslan Vassiliev."

I see all the color drain from his face instantly.

I don't believe there's a living man in this part of the world who hasn't heard of my grandfather. Ruslan is feared and respected in equal measure.

"What is she to him?"

"No more questions. I need to know the rest." I nod to one of my men. "Send her to bed. It's late and her day will be full tomorrow."

The man goes to carry out the order, and my host asks:

"Full how?"

"As I said, no more questions. You're still breathing, Abramov, which means your story has convinced me so far. Don't test your luck. Let's talk about your past now."

"What do you want to know?"

"First, I want to know who you are. Why is there no record of this property in your name and how the hell did you live with her for the last... three years, you said?"

From the date he gave me, he rescued Taisiya just a month after she was kidnapped.

"This house belonged to an aunt of mine. I never transferred it to my name, and to be honest, I don't even know if it's legally registered. I believe the government doesn't even know it exists. As for the other things you asked, it was just that: I found her inside a house when I went there to steal. I've always survived by small thefts in the region."

"What did you think when you saw her?"

"I thought she was dead, given the number of bruises on her back. Whoever did that whipped her more than once."

I feel my jaw clench. Ayrtom Stepanchikov is going to die, and it won't be a good death. I assume that as the head of Taisiya's family, Maxim will want to do *the honors* and send the bastard to hell, but I plan to spend some time with him as well.

"Continue."

"She was unconscious. In fact, I think if she hadn't been rescued that day, she wouldn't have survived."

"Was it that severe? The injuries, I mean."

"Yes, they were. Before going to the basement, I checked the rest of the house. It seemed like no one had been there for a few days, which might mean that *he*, the captor, wasn't from the area, just kept the property. He might have had to work somewhere else. That, of course, was lucky for my girl. If she had been beaten daily, she'd be dead."

"How could she go so many days without eating or drinking water? Are you telling me that the supposed owner of the property—" I say, without giving any hint that I know who it is—"didn't come around often? So, who was taking care of her?"

"I thought about that too. There had to be an accomplice, or she wouldn't have survived. The person who mistreated her wasn't the same one who fed her."

"A woman?"

"I don't believe so. The place is inhospitable for women. In my opinion, it was the work of at least two men."

I mentally file this information away to check later.

"Why get involved in this? Didn't you think about the mess you'd be in if the person who captured the girl caught you?"

"A few minutes ago, you asked who I was. I am a former Orthodox priest and also a killer," he says, seeming indifferent to what I might do with the information.

"What kind?"

"What?"

"You said you were a killer. What kind?"

"I killed another priest who abused boys in our parish. He was reported by the boys' families, but nothing happened, until the day a teenager disappeared. He helped at the church and always stayed there after school, almost until dusk."

"I will check your story. You know that if you're lying, you're dead, right?"

"I'm not lying, but as I told you before, I don't have a problem with dying. I'm just breathing. I no longer live since I committed the greatest of all sins: taking a life."

"Tell me the rest."

"The boy who disappeared was studious, credulous, helpful. One day, he entered the church and never came out. I investigated. It didn't take me long to find out who was responsible. I think many other priests suspected, but the church not only covered up the case but also started spreading the rumor that he had run away. That, of course, fell apart when the body was found in a stream, five days later."

"And from then on, did you become the defender of innocent youth?" I ask with cynicism.

His story might be real, and if it is, the son of a bitch got what he deserved, but from everything I know about human nature, most people are cowards and selfish. Few would risk their own necks to save a stranger, and not just any stranger, but one who was in the captivity of a rich man like Taisiya was.

"I am far from being a hero, but I live according to my conscience. I thought that *She,* the girl you came looking for, was a prostitute, to be frank. There are many like that in these remote corners. They are sold by their families at ten or twelve years old. The teenager who was killed at the church came from an adjusted home with relative means, so what crossed my mind was: if the dead boy had no chance against the power of the church, the one I rescued wouldn't be taken seriously if she was indeed a prostitute. The most likely thing was that the authorities would send her back to the captor in exchange for a "reward."

"Did you tell Taisiya that you thought she was a prostitute?"

"Taisiya..."— He smiles, testing the name. "For a long time, I tried to imagine what her name was. As for your question, the answer is: no. She only knows that I rescued her, but we never discussed it. The girl is aware that she came to me hurt, but we never went into detail. I just took care of her."

"You want me to believe that you had a beautiful teenage girl in your possession for three years and never touched her?" I say, more to push him, because intuitively, I am almost certain that he is telling the truth.

"*She* lost her memory of the past, but from the day I rescued her until now, she remembers everything. Interrogate her. You'll get the answers to what you're looking for."

Again, he doesn't seem the least bit shaken.

"I will do that as soon as she wakes up tomorrow."

He shows no concern about the fact that we'll be staying in his house, perhaps because he knows he has no choice.

"What will happen to her?"

"If she is indeed who I'm looking for, I will take her away." He nods, agreeing. "Aren't you going to protest?"

"Would it make a difference?"

"No."

"I knew she wouldn't stay here forever. She's young. I thought sooner or later, she would want to leave. I had no idea they were looking for her."

"If the DNA result is what we expect, we'll leave immediately. You, however, will remain under surveillance."

He doesn't ask why.

"Can I lie down? I don't even need to say make yourselves comfortable, because you already are," he says, with a hint of irony.

I nod, and one of my men positions himself to accompany him.

"Don't do anything stupid and you might survive," I warn.

"I don't intend to confront them, if that's what you're insinuating. My only concern is with the girl. I should assume, given the care you have with her and who sent you to us, that she will be safe with your men here?"

"Whether she is who I'm looking for or not, while she is under my care, the girl is mine. Yes, she will be safe."

Chapter 11

Taisiya

It has been more than an hour and a half since they sent me to the room, and yet, I can't sleep. My heart won't slow down, and it feels like my nerves are connected to electric currents.

I tiptoe and try to listen for any sound in the hallway, but there is nothing.

Could they have left? I'm not sure if that's what I want. Although I didn't like at all the way *Thor* spoke to Grandpa, he looked at me as if he knew me, and a glimmer of hope, though surrounded by a lot of fear, appeared in my heart.

I place my hand on the doorknob, uncertain if what I'm about to do is right, but then again, if those men were bad people, wouldn't they have already come here to hurt me?

I heard Grandpa's footsteps going to his room, which means they let him go to sleep too. It seems like a good thing, so I decide to take the risk and see if they're still here.

I put on an old, thick, checkered coat that belonged to my grandfather and which he gave to me.

I don't put it on because I'm cold. The house is small and warm, and yes, because in the rush of leaving the room the first time, I was just in sweatpants and a T-shirt. Grandpa says I'm a young lady, almost a woman, and should dress modestly.

I dig my nails into my palms, praying that I'm not making a mistake by sneaking around.

"God, please help us. Don't let them harm us."

The floor, of course, creaks, giving me away. Two seconds later, an armed man appears in the hallway.

Guns don't scare me. I know all about them because Grandpa has several, but the man is looking at me as if he's going to kill me.

I stare back at him, pretending to be calm, as if my knees weren't so weak they're knocking against each other.

"I want to talk to the blonde man. The big one."

No one needs to tell me that Thor is the boss. I don't know much about life outside this cabin, since I don't remember the past, but his demeanor, like that of a king, made it clear that he is in charge.

The stranger stares at me for more seconds than my cowardly heart can handle; I start seriously considering turning back and going to my room when he finally moves.

"Come with me."

As I pass through the living room, I see that the others are sitting in the armchairs as if they own the place. One of them, who introduced himself as Keiron, asked me for permission to swab inside my cheek earlier today, and is standing by the window. He doesn't turn to face us, even though I'm sure he hears our approach.

I know he can't see anything outside. It would be impossible at night because we are the only house for miles. What goes through my mind is that he prefers to stay like this, not interacting with the others.

When we finally reach the kitchen, the giant has a laptop open in front of him on the table.

He is sitting, facing the entrance, so he sees me arrive but only raises his eyes from the screen, over the edge of the computer.

He doesn't say anything. He just stares at me, and if I were smarter, I might run, but there must be something very wrong with my brain because my foolish heart tells me that next to the blonde man, who as far as I know is an intruder, I am safe.

"I wanted to talk." I gather the courage to speak, finally.

He gestures for the man who brought me to leave and then returns to staring at me with those intense blue eyes.

"You should be asleep, Taisiya."

"Why do you call me that?"

"Because it's your name."

"How can you be sure?"

"I was looking for you. We'll have confirmation soon. We did a DNA test."

I look at him, confused.

"The swab one of my men took from your mouth."

"Oh..." So that was it. I was wondering if it was some kind of test, I just didn't think they would try to confirm my identity so soon. Grandpa explained to me about DNA and said that nowadays many old cases are being solved this way, because laboratories, especially American ones, can investigate crime evidence left by the killers. "Did you have a photo of me from before? I'm asking because you came calling me Taisiya as if you knew who I was."

He nods, and I'm now certain that getting information will be difficult. The man doesn't seem to want to talk to me.

I take a step closer and his eyes follow me like a wild animal assessing its opponent. It's as if attacking comes naturally to him. Even though I don't feel threatened, my instinct tells me he is someone used to violence.

Shouldn't I run? Of course, I should, but instead, I take small steps until I'm very close to him.

"Can I sit down?"

"Go to bed. It's late, and if the result is what I hope, I'll take you away soon. Maybe even tomorrow."

"What?" I ask, almost shouting and suddenly feeling the kitchen spin around me. "You can't take me away from my grandfather."

"He's not your real grandfather," he says, sounding indifferent. "You have someone looking for you."

Now, I feel my heartbeats in my ears. Torn between loyalty to the man who's cared for me for the past three years and the anxiety of knowing that, no matter what has happened to me in the past, there's someone who cares enough to send people after me.

"Who is looking for me?"

"Sit down," he says, with a sigh that sounds more like a lion's roar. It's clear he didn't want company, but maybe he noticed that I can barely stand from nervousness.

I slowly pull out the nearest chair to him. Only God knows why I chose this one when there are four others at the table.

The only explanation I can think of is that I feel a connection to the grumpy stranger.

"Because he might have answers for me," I try to justify to myself.

As if reading my thoughts, he says:

"You shouldn't approach strange men like this, Taisiya. I could harm you."

I feel my cheeks warm as I confess:

"I don't know much about social behavior. I only interact with Grandpa, but I trust my heart, and it tells me you didn't come to hurt me. You came to protect me. Am I wrong?"

Chapter 12

Lorcan

"Tell me what you remember," I say instead of answering her.

It surprises me how almost instantly I felt a connection with the girl, an abnormal need to protect her, given that I never get personally involved with my work at the Syndicate—and Taisiya, although I'm here at Ruslan's request, meaning for the benefit of the Russian Organization, is just a mission.

I don't like that she has also noticed that I care.

From everything Abramov told me, I know she must have gone through hell, but I don't want any responsibility for the teenager beyond the promise I made to my grandfather.

She was staring at me but looks away after what I say.

"I don't remember anything. Did my parents send you to find me?"

"No."

"Do I have parents?" she asks, her voice full of sadness. She may not remember the past, but she's an intelligent girl and is starting to piece things together.

"Do you remember anything about them?"

"No. I just feel in my heart that I'm alone in the world."

I could lie to ease her discoveries from here on, but it's not in my nature.

"Not completely alone," I say, without actually explaining anything. "There is someone, and it's because of her that I came to find you."

"The girl with golden hair?"

"What?"

"I don't know her name, but she always appears in my dreams. Smiling and beautiful. I know we have some connection, but I don't know what it is."

"Her name is Anastacia."

I could wait for the results of the test before starting to reveal facts, but I know I have Taisiya in front of me. She's still as beautiful as in the photographs I was given, and although she no longer has the childish face she once did, her eyes and smile are the same.

"Grandpa says I shouldn't hear about the past from others. I have to remember it on my own."

"He's not your grandfather, as I've already told you. He's also not a doctor."

"I don't care that we don't share the same blood, sir. He took care of me."

"Just took care of you?" I ask directly, because despite the conversation I had with Abramov, Taisiya will undergo a full physical examination to see if she was harmed in any way.

"I didn't understand," she says, and there's so much innocence in her face that I already have my answer. "He... um... also taught me how to shoot."

No, the old man didn't abuse her, though that doesn't mean it didn't happen while she was held captive.

"You'll have to remember the past sooner or later," I say, changing the subject. "But for now, you need to know that if the DNA test I had done comes back positive, you'll come with me."

Her face now shows anxiety.

"I don't know you."

"But you trust me, or you wouldn't be here at this hour. You didn't go to speak with another man; you came to stay with me."

"Maybe because I'm not a good judge of character."

"Or maybe because you have good instincts. Even so, it shouldn't happen again. Don't do this again, Taisiya: staying close to a stranger in the middle of the night just because he *seems* like a good person."

"I didn't say you..."

"You."

"I didn't say that *you* seemed like a good person," she says, and a corner of her mouth lifts in a hint of a smile.

She's a precious and sweet little thing, which isn't good for her. Something tells me the girl in front of me is her true self. When she remembers the ordeal she went through, the suffering will be even greater.

"As I said before, you have good instincts. Now, let's clarify something, Taisiya: don't think you have a choice. You'll come with me if your identity is confirmed. I crossed the world to find you and promised someone important to me that I would take you back."

"My grandfather will miss me," she says, sounding sad.

"Anastacia misses you much more. Your place is protected, with family."

"So she is family then?" she asks, but before I can answer, she continues: "Grandpa always said that one day I would have to remember the past and then leave, did you know?"

"And has it ever happened? Remembering the past, I mean."

"No. I have nightmares about fire and smoke. I almost smell it, and that's why I'm sure something serious happened to me, but I'm too scared to try to examine it further."

Jesus, she really has no idea what happened.

"Hiding won't help you."

"I'm not hiding, I'm protecting myself. I'm afraid of suffering."

"It's the same thing. If you let fear control you, you become weak."

"You never feel afraid of anything?"

"No. Fear is a useless emotion."

"And since when is feeling afraid a choice?"

"Feeding it is a choice. Starve it, and it will disappear."

"How?"

"By facing it."

"You're very angry," she says, almost smiling and catching me off guard.

I've never dealt with girls on the brink of adolescence. My family is made up of men.

Besides, I don't want her smiles or friendship. I don't want to form a connection with her.

"I'm just direct."

"Can you try to be direct without being so frightening?"

"Are you afraid of me?"

I don't know why, but thinking about it gives me a fucking unpleasant feeling.

"No, although I think I should be. I'm just asking you not to talk to me as if you're going to bite me at any moment. If you're going to take me back to my family..." she says, and her expression falls, making her look away again—"or to whoever might be left of them, can we be friends during the process?"

At this moment, I almost wish she never recovers her memory. The girl is the image of an innocent angel. Only someone completely unaware of the past could be so credulous after what she's been through.

"So, can we be friends?" she insists.

I grunt something, not giving a specific answer.

"Was that a yes?"

"I'll take care of you. I wouldn't call it friendship."

"A bodyguard?" she says, frowning as if recalling something. "I think I had one at some point in my life."

Of course she did. Her father was a respected member of the Organization, according to Ruslan, and he surely kept a close watch on his daughters.

"I'm not a bodyguard. I'll be your guardian, which is different. It means you owe me obedience."

"I don't like the word 'guardian.' It sounds like I did something wrong, and you'll be on guard as if I were a prisoner."

I'm legendary for my bad temper, but at this moment, I'm smiling internally. She's a character.

"You're not a prisoner, but you're also not free to make choices at the moment."

"I'd rather you be my protector. I'd feel safer that way," she continues, apparently ignoring what I said. "But for that, I need to know your name."

"Lorcan."

"That's not a Russian name. Grandpa and I are Russian."

"It's an Irish name."

"If it's Irish, how did you find the girl with the golden hair... Anastacia, you said her name was, right?"

"You'll know everything in due time, Taisiya. Now, go to sleep."

Chapter 13

Lorcan

When she finally does what I told her, I refocus on what is necessary at the moment.

I grab one of the secure phones my grandfather gave me, courtesy of Odin Lykaios, a friend of Grigori who also happens to be the world's leading information security expert today, and complete the call.

I only use the device to talk to Ruslan because our conversations are never about flowers or how the day is going. We discuss matters that we don't want any authority to know about.

Even though my grandfather assures me that the phone can be used safely even for matters related to the Syndicate, and could even provide us with devices, Cillian would never accept a favor.

He has his own specialist handling that for us.

The phone barely rings three times before he answers. I know he stayed in the United States, but no matter what time zone he's in, my grandfather is always alert.

"I found her. I'm just waiting for the DNA test results. I had one of my men send it to a lab here in Russia. Maybe you should use your influence to expedite the result."

"I'll do that. Give me the details of which lab it's at, and by the end of tomorrow, at the latest, we should be able to resolve the issue. Actually, I was already expecting this, but I thought you might send me to do the test since you don't know many people in my country."

"I don't like waiting. And as for not knowing many people in your country, I have strategic contacts all over the world, grandfather."

"You may have only a bit of Russian blood, Lorcan, but you're my grandson to the last strand of hair. Arrogant, stubborn, and doesn't like asking for help from anyone."

"Yeah, I can't deny that. The other reason for the rush is that Cillian is uncomfortable with me being here. Even though you're my grandfather, this is, for us, an enemy country."

"You're not in danger. You have my protection on Russian soil, but it wouldn't help to tell your Boss because he wouldn't believe it. Are you sure it's her?"

"Yes, it is. There's no doubt in my mind. She has the same eyes as the photographs you gave me."

"And how is she?"

"She lost her memory. She doesn't remember anything, except vaguely for a girl with golden hair."

"Anastacia."

"Yes, and she also has nightmares about smoke and fire. Other than that, she doesn't even know her own name. The man who rescued her refers to her as 'She.'

"The man who rescued her?"

I explain in detail everything I've discovered about Abramov, and when I reach the part where I reveal the identity of Taisiya's kidnapper and what he did to her, my grandfather roars:

"Son of a bitch. Damned."

"You need to inform Maxim. I know he'll want to settle the score personally, but I need you to give me some time with Ayrtom first."

"Granted, as long as Maxim gets to finish the job. Let's think about the next steps. The DNA results should arrive within forty-eight hours at the most, because I'll set fire to the lab if necessary, but I want Taisiya reunited with her sister as soon as possible."

"Alright, but I think she should be examined first. A trusted doctor. She's been in Ayrtom Stepanchikov's hands for only a month, but she's been in Siberia for three years. I'm not talking just about a basic exam to check what was done to her, but also about her overall health."

"Does she seem well?"

"Yes, on the outside, she seems like a healthy teenager. Perhaps the memory loss, coupled with having lived in isolation, has removed some of her inhibitions because she wasn't afraid of me, or if she was, she didn't show it."

"I don't understand anything about adolescent issues. Especially in her situation. I'll talk to Talassa and Lara about it."

I know that Yerik and Grigori's wives, who are also best friends, were victims of sex trafficking, and if there is proof that we, humans, can go through all sorts of shit without breaking, it's them.

"When do you think you'll have that bastard Stepanchikov in your custody?"

"Today. As soon as we hang up, I'll have him dragged out of bed. I hope he had a good dinner last night. A fitting farewell, because it will be his last."

"After the result, we'll need her documentation."

"I'll arrange that. Now, let's talk about practical matters: I want you to stay at my house in Moscow, Lorcan. I'll have to deliver the news to Maxim in person about finding Taisiya, so I'll take a few more days to return to Russia. Keep me informed. I also need your location. I'll send someone to pick you up."

"I came with a friend's plane."

"Thank him, but it's no longer necessary. Once you're in Moscow, I want you to be protected. Not just for Taisiya, but for you as well. You're Irish, and few know you're my grandson."

"I don't want Russian bodyguards."

"Stick with your own, but I'll have my men ensure your safety as well. You'll let me take care of you. It's my blood, Lorcan. I'll protect you even against your will."

TAISIYA TOOK MY ORDER to avoid being around strangers very seriously. For the entire following day after our meeting in the kitchen, she didn't leave the room.

It's either that, or she's already saying goodbye to Abramov, because I heard them talking in the hallway and then him bringing her breakfast, but I haven't seen her since.

The DNA test results are expected today. As promised, Ruslan managed to get the lab to expedite the process. In the United States, given our influence there, we could get it in twenty-four hours, but I wasn't very hopeful they would be that fast here in Russia, due to the difficulty we had sending the material to the lab.

I'm eager to leave, but not for the usual reason — that staying in one place for too long bores me — but because I received a message from my grandfather saying they already have Ayrtom. I don't like to delay settling scores in general, but I can't wait to face that son of a bitch.

"Will I get to see her again?" I hear Abramov's voice behind me.

I was watching the night fall outside and at the same time, wondering how anyone can live in such a godforsaken place and not lose their mind.

I don't like people most of the time, but I like the noise they make. Voices, horns, I need to feel life outside of me, maybe because inside, I'm like a mere spectator of the world.

"If her family allows it. If Taisiya wants it. If you've told me the truth and I let you live. There are several 'ifs' in your path, Abramov."

He doesn't seem disturbed by the implied threat. What he might not know is that it wasn't just a threat. Once we confirm her identity, Taisiya will be taken for both medical and psychological evaluations.

She will undergo clinical tests to determine the extent of the abuse, but she will definitely see psychologists, and I hope to finally find out what happened.

"As I told you before, I didn't lie. I didn't have to confess that I'm a killer, but I did. I just want to know if she will be okay."

"People confess to anything when they want to save their own skin. I'm an expert at convincing others to tell the truth," I reply with irony. "Regarding Taisiya, yes, she will be fine. She will be where she belongs. If what you did for her is confirmed, you will be rewarded and protected as one of ours. If you lied, you'll wish you were dead. Either way, someone will be on watch to ensure you don't escape."

"Escape to where? I have no desire to go anywhere else. I just want my girl to be okay. I hope that God can forgive some of my past sins for taking care of her all these years."

Chapter 14

Taisiya

"**D**on't cry," Grandpa Abramov says, hugging me.

I don't want to make him sad, but I can't help it. About two hours ago, Thor came to see me here in the room and, as if he were talking about what's for dinner, told me that I am indeed the girl he was looking for.

The test results have arrived, and he seems eager to leave.

"I'm scared. I feel safe with you," I confess.

"Feeling safe isn't healthy at your age. Not if it means being afraid to take risks. You're at the perfect age to make mistakes."

We're sitting in my room. I'm on my bed, already ready to leave. He's in the chair, which, along with the dresser and a bedside table, are the only pieces of furniture in the room.

I look around the simple room, but it's my refuge in the world. A place I've learned to love because it gives me the feeling of being protected from a past that, to me, doesn't exist, since I don't remember it.

"I think I understand what you're saying, and to be honest, I'm looking forward to meeting the girl of my dreams, the relative. But I feel sorry to leave you here alone and am also very afraid that at some point I might remember the past, and it will be too horrible. What if I can't handle who I was before coming to live with you?"

"Don't underestimate yourself, Taisiya. I think I can call you that now, since you've got your name back," he says, reaching out to take my hand. "We, human beings, are strong. Capable of overcoming situations we never imagined we could. We've talked many times before, and you knew that your life here wasn't 'forever,' and now that you know there's someone waiting for you, it's even more important that you reunite with your family."

"You're my family too."

"Yes, and I always will be, but I'm not going anywhere. You can visit me whenever you want."

"They won't hurt you?"

"No. Lorcan gave me his word that if I was telling the truth, I would receive protection. I trust the young man."

"Me too. Does that make me a fool?"

"No, my daughter. It means you have good judgment. I would never let you go if I thought they could harm you. I would die fighting to protect you."

"I don't like it when you talk about death."

He shrugs.

"It's inevitable for all of us, especially for me, who am much closer to the end than to the beginning of the road. You, however, have your whole life ahead of you." He pauses for a moment, as if thinking about how to tell me something before continuing: "I spoke with the godfather of this girl, Anastacia, on the phone earlier today."

"Her godfather?"

"Yes, ultimately, he was the one who sent these men to save her. Thor, as you call Lorcan," he says, hiding a smile, "is his grandson."

"Oh! So we're related by affinity? I mean, the man you spoke to is Anastacia's godfather, who is also my relative, and Lorcan is his grandson. It seems like we're part of the same family."

"I don't think it's that simple. The godfather I mentioned is Russian. A very important man here in our country, in fact. To be honest, it's a bit of a puzzle to me how he can have an Irish grandson. But that doesn't matter right now; what matters is that I'm sure you will be protected. No one will touch you knowing you're connected to Ruslan."

"You could buy a cell phone. That way, we could talk from time to time," I say, unable to imagine what it will be like not to hear his voice every day.

"I don't like modern conveniences."

"Not even for me? I can ask Lorcan to get one for you."

"Alright. For you, I'll use a cell phone. Now, get up. It's time to leave, my angel."

I get up from the bed with no enthusiasm. The coward in me wanting to hide.

"Everything will be alright, my daughter."

As if to confirm, we hear a knock on the door, and when I answer that they can come in, seconds later, I see Thor standing in the doorway, filling the entire passage.

He looks at me in silence, as if he were looking inside me. Since our conversation in the kitchen, I've practically stayed in the room and haven't spoken to any of them.

After the initial surprise of having strangers in my home, I resented those men appearing out of nowhere to turn my life upside down.

"There's someone who wants to talk to you," he says, showing me a cell phone, and at the same time, Grandpa leaves.

Lorcan, however, doesn't seem the least bit willing to give me privacy and after handing me the phone, leans against a wall and crosses his arms in front of his chest.

"That's right, make yourself at home. Pretend the room is yours."

In my head, I'm rolling my eyes.

The man certainly needs a lesson in manners.

"Who is it?"

"Answer, Taisiya."

Annoyed that he's treating me like I'm his property, I turn my back and walk to the window.

"Hello?"

"Taisiya, my name is Ruslan. My grandson told me you've lost your memory, so I'm calling to let you know that you'll be safe with him."

Jesus, talk about being direct.

"Good morning, Mr. Ruslan. Just out of curiosity, would I have had any options if I didn't want to go?"

"No. I'm informing you out of courtesy."

"Thank you." I can't hide a hint of irony. "When will I see Anastacia?" I ask, because although I don't remember her beyond the dreams I've had, she seems to be the reason I have to leave with strangers.

"Do you remember her?"

"No, but your grandson gave me the basics."

"She's in the United States. Lorcan will take her to Moscow, where she'll see doctors, and then I will arrange her documentation. After everything is ready, we'll bring her so you can meet her."

After that, he ends the call with a kind of growl and hangs up.

Chapter 15

Taisiya

"You're very quiet," Thor says, after about ten minutes since the helicopter that came to pick us up took off.

I think for a moment about how to respond because I need to remember that I'm no longer with Grandpa; I can't say everything that comes to mind.

Finally, I sigh, knowing that it won't work because I can't fake it.

"Aside from going with a stranger to a place I have no idea where it is," I say, looking out the window, "I'm terrified of flying."

"Look at me while we talk, Taisiya."

I obey, and a strange sensation, a fluttering in my stomach that has nothing to do with being in a metal box many meters up, hits me.

"I thought you didn't want to talk."

"It's not personal. I'm just not much of a talker, generally speaking."

"No one at all?" I ask, surprised. "How do you manage? Grandpa says I'm capable of setting records for words per minute."

It might be my imagination, but for the first time since we've talked, I think he almost smiles.

In a second, however, the shadow of the smile disappears.

"You don't need to be afraid; helicopters are one of the safest modes of transport."

I look back out the window, frustrated again, and struggle hard not to cry.

I need to be strong, or something tells me I'm going to suffer a lot. The world I knew is gone. Grandpa is left behind, and now, all I have left is to endure this grumpy giant until it's time to meet the smiling girl.

"It's easy to feel scared when we don't remember anything. When everything seems uncertain. My only point of reference is gone."

"Are you talking about Abramov?"

I nod, without looking back at him.

"Deal with one of them at a time."

"What?"

"Since you can't avoid feeling scared, deal with one of them at a time."

The words seem like a kind of warning because soon after, the helicopter jolts, making my stomach hit my brain. Breakfast is seriously threatening to come out in a not-so-elegant way.

I try to take deep breaths to control the panic, but when two seconds later, another maneuver throws me almost onto Lorcan, I grab his hand as if my next breath depends on it, forgetting that the man didn't respond when I suggested we could be friends.

Fear and dignity travel separate roads. At the moment, I want the security that the big guy can give me.

He doesn't try to pull away from my grip but stays rigid, and when I turn to look at him, he's focused on our intertwined hands.

I feel awkward and try to let go, but he tightens his grip instead of letting me go.

"If it'll calm you down..." he says, not finishing the sentence.

"My heart is racing so fast I feel like I'm going to have a heart attack, so yes, if you can hold my hand, I'll calm down."

It's his turn to look out the window, and if I weren't so afraid of dying, I would let go, but I prefer the embarrassment of depending on a stranger's safety rather than keeping my pride intact.

Lorcan doesn't say anything more, and about twenty minutes later, the helicopter lands in a place full of airplanes.

An airport?

Just like with the bicycle, I know instinctively that I've flown many times before. They're not specific memories. What makes me sure is that aircraft, men signaling on the runway, carts moving around—everything is familiar.

Lorcan surprises me by unfastening my seatbelt and after we get out, without waiting for me to follow, he grabs me by the waist and sets me on the ground.

There are other men waiting for us, and as we approach, they try to speak to him in Russian, and he says a word or two but it's clear he's not very comfortable with our language.

We head toward the plane, and I pretend not to hear when Lorcan says that only the men who were in the cabin with us will board the aircraft.

Why? It doesn't make much sense to me.

Then I remember that everyone at Grandpa Abramov's house was Irish. The ones waiting for us now are Russian.

Is that it?

Jesus, what a mess.

"They are Ruslan's security, not mine," he says as soon as we enter the plane, as if reading my thoughts.

"I don't understand."

"And you don't need to. Just know that while you're with me, I'm the one who will protect you, not the Russians."

THE TRIP WAS LONG, about twelve hours. I was so exhausted from being tense the entire flight that when I arrived at the huge house, which looks more like a luxury hotel, I barely remember walking to the room.

Thirty minutes later, a maid knocked on the door and brought me new clothes. I took a shower and crashed, until the phone I asked Lorcan for rang.

"Daughter?"

"Grandpa Abramov!" I reply, excited. "Sorry I didn't call earlier. I fell asleep. I already miss you."

"You don't need to apologize. I just called to make sure you arrived safely."

"Yes, I arrived. I was terrified of the helicopter and the plane, but now I'm on solid ground. I'll be fine. And you?"

"I'm fine, Taisiya. And I'll continue to be, don't worry. The reason I'm calling is to say that my thoughts will always be with you, but I think we need to stop talking for a while."

"Why?"

"Because you'll feel torn and guilty. It's not fair. Go back to your world. I'll be here, and when you've adjusted to your new reality, we can talk again, but you need to fly solo, my daughter, and as much as I adore you, this has to be a solo flight."

We talked for a few more minutes, and like every time we speak, his advice calms me, even though my head is still quite confused.

When the same maid knocks on the door some time later, asking if I want to come down for a meal, I shake my head and go back to lying down.

Lorcan told me that tomorrow I'll see a doctor. I'll try to rest and give my mind a break.

There's too much going on, and I'm not handling it all well.

Chapter 16

Lorcan

"**C**an you wait here for a moment?" I say to her, watching her cheeks flush with embarrassment.

Taisiya has spent the last two hours locked in a room with a doctor and two nurses who specifically attend to the women of Ruslan's Organization.

I know that several tests have been done, mainly blood, urine, and some imaging tests, the results of which will come out in a few days. But what I want to discuss with the doctor can be answered today.

I feel like I'm invading Taisiya's privacy; however, I'm responding to another request from Ruslan, and what he wants to know isn't out of mere curiosity but to close gaps in the story of her kidnapping.

Taisiya nods and then goes to sit in an armchair in the waiting room.

Although I know she is safe here, as Ruslan ordered the clinic to be emptied today specifically to attend to her, two men stand guard while I go to speak with the doctor.

Twenty minutes later, I emerge with my nerves jumping inside my body. On one hand, I'm relieved that she hasn't suffered any sexual assault, as the doctor said her hymen is intact—which, given the effort he put into kidnapping her, I still can't understand—but on the other hand, I want to go straight from here to kill Ayrtom

75

because, although he didn't rape her, he abused her body with physical torture.

The doctor told me that the scars from the lashings on her back can only be removed with plastic surgery.

When I return to the waiting room, she is sitting where I left her, looking at her hands in her lap.

Against everything I promised myself, that I wouldn't get personally involved, since she, despite being Ruslan's protégé, is Russian and belongs to Yerik's family, I say "screw the rules" and kneel in front of her.

Taisiya doesn't lift her face.

"I didn't look at myself in the mirror. I didn't know there were so many. The doctor said I'll need plastic surgery." She tries to be strong, but her lower lip trembles. "Why did they do this to me, Lorcan? Was I a bad person?"

I know my men are paying close attention to the conversation, so I stand up and walk over to them, telling them to wait in the hallway.

As soon as they close the door, I return to her and hold her hands.

I'm terrible at comforting. I cause pain, not heal it, but I try my best.

"No, you weren't bad. And whoever did this will pay, Taisiya. You have my word."

She stands up and, catching me completely by surprise, hugs me.

At first, just like when she gave me her hand on the helicopter, I freeze. Reason tells me to back away because Taisiya shouldn't form an emotional bond with me. As soon as we get to the United States, our paths will separate.

"Can you give me a hug?" she asks when I continue to stand still.

I fight an internal battle, but in the end, I pull her towards me.

Taisiya is small and gets lost in my arms.

She holds me tight.

"I'm so scared of remembering..."

Damn it! An adult in her place would be scared, let alone a girl so young.

I let my hands run over her back, trying to comfort her, but I realize it was the wrong move when I feel the raised scars through the thin fabric of her dress.

Jesus Christ!

I don't remember ever feeling so shaken in my life, but my body is unstable, so intense is the hatred spreading through my veins.

I hold her tighter.

"For reasons you don't need to know now, we can't be friends when we get to the United States, but here's a promise: no one will ever hurt you again. I will always be watching over you."

She pulls away a little and lifts her face to look at me.

"That's not enough. Watching from afar, I mean. Be my friend, not just my protector."

"I can't promise that. You'll understand when you talk to Anastacia."

"And by phone? At least I can hear your voice? I know the girl you call Anastacia is my relative, but I don't remember her except for dreams. Yesterday, Grandpa Abramov told me that we'll need to stay silent for a while so I can readjust to my life. I didn't want to, but I would make him sad if I refused, as he'd think I couldn't move on, even though deep down, I'm not sure I will. As you can see, I have no one, so risking embarrassment, I'm still asking for your friendship. Be my friend, Lorcan."

"Taisiya, you'll meet people your age, make new friends."

"You talk as if you're old."

"To be your friend, I am. I'm thirty-five."

"Friends don't have an age. Can you at least think about it? I'll feel calmer knowing I'll hear your voice when I'm feeling lonely."

"Taisiya, it's not going to work."

She pulls away, her eyes shining with tears.

"I'm going to use the bathroom before we leave, okay?"

Without waiting for a response, she exits almost running, and I feel like a bastard for hurting her even more. But, in the real world, a Russian mafia princess can't be friends with a member of the Irish Syndicate.

As if life is confirming my thoughts, my second phone rings, and I see it's Cillian.

"I heard everything went well with the girl. When are you coming back?"

"Only when she can leave too."

"Fuck, that's not what we agreed on. And the fight?"

"I'll get there in time, but I'm not leaving her alone here."

"She won't be alone. Her grandfather will be around."

"Taisiya is my responsibility, cousin. I will only leave her side when I hand her over to Anastacia."

"Don't complicate things by getting attached to the girl, Lorcan."

"What are you talking about? She's only seventeen. She's a child."

"At some point, she'll be eighteen. Don't make her fall in love. You know a relationship between you two would be impossible."

"Where the hell did you get that? I came to rescue her, and now Taisiya is under my protection. That's all."

"I want your word that it will remain just a mission."

"No, I'm not giving it. What you're saying is ridiculous. The girl went through a fucking nightmare, and if I'm still here, it's because of my sense of duty. There's nothing more to it. Was that all you wanted to say?"

"No. About the Mexicans too. Shit has already started flying. Watch your back."

I hang up the phone and hear a noise behind me. When I turn around, Taisiya is staring at me. I don't need to be a fucking body language expert to know she heard everything.

Damn, this is just getting more complicated.

"Ready?"

She doesn't meet my gaze and just nods, heading straight for the door. Her shoulders are slumped, and I know I'm responsible for that, or at least worsened how she was feeling after the exam.

"Taisiya."

"I want to go home, Lorcan. I'm tired."

Chapter 17

Lorcan

Two Days Later

I enter the warehouse where they've brought him and shake my head in disapproval at the men guarding Ayrtom Stepanchikov.

He's bent over a piece of equipment that closely resembles a gymnastics horse, and given that he's naked, I don't need to be a genius to know what's happened.

But how the hell do they expect me to work on him like this?

"Get him on his feet, wrists chained."

I take off my leather jacket while waiting for one of the men to follow my order. Once he's secured, I tell them to leave.

I snap my fingers to warm up and, in the meantime, study the face of the bastard.

Looking at him, no one would guess the kind of fucked-up sicko he is.

With his well-groomed hair, trimmed beard, and a face slightly damaged at the moment—as expected—he would look like a respectable man in a fine suit, not a sadistic torturer of young girls.

As I circle around his body, I notice he's already been given a "warm welcome" by his compatriots, and not in a very affectionate way.

"Ruslan's orders?" I ask myself as I see blood oozing from his ass. Probably. My grandfather favors an eye for an eye, and although Ayrtom didn't rape Taisiya, he treated her like a punching bag.

"I could introduce myself, but I'm not much for small talk. So, you piece of shit, let's get to work."

I grab one of the knives that have been laid out and watch his swollen eyes widen.

"You're not Russian. Why are you here?"

"I'm Ruslan's grandson. So, you could say I have Russian blood, although I prefer my Irish one. Now, let's clarify something: there will be no conversation. I'm not going to kill you because someone else in line needs to honor the family, but there's nothing you can say that will stop me from hurting you." I pause. "Just like you hurt Taisiya."

By the look of desperation he gives, it seems no one has had the courtesy to explain why he's here.

I need to make him understand that everything that's going to happen in the next few hours is retaliation for her.

I know how to inflict pain without making a wound fatal and start slicing the back of both his heels.

He howls in despair, and when I look back at him, he begs me to leave him alone.

"You ruined her back. The doctor told me that even with surgery, it will never be what it was before. You beat a child, you bastard, and for your fucking luck, she survived. I found her, and now you're going to pay for all the pain you caused."

His eyes scan my face, and I can almost hear his brain spinning, looking for an escape, but he knows he's already dead.

I move to the back of his body and slice the soles of his feet.

"Fuuuuuuck! Just kill me already, you Irish piece of shit!"

I drop the knife for a moment and spend about five minutes turning his ribs into a punching bag. A good training for the fight in a few weeks.

"Don't insult my homeland. That would make my aunt sad."

I switch the knife for a pair of pliers and begin one of the most painful and effective tortures: pulling out nails.

"I know you have an accomplice," I say, before pulling out the first one. "I want his name."

"I don't... Aaaaaah, fuck!"

"We both know you'll tell me, it's just a matter of when. I'm not in a hurry, Ayrtom."

And he did. Exactly forty-five minutes later, I had everything I needed, but unfortunately, I had to stop playing with him. I had tried everything non-lethal.

I have to keep my word and leave the bastard for Maxim.

Leaving the warehouse was one of the hardest things I've ever had to do because all I could see in front of me was Taisiya's innocent face.

I can still feel the raised marks of the lashes on her back on the tips of my fingers.

I want to kill him so badly, and to keep my word, I clean the tools I used on him to remove fingerprints with the chemicals left there for that purpose, and then drop them on the floor.

"We'll meet in a few years in hell, you piece of shit. When it happens, you'll be mine. I'll spend eternity causing you pain."

I KNOW THAT BEFORE going to where we're keeping Ayrtom, Maxim visited her. I also know that Taisiya was sleeping. She hasn't left her room since she overheard my conversation with Cillian, and I, who never understood shit about depression, told Ruslan that she needed to talk to someone because even for me, who's a damn insensitive prick, she's not okay.

I'm not the type to not know what to do or hesitate about anything, but this time, I'm lost.

I asked my grandfather if we should let her talk to Anastacia, but he told me that if I think she's depressed, it would be better for Taisiya to speak with a psychologist first.

I enter the house and nod to my men, who are playing cards in the living room.

The bodyguards my grandfather insisted I use are outside. I've been around Russians more in this past week than my entire life. I need a break.

"Where is she?" I ask.

"Upstairs," Keiron says. "By the way, she hasn't come down all day."

I head straight to my room, which is on the same floor as hers. Although I've already left the bloodstained clothes behind to be incinerated, I decide to take another shower before going to look for her.

I still feel filthy.

I've never had a problem with the "hands-on" part of my job, but I don't want Taisiya to have any contact, even indirectly, with that son of a bitch. Not even through me.

Twenty minutes later, I knock on her door, but no one answers. I'm about to open it when a laugh from the stairs catches my attention.

I know it's her, but who is she laughing with? Taisiya hasn't spoken to anyone since we came here, and now she's laughing?

From the top of the stairs, I see that she's talking with Keiron. What's surprising, however, is that *both* are smiling, and my soldier isn't exactly the cheerful type.

"I came to look for you in your room," I say, with her still facing away from me.

I don't know if she had already guessed I was coming closer, but when she turns to face me, the smile fades.

"I didn't know you wanted to talk to me."

"I always want to talk to you... to check if you need anything."

She averts her gaze.

"Thanks, but when I need something, they take care of it," she says, nodding toward Keiron.

"I thought you might like some company for dinner."

My cousins would laugh their asses off if they heard me suggesting something like that because I'm not the type to have meals at the table, except for Aunt Orla's Sunday lunches.

"I'm not going to dinner, thanks."

"You can go," I say to Keiron, not wanting him to continue overhearing our conversation. Once he leaves, I continue: "You need to eat."

"I am eating. I already had an apple. Is it part of your duties to check if I've eaten?"

"I'm not going to apologize for the conversation you overheard in the office. I said nothing but the truth. I'm keeping a promise I made to my grandfather. That's the only reason I'm here. I'm not Russian. What the hell would I be doing in Moscow if it weren't for you?"

"Keiron said that a man, Anastacia's husband, was here earlier. I was sleeping. He's leaving, you're free."

"He'll be back in the United States in a few days. I'll be the one to take you to Anastacia when the documents are ready."

"Does she already know that you found me?"

"Yes."

She nods and starts to head up the stairs, probably back to her room.

"Aren't you coming down?"

"I changed my mind."

"What's wrong?"

"Nothing. Why are you insisting? You've made it clear that you don't want me around. I'm not your friend, I'm your guardian, and I'm here out of obligation. All understood. I made a mental note. I've lost my memory, but I'm sure it hasn't affected my ability to understand. Now, if you'll excuse me."

Yes, I should let her go, but I'm at my limit.

After everything that happened today, from what I extracted from Stepanchikov during the torture session, the need to protect her has tripled.

"I'm not giving you permission."

"What do you want?"

"Company. Let's have dinner."

"You want my company?" she says, as if I've suggested something absurd, which might not be too far from the truth.

"Come on, Taisiya. I'm starving and I get a hell of a mood when I don't eat."

"So this is your cheerful side, then?"

"You almost fooled me, looking like a well-behaved girl."

"I'm almost an adult, not a girl. As for good behavior, I just asked a question," she says, masking a smile.

After what I discovered today, I know these moments will be increasingly rare when she regains her memory, so on impulse, I pull her into my arms. It's her turn to be stiff, but seconds later, she relaxes with a sigh.

"I like you," she says. "Don't ask me why, because I must be crazy, but I like you, Thor."

Thor.

I shake my head, laughing inside at her impudence.

"Until we get back," I say.

"What?"

"I'm proposing a friendship contract until we get back to the United States. After that, we'll go our separate ways."

She lifts her beautiful face to look at me and gives me a smile.

"I accept the deal. I'll be the best friend you've ever had."

"You'll be the only one," I think.

If she knew about the kinds of relationships I have with women, aside from my aunt, she'd run away. She doesn't remember that she wanted to be a nun, but I do. However, Taisiya is not at any risk. She's just a girl who needs protection, and that, I can provide.

Chapter 18

Lorcan

The next day

I listen as Taisiya's brother-in-law recounts what he learned during his "conversation" with Ayrtom.

I know he's aware that I, like his men, had our time with the bastard before he arrived. The deal was to leave him alive for Maxim, aware of the pain he would inflict.

"So, the stepmother schemed to have her stepdaughter given in marriage to the bastard?"

He nods, agreeing.

"She knew the son of a bitch was a pervert with twisted sexual tastes, and still, she conspired to get rid of her stepdaughter," he says, his jaw clenched with rage. "She didn't want Ana to marry and leave the house; she wanted her to suffer because she hated her, jealous of Timofey's first wife, Ana's mother. Ana looked like her mother, I found out. That's why Kristina hated her so much."

"But the plans went off track when her father allowed her to study at the convent?" I ask, remembering what Ruslan told me.

"Exactly. And Ayrtom blamed his cousin, Kristina. Contrary to what Ruslan believed, he knew Anastacia wasn't in the house anymore. He planned to capture Taisiya first, then my wife. Torture them one in front of the other, and then eliminate the younger one."

"That's why she wasn't raped? He was waiting to do that in front of his wife?" I ask, wishing I could go back and make him scream in pain again.

Damn!

"Yes. I have no doubt that, in the end, both would have suffered the same, but he was sadistic. He wanted Ana to watch her sister's suffering for daring to try to escape the marriage contract by moving to the convent until she turned eighteen."

"Anyway, he took a huge risk for revenge."

"I don't think it was just revenge. At first, it might have been, but later he must have become obsessed with possessing both, making one sister experience the other's suffering."

"But he hasn't made any move since Taisiya was rescued by Abramov."

"No. He confessed that when Taisiya escaped, he was afraid of being tracked by the Organization, so he stayed in the shadows for three years. He married someone else and waited until he could safely pursue Anastacia again."

"And the dead nun?"

"He did that to scare her. Frustrated because Ana, even within the convent, was heavily monitored, by Ruslan's orders."

"He intended to take her to Siberia, then? I can't believe he'd be stupid enough to return to where he kept Taisiya prisoner."

"No, not there," he says, taking a sip of whiskey. We're sitting in Ruslan's library. "But he held a high position within the Organization. He must have had other hideouts."

I know that Maxim, unlike me, who made the bastard confess everything without any aids, used a truth serum on Ayrtom.

He needed details about the miserable's plan—which didn't concern me—to know if Anastacia would still be at risk in the future. I only care about Taisiya. It's no longer Ayrtom who interests me, but his accomplice. Once Ruslan arrives in Russia, we'll discuss this.

"With my 'encouragement,'" he says, referring to the drug he administered, "freed from his inhibitions, the depraved man revealed what he planned for her. The idea was to make my wife a prisoner forever, using her whenever he wanted."

"And now, what will happen?"

"I have to go back to the United States, but I ordered that he not be killed until a month has passed. For thirty days, he will receive the same treatment he wanted to inflict on the two sisters. The man responsible for being his 'companion' is used to this kind of care and can be quite creative."

"And what about the execution method?"

"I've ordered him to be burned alive when the time comes. He'll suffer the same fate as my father-in-law."

WE ENTER THE ORGANIZATION'S clinic together.

Last night, Taisiya woke up screaming from a nightmare. It had never happened since I brought her to Moscow, and I didn't know what to do when she panicked, saying she remembered the "house." I have no doubt she was referring to the place where she was kept prisoner.

I called the doctor, and he told me I should bring her in to be examined. In the end, she spent the rest of the night here.

As soon as we arrive, she smiles. Maxim looks confused because his sister-in-law doesn't recognize him. When he realizes she's smiling at me, however, he scowls.

Taisiya doesn't notice his bad mood, her freckled face and bright eyes making it seem as if seeing me made her day better.

"I'll wait outside," I say, but I don't close the door when I reach the hallway and stay close enough to hear their conversation.

Brother-in-law or not, she's mine for now.

I can't say I've fulfilled the promise to become friends because I'm not sure how to make it work, but we have dinner together every night, and she talks non-stop, asking me a million questions.

Strangely, since I'm not one for small talk, spending time with her doesn't tire me, and sometimes I even find myself having to stifle a laugh at her curiosity.

"Are you also friends with Grandpa?" she asks Maxim.

Her voice sounds childlike, and I've noticed it always happens when she feels insecure around someone. When she's with me, she acts more relaxed, but with a stranger, it's as if she mentally regresses.

"He's not your grandfather," Maxim says, although I've already told him that she knows this.

"I know he's not. But he saved me from that house," she replies, as after last night's dream, she remembers her captivity.

When we have to face the authorities, since after being presumed dead for three years she will have to "come back to life," Ruslan said the story to be told is that she was found disoriented and doesn't remember anything. A half-truth without pointing fingers. The police could never give Stepanchikov the punishment he deserves, and besides, we prefer to handle the revenge ourselves.

"What do you remember from there?" he asks.

"Nothing. I just know I was imprisoned and hurt, and still, I pieced together the story. The doctor examined my back, and I dreamed of the house and the chains I was kept in last night."

"Do you know who hurt you?"

"No. Who are you? You didn't introduce yourself."

"I'm your brother-in-law. I'm your sister's husband, Anastacia."

"I have a sister?"

"Yes, you do. Didn't they tell you about her?"

"Kind of. They told me about Anastacia and that she sent for me. I assumed she was my sister, but I still can't believe it. For so long, it's just been me and Grandpa."

"Anastacia is very eager to see you. Would you like that?"

"And my Grandpa? Will he be okay alone? They won't hurt him, right?"

"I'll make sure he is," Maxim reassures her, reinforcing what I had already promised her.

"Do I have a father and mother?"

She's seeking confirmation of what she had already asked me. I never directly said they were dead, only that I didn't have any family.

"No, they're deceased, but you have your sister, and she adores you. We want you to come live with us, Taisiya."

"That blonde man out there, Lorcan, the day he came to our cabin and pointed a gun at my Grandpa, he also called me that. Is that my name? I haven't seen any documents to prove it."

"Yes. That is your real name."

"You're my sister's husband," she repeats his words, and I can hear her footsteps as she approaches the Russian.

"I am."

"What's your name?"

"Maxim."

"If I agree to go with you, Maxim, will you promise that whoever hurt me won't do it again?"

"Never again, little girl. You're safe now. I won't allow anyone to hurt you again."

"I believe your word."

Chapter 19

Taisiya

"Why didn't you stay in the clinic room when Maxim came?" "Because he's your relative, I'm not. I wanted to give you privacy, despite..." He pauses, and I could almost swear he's smiling.

I said he looked like Thor, but that's not true. The giant blonde is much more handsome.

"I heard everything from outside."

"Oh my God, that wasn't polite, sir," I say, nudging him with my elbow.

I'm feeling happy because half an hour after Maxim left, the doctor said I could go home. I've concluded that I hate hospitals.

"I've never been mistaken for someone polite, Taisiya. I'm usually called rude."

"Not with me, because we're friends."

"We're not. It's a temporary friendship arrangement."

"I don't care how long, Lorcan. For now, you're my best friend."

"But you asked him for protection," he says as we reach the garage.

I shiver, and he notices. Before I can blink, he takes off his leather jacket and puts it on me.

"Thank you."

He shrugs with that "few words" attitude I'm starting to get used to.

"Did you overhear my conversation with Maxim? Is that why you asked if I requested his protection?"

"Yes, I heard everything."

"That man, my sister's husband, wants to take me to live with him and Anastacia. I won't have Grandpa or you around. I have no choice but to trust this new family I don't even know. So yes, I asked him to protect me. Especially now that I remember the place where I was kept prisoner."

"What do you remember?"

"I don't want to talk in front of them," I say, referring to the bodyguards. "Can we talk when we get home?"

"Sure."

I get in the back of the car, and he follows me.

I notice the security not only in the vehicle we're in, in the front seats, but also in the cars around us. There are so many that I feel like we're royalty.

"Your voice changed when you were talking to Maxim," he says, after checking if my seatbelt is fastened.

"Changed?"

"Yes. It became more childlike. Different from when you talk to me."

"It wasn't intentional. Do you think it could be because of the memory loss, as if I were two different people?"

"I don't know, Taisiya, I don't understand anything about psychology. My mind is linear. I want something, I take it. Something displeases me, I destroy it."

I look at him to see if he's joking.

He's not. Lorcan never jokes. He seems to speak intentionally about everything.

"Was that what you did the day we agreed to be friends?"

"What?"

"The night you found me on the stairs talking to Keiron, the knuckles of your fingers were injured." I take one of his hands and bring it to my lap, gently stroking the scars. "They're still injured."

He doesn't try to pull his hand away but keeps it closed in a fist.

"What do you want to know, Taisiya? Ask me directly."

"You said when something displeases you, you destroy it. Does that apply to everything? Does it mean you're a violent man?"

"Only when I need to be. Against enemies."

I stare at him, wanting to ask something but lacking the courage. And before I can decide, he says:

"I fight. In an MMA circuit, similar to the UFC. Do you know what that is? Much of the anger I keep inside, I release in the ring."

I'm at a loss for words for a moment, but then the image of a mustached man laughing and watching a competition of two guys fighting in a ring comes to mind.

"My father liked MMA."

"What?"

"He liked to watch the fights. I mean, I can't see his face, but I assume it's my father because I'm sure it's someone older. Maxim told me they're dead. Both of them. He didn't say how they died, though, but I..."

"What?"

"I'm starting to piece together the clues. They're not memories, just logical deduction. Did you get upset with the questions I asked him?"

"About your name actually being Taisiya?"

"Yes, and about Anastacia being my sister. You have to understand that I only have your word and that man who spoke to me, Ruslan, that I am indeed Taisiya. They didn't even show me the DNA test results."

"I wasn't upset. You're right not to trust me."

The driver parks the car at the house where we're staying, and after helping me out, he walks beside me.

"I didn't say I don't trust you. Just that I wanted to be sure of the truth." I stop walking and look at him. "I feel guilty, Lorcan."

"Guilty about what?"

"When Maxim told me my parents were dead, I didn't grieve because I don't remember them. I know I should feel sadness because they were my parents, but I don't even remember their faces. How can I miss people I don't remember?"

He puts an arm around my shoulder and pulls me close.

It's not enough, and I hide my face in his chest, sobbing softly.

"Don't force yourself. Your memory will come back."

"And when it does, will I suffer?"

"I don't know if you're ready to hear the answer."

"I don't want you to lie to me. You're my safe harbor now. I need something to hold on to or I'll drown, Lorcan. When I had the nightmare last night, I panicked. The images were jumbled. The dirty house. Darkness and chains. Nothing more than that, but I know from the marks on my back that when the memories return, I'll suffer."

"I can't take that away from you, Taisiya. I don't have the power to erase your memories or stop them from coming back completely, but I'll always be just a phone call away."

"Why not be present, by my side?"

"You're not ready yet to know who we are, little one. At some point, everything will become clear."

Chapter 20

Taisiya

A Few Days Later

Lorcan had to travel, and now, in addition to the Russians and Irishmen who watch over me, there are two women, nurses, staying at the house. I think he sent them because, even though he trusts his men, he doesn't want me to be alone with them.

Lorcan calls me before I go to sleep to check if I'm okay or if I've had nightmares. Despite what he said before, that our friendship was temporary, I think that when I go to the United States, we'll still be friends.

Yesterday, the man who spoke to me on the phone while I was still in Siberia, Ruslan, called to say that my paperwork for going to the United States was ready. I felt both sad and happy at the same time.

Happy because I will finally meet my sister, and sad because I will be even farther from Grandpa Abramov.

I called him and asked how he was. We talked for almost an hour, and when I hung up, I concluded that he seemed fine, despite the usual pains.

One day I plan to go back to visit him, and I hope Anastacia agrees to it. I found out through Ruslan that she is the older one of us two, so, theoretically, she is in charge of me.

Today, we're going to talk on the phone for the first time. It was only this morning that I learned that it was the medical team and also the psychologist I've been consulting with for a few days who didn't authorize us to speak earlier, fearing that Anastacia might tell me something I wasn't ready to know yet.

I hold the cell phone tightly. I'm very nervous.

I press the screen to complete the video call, and the seconds it takes for her to appear on the other side make me so anxious that I feel nauseous.

When I finally see the girl from my dreams in front of me, I become so agitated that I end up spouting a huge amount of words without any idea of what I'm saying.

"Anastacia? Hello. Your husband told me we are sisters."

My God, is that how you greet someone?

She looks at me in silence, and as the initial anxiety starts to fade, I study her face calmly.

The golden hair, her trademark in my dreams. The eyes identical to mine are now filled with tears. Somehow, it feels wrong.

Anastacia crying, I mean.

And then, a memory comes back.

I close my eyes for a moment and clearly see a raven flying over our heads. We're outside a house, talking.

Ana saying that ravens were signs of bad omens, according to our grandmother.

My sister is superstitious, I'm sure, and really believed in that.

I laughed in response, mocking that there was no scientific evidence against the poor bird.

And then, in my recollection, she starts talking.

"Papa will never allow it, and besides, it will ruin my dreams of being a famous ballerina and traveling, performing all over the world," Ana said.

I looked at her pityingly because I knew she would never fulfill that dream because... we are mafia princesses.

My God!

Mafia.

We were raised in the Russian mafia!

I force myself to focus on the memories.

We have no choice about marriage, and it's certain. It will happen as soon as we turn eighteen. Maybe sooner. So, her plans to travel with a ballet corps were unrealistic.

"You'll never know if you don't try, Ana," I told her.

"Taisiya, you're the one who wants to be a nun, not me. Although you'd be the craziest nun in the country."

I wanted to be a nun? So we are Roman Catholics and not Orthodox, like most of the Russian population? And how do I know that?

Information begins to flood my brain, like a storm that can't be contained.

She continues speaking, in my memory, about how I wish to be a bride of Christ, but that she wants a different life for herself.

"You won't be a nun, you silly," I joked. *"You'll just pretend to want to be one and then, later, you can escape the country."*

"You definitely aren't okay, sister. Where would I go? Daddy would bring me back in no time and be very angry."

"As if he gets angry with you for more than five minutes, huh? If the Organization's men knew how good he is to us, they wouldn't fear him so much."

"For your mother, he would be stricter."

My mother? So we're not daughters of the same mother?

"I'm sorry, sister. I shouldn't have said that."

"It's okay. I love you out of obligation, but I know that Mom is very cruel to you."

Oh my God!

"Why bring up the convent story just today?" she asked.

"I don't want to tell you the reason to avoid making you sad."

"Impossible. I'm the smiley girl. I need to be in order to show off my gap-toothed grin. It's my charm," she said, and I laughed. *"Tell me what's wrong, Taisiya. I know you. You wouldn't bring up the convent without a reason."*

"I heard my mother talking to Daddy. She wants him to betroth you to one of her cousins."

"What?"

"He's also a member of the Organization. A high-ranking member, Ana. Daddy can't refuse because he's a great match, according to Mommy."

"Maybe this man, my future husband, will let me continue dancing and performing in theaters here in Moscow," she said, sounding resigned, because she knew we had no control over our own lives. *"Not for the money, just for the pleasure."*

"He won't let you, Ana."

"Why do you say that?"

"Because I heard him talking to Mommy. He wants heirs as soon as they're married."

She shuddered as if she felt disgust, and now I understand our conversation. I'm trying to convince my sister to escape with me to a convent to avoid an arranged marriage.

"How old is he?" she asked.

"Much older than our father. I'd guess around sixty."

"Oh my God!"

"That's why I'm suggesting the convent alternative. Say we'll go together."

"Daddy will never fall for that. He knows I don't want to be a nun."

"Calm down, I have it all planned. You'll tell him that you want to live in the convent to be near me, but that as soon as you turn eighteen, you'll leave to get married. Once we're there, you'll run away."

"Are you feverish? You must be delirious, Taisiya. I wouldn't survive a day on the streets. We were raised as true ladies, we know nothing about the world."

"I know, Ana, but you need to trust me. We'll figure something out. I can't let you go live with that man. He makes my stomach turn."

"What aren't you telling me?"

"This Ayrtom isn't a good person, Anastacia."

"How do you know that?"

"The things he and my mother talked about... I didn't understand much, but I didn't like what I did understand. Mommy doesn't want what's best for you. This marriage won't benefit you."

"Then why would Daddy allow such a thing?"

"You know the reason. The Organization always comes first. It's above family, even."

"You seem older than me. More prepared for the world, too. How is that possible?"

I remember Ana always saying that I seemed more mature than she was.

"Our cook said the other day that I'm an old soul. She was explaining to me, away from Mommy's ears, some of her beliefs, and she told me that in her religion, people reincarnate, so she's sure I'm in my last reincarnation because my heart is old for my age."

"You're an angel, Taisiya. If I go away, if this crazy plan to escape actually works, I'll die of longing. Not seeing you anymore will be like losing half my heart."

"It's only until you're safe. Then you can come back to find me."

"It's not what I dreamed for myself. Not the convent and definitely not a husband. I want a stage and my ballet slippers."

"Trust in God. You'll have all that. Let's go together to talk to Daddy. He won't deny us this request. That way, we'll have three years to figure out what to do. Who knows, by then, he might find another bride and you'll be free?"

"I won't be free forever. You will only achieve this because your calling to faith is true, just as mine is to dance, but even if it isn't this Ayrtom, at some point, I will be promised in marriage to another man."

"Let's not think too far ahead. One day at a time; the most important thing is that you know I will always love and protect you, Ana. Even if we're far apart, I will protect you."

"Taisiya?" Anastacia calls, bringing me back to the present.

When I open my eyes, she's crying, and my heart aches.

I can't hide what I'm feeling as I look at my sister. I don't remember much beyond this conversation we had in the past, but I know I am in front of the most important person in my life.

"Don't cry, Ana. You are the smiling girl."

"You remember."

"Not everything. Just one of our conversations. I wanted to be a nun, and you, a ballerina. Neither of us got what we wanted."

"Let's talk about that in due time, sister. For now, I just need you to promise me you're okay."

"I am, but I'm also sad that I don't remember anything."

We talk for about half an hour, and she asks me general questions, nothing about the past, although I think she wants to know much more but is holding back.

"I hope that when I meet her, my memory will return."

"Don't push yourself. The psychologist said it's not good to do that."

"I'm not in a hurry to remember, but I need to tell you something."

"What?"

"When your husband came to see me, he talked about me moving in with you, but I'm still confused. Very much so, Ana. And it got worse after I remembered I wanted to be a nun. So, I've just decided that I want to join a convent."

"Oh my God, Taisiya, I don't want to be separated from you now that we've finally found each other."

"It doesn't have to be far from your home, but you need to understand that I am very frightened by everything. I need some time alone to clear my head. I don't think living with you and your husband will help with that."

"Can we leave the decision until after you arrive in the United States?"

I nod in agreement, just to keep her from being sad, because inside, I already know what I want and I'm not changing my mind.

Chapter 21

Lorcan

"Are you telling me that you managed to get from Ayrtom that he had an accomplice and didn't tell Maxim anything?"

I shrug.

"His revenge was against Stepanchikov, and he already got it. I want this second man. I will take care of him personally."

"What are you not telling me, my grandson?" Ruslan asks. "Who is this son of a bitch? Someone from the Organization?"

"No. He has a connection to Ayrtom, but if the bastard hadn't confessed who he was, we would never have guessed. I looked him up. He's someone completely off the radar."

"Why didn't Maxim find out about the accomplice? I know he administered the truth serum on the bastard."

"Because he didn't ask the right questions. Maxim didn't suspect the accomplice. I was the one who came to that conclusion after Abramov told me she wasn't beaten every day. If Ayrtom had been with Taisiya throughout the entire month she was imprisoned, he would have killed her, considering the cruelty he showed. It wasn't him, but there had to be someone who fed her and gave her water, or she would have died of thirst and starvation."

"I don't like mysteries."

"It's not a mystery, grandfather. Trust me. The man who was there is someone famous and hard to reach, but I'll catch him as soon as I ensure she's safe."

"And how the hell was he related to Ayrtom?"

"He came to Russia on vacation. They are related by affinity. He was here by chance, and the son of a bitch Stepanchikov decided to let his friend have some fun with her, torturing her too, just to pass the time."

"Damn sickos. But he took a risk. The accomplice could have sexually abused her."

"No, because Ayrtom threatened him. He needed Taisiya intact to cause even more suffering to Anastacia when she was captured. He wanted her to see the younger sister lose her innocence."

Ruslan makes a hand gesture and grabs his phone. He speaks briefly in Russian, then hangs up.

"What happened?"

"What I ordered for Ayrtom was not enough. I knew he was a damn depraved bastard, but not this much. He will spend every remaining hour on this planet screaming in pain. I asked them not to rush his death. I want him conscious and suffering. His screams will be a tribute to the two sisters."

"I WANTED TO TALK TO you," she says, without looking at me, as soon as I enter the house.

Ruslan went to a meeting with Organization associates, and I went straight to see her.

Just to check if she's okay, of course. Taisiya will be my responsibility for a few days from now. Soon, she'll be reunited with her family.

"So, you waited up for me?"

She shrugs.

"It's not that late. I don't sleep before eleven anyway. Have you had dinner?"

"I had a sandwich."

"So you're not in a bad mood then?"

I move closer and tuck a strand of her hair behind her ear. She still doesn't look me in the eyes, and I wonder why.

"Not enough to kill someone," I say, partly joking, partly serious.

"But that wouldn't be unusual for you, right?"

I furrow my brow, trying to understand where that's coming from.

"What do you mean?"

"I talked to my sister on the phone yesterday."

"Yes, I heard. How did it go?"

"In the middle of the call with Anastacia, I remembered a scene from the past. A conversation we had at our home. I was planning a way to save my sister from a marriage of convenience."

"I knew that. Go on."

"It was a crazy plan. She would hide in a convent with me for three years, and then I would try to help her escape."

"What? I knew you planned to go to the convent together, but I didn't realize the intention was to escape. How did you think you could pull off something like that, Taisiya? You were practically children."

"I don't know. I don't have answers for you, just that I overheard a conversation about Ana's future marriage to a much older man and knew my sister would be unhappy. However, that wasn't what made me more agitated."

"Remembering your sister and those plans, you mean?"

"Yes. What's tying my mind in knots is that I discovered both Anastacia and I are Russian mafia princesses. That's why my sister would never have a choice about her husband. She would have to marry that man if our father decided so. My plan was born out of sheer desperation."

"Do you understand now why I said we can't be friends?"

"No."

"You belong to the Russian mafia elite, Taisiya, and I belong to the Irish. We are enemies."

She pales.

"If that's true, how could you come after me?"

"It was a temporary pact between the organizations, just a personal favor for Ruslan, but it's short-term. It will end as soon as we return to the United States."

"I don't want that."

"There's no choice in the matter. You can't go against your family for a friendship."

"It's not just any friendship, it's you."

"You barely know me. Don't create fantasies in your head. I'm no saint."

"Are you evil? I don't care. You already have a piece of my heart, Thor."

I pull her into a hug, and for a few seconds, we stay like that.

"Live your life. You're young and have already had years of it stolen. Enjoy from here on out."

"I'll never be able to enjoy anything. There's a shadow in my past. Something I fear and don't remember, but that threatens to explode at any moment. I don't want to say goodbye to you, Lorcan."

I pull away and take a step back.

"Your wants count very little. As you said, you're a Russian mafia princess. We come from different worlds."

"That's not all."

"What?"

"There's more behind it. You don't want me around. Why? Is there a girlfriend who'll get jealous? If so, tell her I'm just a silly and needy girl."

"There's no one. I'm not dating, I... I just go out with women. No commitments or ties."

"Oh! In that case, there's nothing stopping us."

"Aside from two criminal organizations, of course," I say sarcastically, "but that's nothing much."

Her beautiful face now shows anger.

"You don't want my friendship. You don't even want to try to make it work. Fine, I don't need it anyway. Not for where I'm going. You didn't even wait for me to finish talking before saying 'no.' I didn't just come to tell you about my call with Anastacia, but that I've decided that when I return to the United States, I will follow my initial plan and join the convent. I'll be a nun, so as you see, I won't be part of any mafia."

I try to mask the shock her declaration causes me. Of course, I knew about her plans before the tragedy destroyed her life, but it never crossed my mind that she would still want to become a nun.

"You don't need to go to a convent. Your sister said she would take care of you."

"Yes, she did, and I plan to stay close to Ana, but I also need to be alone for a bit. Forget what I told you before, Lorcan. It wouldn't work anyway. Brides of Christ and mobsters aren't friends."

Chapter 22

Lorcan

"She's very quiet," Ruslan says.

About an hour ago, Taisiya asked us for permission to go to the plane's suite.

"She must be contemplating life, the future," I offer as a cover.

He makes a face of disgust.

"Given everything she's been through, I understand she'd want to retreat to the convent, but I'd prefer if she stayed with us."

"She's almost of legal age. She has the right to choose."

"You know perfectly well that, being who she is, the choice isn't really in her hands. I think she should see a psychologist or something and then, make a good marriage."

"What?"

"It's the norm. She's young and beautiful. I'd like her to put the past behind her. Turn the page and move on."

"She doesn't want to get married."

"How do you know that?"

"She's still a little girl."

"Ana got married with just one year more than she is now."

"But from what you told me, it was initially a marriage for her protection."

"It ended up being very real. She and Maxim are happy. They're good for each other. It's the natural order: be born, procreate, die. It's part of the life cycle."

"No."

"No, what?"

"This kind of arrangement isn't right for Taisiya."

He looks at me as if he sees more than I'm putting into words.

"Are you interested in her?"

"Of course not. She's a child."

"Well, Maxim is practically twenty years older than Anastacia. But it's not just because of that you're not right for Taisiya; it's because hell would break loose if there was a marriage between you two. Yerik and Cillian would go mad."

"I'm not applying to be anyone's husband, much less a Russian princess's."

"You have feelings for her. Will you deny it?"

"I neither deny nor confirm. I've formed a bond because I consider Taisiya my ward. If we weren't who we are, I would continue to visit her to make sure she's okay."

"I can arrange that if you think it will do you both good."

The idea is tempting, but I keep a stoic expression.

"It wouldn't work. As you said, Yerik and Cillian would hate our closeness."

"Taisiya is a neutral element. A Russian princess who's going to become a nun isn't much use to the Organization. We'd only be concerned if she were to marry. If she changed her mind about the convent, then we'd have to find a suitable candidate."

I stand up because this conversation is driving me crazy.

I wasn't happy when she told me she was going to join a convent, but the idea of her marrying some Russian bastard is even worse.

"What's wrong?" he asks.

"Nothing. I think I need to fight. I get like this when the moment approaches, and I have a fight coming up soon."

He looks at me as if he didn't believe a word I said.

"Whether she's going to the convent or not, we'll have to keep an eye on her not only while this war against the Mexicans lasts but until you catch Ayrtom's accomplice as well. I'm giving you a vote of confidence, Lorcan, believing you'll eliminate that bastard."

"He's already dead, Grandpa. He just doesn't know it yet."

"Do you want a drink?" he asks. "You look like a caged lion."

That's exactly how I'm feeling, and I can't even explain why.

Before I can respond, we hear a cry, and I start to walk toward the back of the plane.

"You shouldn't go into her room."

"I shouldn't even be here in the first place, and yet, you're the one who assigned me to this mission, Ruslan. Until I hand her over to Anastacia, Taisiya is mine."

I don't wait for a response and enter the room.

She's in bed, tossing and turning in the middle of a nightmare.

"Hey," I call, sitting down and pulling her into my arms. The first time this happened, I didn't know what to do, but this is already the third time I've witnessed it.

"No." The denial isn't for me, I know. It's for whoever is hurting her. Her voice sounds low and weak because in her mind, she's still trapped there.

"I've got you, little one. No one will hurt you again."

I repeat this while running my hand over her back until I feel her body relax against mine. She doesn't wake up, and I should lay her down again and leave, but I don't.

In a few hours, we'll be saying goodbye, so I throw common sense to hell and lean back against the bed's guard with her in my arms.

I dry the tear-streaked cheeks and watch the face that looks as if it was crafted by a sculptor, so perfect. Her long, dark eyelashes, darker than her hair, are closed, but I don't think she's asleep. She's just letting me hold her, though we both know I shouldn't be here.

"I'll keep sending you messages," she says, without opening her eyes. "I don't care if you reply or not. I'll do it anyway because I need to know you're on the other side."

"Just because I won't be there doesn't mean I won't think of you, Taisiya. Do you really think I'll forget you?"

"I'll be fine. I'll be imprisoned this time, by choice."

"Why go there?"

"Because it's my calling. Besides, what's left for me outside?"

"Anastacia."

"My sister is newly married. Soon, she'll have her own family. I need to take care of myself."

"Open your eyes."

"No. It's easier to talk this way. I feel braver."

"You're fucking brave. Don't let anyone convince you otherwise."

"I don't feel brave and I don't care about that. I'll serve God and try to deal with the past when the memory comes back."

"Don't send me messages. You'll get into trouble with your brother-in-law."

She opens her eyes, and for a moment, I say nothing, focused on all the blue-green hues of her iris.

"Say you don't want me to send messages because you don't care about me."

"That would be a lie."

"You don't lie?"

"If necessary, yes. But only about business, not about my personal life."

"Say you don't care about me, Lorcan."

"I care about you."

"Then I'll keep sending you messages until the day I die. You don't need to reply. I just want to share my day with you."

"After you become a nun, will you be able to have a phone?" I ask, more to steer the conversation away from the dangerous path it's heading. I don't want to analyze what she said because her stubbornness, instead of annoying me, makes warmth spread in my cold chest.

She smiles.

"I don't know. If they forbid it, you'll have to put your mafia skills to use and find a way to get one to me."

"Will you be a sinful nun?"

"For trafficking a phone to talk to you? Maybe."

"Alright, here are the rules. Never call me. Send messages instead."

"Why?"

"I might be in the middle of an operation. I don't want to put you at risk if I get caught."

"I'll send short messages then: 'hey, I'm alive.'

"No. Since you're going to send them, I want more details. And, most importantly, whenever you remember something and can't deal with it, tell me."

"For what?"

"Because maybe you won't be able to handle everything alone. The memories, I mean. And I'll share them with you."

Chapter 23

Taisiya

It might be madness in my head, but the man who is my sister's godfather, Ruslan, has been looking from me to his grandson as if he's thinking about something since we got off the plane.

During the car ride to his house, where I'll meet Anastacia, he asked me questions about my vocation: if I remembered that in the past I wanted to be a nun; if I thought I'd be okay alone in a convent; if I'd prefer to wait a bit longer before moving there.

I told him the truth, that I didn't remember wanting to be a nun, except for the conversation with Anastacia. I don't know if I'll be okay, but I want to try, at least. And yes, I'd rather move right away than wait—I didn't confess it, but the truth is I'm afraid I'll lose my courage if I don't do it soon.

Even though my sister has shown a desire for me to stay with her, I don't want to be a dead weight to anyone.

After a few phone calls, I gradually got familiar with Anastacia, and the atmosphere between us is becoming more natural.

She wasn't very pleased when I said I hadn't changed my mind about the convent, but she was understanding when I told her I chose one near Boston, which will allow us to see each other frequently.

"I spoke with the Mother Superior of the convent you're moving to, Taisiya," Mr. Ruslan says, "and I asked her to be more flexible with you. You'll be able to leave whenever you want to see your sister."

I look at Lorcan, who is watching me silently.

"And can I have a cell phone?"

I see a corner of his mouth lift in a hidden smile, and then he shakes his head from side to side, unnoticed by his grandfather.

"I'll arrange that too. There's no way she can deny it. I won't allow you to be unreachable."

I could argue that I wouldn't be unreachable because there's probably a landline in the convent, but I keep quiet because I really want a cell phone to send messages to my reluctant best friend.

My God, I haven't even joined the Order yet, and I'm already sinning.

The elevator seems to take an eternity to reach the floor, and during that time, I'm thinking about the next steps in my life from now on.

Regardless of the convent, Anastacia has arranged for a psychologist for me to continue therapy. Apparently, she's from New York, works with a friend of Ana's, and will come to Boston once a week for us to talk.

She works exclusively with women from the Organization.

I now know that's the name of the Russian mafia my father was part of. My sister explained some things about it, mainly regarding our social conduct. The rest is a blank space for me.

I've already had an online consultation with this psychologist once, back in Russia, and when I asked her if there was a chance my memory would return, she said yes, but there's no way to determine when it will happen, as some traumatic events can be completely erased from our minds, and there's a good chance that's the case for me.

Unlike everyone else I've talked to, the psychologist told me I shouldn't feel obligated to do what others want. If I want to go to the convent, I should go. It was a relief to hear that, as everyone seems more than determined to make choices for me.

We finally reach the floor, and I see bodyguards outside the apartment. I've gotten used to them. They're everywhere.

The door to the apartment opens, and before I have time to brace myself, I'm face to face with my sister.

Neither of us speaks, examining each other eagerly, as we've only talked via video call once.

Ana is short, much smaller than I am, but otherwise, she's exactly like the girl from my dreams.

I don't know what to do, and I sigh with relief when she hugs me. It's not a loose hug, but one of those "I really want to hug you" kind, and my heart, which had been anxious throughout the trip, immediately calms down.

I can't return the hug, not because I don't want to, but because a strong surge of emotion paralyzes me.

Ana doesn't seem to mind. She strokes my hair and kisses my cheek.

Almost two minutes later, I finally relax and return the affection.

"I missed you, Ana."

"I missed you too. We have so much catching up to do."

"Anastacia," her godfather says, "I want you to meet my grandson, Lorcan. He's the one who brought Taisiya back to us."

After my sister kisses Ruslan's hand, she looks at Lorcan, but doesn't approach him.

In turn, he doesn't look at her either, but at me. He seems focused only on my face, as if only I existed.

"Nice to meet you, Lorcan," she says, and only then does he shift his gaze to her.

"Nice to meet you, Anastacia," he replies, without any emotion in his voice. "I have to go."

He comes over to where I am, and I release myself from Ana's arms.

He touches my chin, and I really want to hug him, but I feel shy because of the "witnesses."

"Are you going to be okay?" he asks.

I smile.

"I will. Don't forget what you promised me; I'll hold you to it."

"You have my word that I'll always answer your calls," he says, seeming indifferent to whether Ruslan and Ana are listening.

"But you won't come to see me."

He doesn't respond, and I try to pretend it doesn't sadden me.

He takes another step forward.

"I'll always be around, keeping watch. You know that, don't you?"

I nod and, stepping away from the others, lead him to the door we just came through.

"I thought our arrangement was supposed to be secret," I say as we reach the entrance of the apartment.

"I don't have to answer to anyone. It's just a phone call."

"One, no. Several. I had proposed messages. You mentioned calls. Now you can't go back."

"Send a message first, and never during the night."

"So you don't disturb girlfriends?" I ask playfully, but as the words come out, a murderous jealousy takes over me at the thought of him with someone.

"Why are you scrunching up your nose?"

"I was thinking of you with a girlfriend. I didn't like the idea. When you get married, I'll help choose the candidate."

"I'm never getting married, so don't worry. Now, promise me you'll tell me if you have those nightmares again."

"I promise. You're my best friend. How could I not tell you?"

"I'm not. We're colleagues. Just that."

"Best friend. Protector."

"You're a pest, Taisiya."

"I like you, Thor. My heart has already chosen you. I'll never leave you in peace."

I expected him to say something mocking, but instead, he surprises me:

"Don't leave me in peace."

"You can't be serious. I almost forced you to accept my friendship."

"Nobody forces me to do anything I don't want to."

"Speaking of doing, are you traveling again soon?"

"No. I have the fight, remember?"

On the plane, he told me about his sport, and I really wanted to go watch, but I think MMA doesn't suit a novice, especially given the Irish mafia. Ruslan explained that I now owe allegiance to Yerik, the Pakhan. I imagine he would never allow me to watch a fight of Lorcan's.

"No, I haven't forgotten. I wanted to watch, but since I won't be there, promise you'll win and record a message for me from inside the ring."

"Bloodied?"

"Oh my God! Do you get hurt?"

"No, princess. I don't get hurt much. I won't promise the message. I don't like videos. I'll feel a bit ridiculous doing that, but I can send you a photo of the knocked-out opponent."

I roll my eyes.

"Confident, huh?"

"Yes, I'm a horrible human being. You should run away."

"I won't. Our paths have crossed. I'll bother you forever."

He steps closer and holds my face with those huge hands.

"Take care, but if you're feeling overwhelmed, send me a message. I'll call back as soon as I can."

Chapter 24

Taisiya

"I'll be in the library," Ruslan says after I return, then leaves. "I'll leave you two to yourselves."

"Are you hungry?" my sister asks, and I force myself to return to the present, despite feeling a bit melancholic about Lorcan's departure.

Was that the last time I saw him?

"Yes, I barely ate on the plane. I could go for a hot chocolate."

Something tells me I've always loved sweets because every time I think of chocolate, my mouth waters.

"And a cake to go with it?"

My smile widens.

"That sounds perfect."

Half an hour later, the conversation is flowing even more naturally than on the phone, perhaps because I'm well-fed, but I think it's also because Anastacia is a genuinely easy person to like. Even though she seems careful in her speech, as if weighing each word, she smiles almost constantly. She touches and caresses. My sister is gradually making me remember her, if not through specific memories, then through her wonderful personality.

"You seem to like him," she says suddenly.

"Like who?" I ask, pretending not to understand.

"Lorcan."

"Oh!" I feel my cheeks flush. "Yes, he was very good to me and to my grandfather. Maxim too. Your husband is a great person."

I'm changing the subject because I don't want to share how I feel about Lorcan, not even with her.

"They're not superheroes, Taisiya. Not even my husband, who is wonderful to me, nor Lorcan."

"I don't think he's a hero. I just adore him."

"I don't want to play the wicked older sister, but you shouldn't adore him."

"Because he's in the Irish mafia?"

"Yes. Right now, we Russians and the Irish are not enemies, but that could change in an instant."

I know she's trying to look out for me, because in our conversations, Ana explained without going into details that we both grew up in a protective bubble created by our father, and now we're both alone in the world. Even though she has her husband, I intuitively understand that we need to stand on our own.

She told me she has matured a lot since arriving in Boston and that I'll also need to face the real world, even if I stay in the convent forever.

"Lorcan told me, as you yourself could verify, that he won't be able to visit me, but we'll talk on the phone, Ana. I don't have anyone besides you two, and I don't want to end my friendship with him."

She sighs.

"I'll tell Maxim about this to avoid problems."

"What's wrong with us being friends?"

"I don't know the details of the situation between the Organization and the Syndicate, Taisiya, but I know there's no friendship between them. Even for you two to talk on the phone, I'll have to get Maxim's permission."

"I don't want to discuss this. In a few days, I'll be where I've always wanted to be: serving God. These mafia war issues won't concern me."

I'm not giving up my friendship with Lorcan, but I don't want to turn my first meeting with my sister into a battlefield.

She looks at me as if she could read my mind but doesn't say anything more.

"Tell me about the convent you'll be going to. I'm glad you chose one in Boston."

I explain everything I've researched about the Order I'll be serving. She doesn't seem to be paying attention to what I'm saying, but rather to me.

After a while of letting me talk without asking questions, I say:

"I won't disappear from your life again, Ana. Don't be sad. I just need to fulfill at least one dream."

"I will never stop you from following your dreams, Taisiya, but my husband's job... which was like Papa's, requires that we stay protected, even if you live in a convent. There will be people watching over you and ensuring nothing happens to you."

"I'm not going to rebel against that. I just want to follow my vocation."

She agrees, though her face seems to say: *don't go, I need you with me.*

I want her close too, but I need some time alone first.

"In a few months, I'm getting married," she says.

"I thought you were already married."

"It's a long story. One you might not be ready to hear yet because it involves our past. It was a proxy marriage I had; now I want a real one, with a wedding dress. Will you come?"

"I wouldn't miss it for anything."

A Week Later

I WAS TAKEN TO ANA and Maxim's house the same night I arrived, but tomorrow, I will go to the convent.

I've been texting Lorcan every day. He doesn't write more than a word or two, but I don't accept his silence, and after enough persistence, the other day I even got a smiling emoji.

I don't mind if he's laughing at me; he's responding, which means our friendship deal is still on.

I'm at the window of my room when I hear footsteps.

When I turn to look, I see Ruslan.

He didn't return to Russia. He said he would only do so when I was in the convent. I learned from my sister that he alternates between our homeland, several cities in the U.S., and an island in the Caribbean.

"Thinking about something?"

"Yes, sir."

"May I ask what you're thinking about?"

"I don't know if I should say."

"Tell me, Taisiya," he commands, stepping inside.

"I'm thinking about your grandson. I miss Lorcan, but he told me I have to be obedient to the Pakhan. Why? I'll be a novice, not a mafiosa. I don't have enemies, at least none that I know of."

"They're rival organizations. We and the Irish have never sat at the same table, girl. This truce has been in place since they discovered Lorcan is my grandson, but it's not a common thing."

I nod, agreeing.

"What are you thinking?"

"I've run out of arguments, sir. All I had in my favor was that I'd be a nun, not a mafia member."

"But you belong to us."

"I miss Lorcan. I don't want Ana to know because she'll be sad, but I can't control my heart. Your grandson already lives there."

"Your friendship is the strangest thing in the world. You don't match, my dear. I'm sure that when you join the convent, you'll find people with similar goals to talk to."

I disagree, but once again I remain silent and just nod, like the good girl they want me to be.

"I'm going to call you."

Thor: "I didn't say you could."

I DON'T WAIT FOR PERMISSION and complete the call.

It's been ten days since I arrived at the convent, and despite what he told me at Anastacia's house about finding someone with the same goals and not Lorcan, Ruslan arranged not only for me to have a room to myself but also for me to be allowed to use my cell phone, giving me more privacy for conversations with his grandson.

I have no idea what he said to the Mother Superior, but the woman seems almost afraid to talk to me.

"I want my video," I request, because he sent me a message a few minutes ago saying he won the fight.

"No videos. You know that's a restricted circuit."

He explained that he fights clandestinely, as the competition he's a champion in is unregistered and the rules are much more brutal than the WCC.

"Video of your bruised face. Or a video call. You choose."

"No. Be content with my voice. Now tell me: did you have nightmares again last night?"

I sigh, not wanting to waste the precious time of the call talking about that. He rarely agrees to talk on the phone.

"Yes, but the same old thing. Smoke, heat. No explanation."

I hear voices talking behind him. They sound like men laughing and swearing.

"Are you going to celebrate?"

"That's none of your business. You're a nun. You shouldn't know about parties and beer."

"You just told me you're going to a party with beer. I can connect the dots."

"Yes, I told you and do you know why?"

"No, and from your tone, I'm not sure I want to know."

He sighs and I feel my heart sink. I can guess, before he even speaks, that he's going to tell me something bad.

"You're confused, Taisiya. You see me as your hero, but I'm not. I'm a monster. Don't fantasize about me. You have your faith, hold on to it. The world out here is a mess, and I'm one of the worst humans you'd want around."

"Love the sinner, not the sin."

"I'm not just the sinner, baby. I'm the sin too. And, above all, I am death."

"Are you ending our friendship? This conversation feels a lot like the one Grandpa Abramov had with me in Russia."

He doesn't say anything, and I feel my throat tighten.

"I understand now. Goodnight, Lorcan. I won't call again."

"I'll always be around."

I hang up without responding. I don't want to think about him anymore. I'm tired of people removing me from their lives as if I were a piece of clothing that no longer fits.

It's time to turn to God alone. He will never abandon me.

Chapter 25

Lorcan

Almost a Year Later

"One day you told me you wouldn't leave me alone and that you would always pursue our friendship. I had to let you go, but you are always with me, little one. Happy birthday."

I don't expect her to reply. It's been about a year since I cut off all communication, although I know almost everything about her life.

The *almost* refers to what I think she doesn't reveal to anyone: her fears and nightmares.

Ruslan keeps me informed, though not willingly. I think I've spoken to my grandfather more in the past year than in my entire life.

I know, for instance, that Taisiya only leaves the convent on rare occasions, such as when the Mexicans threatened to bomb the country in the war against the Russians—and that was one of the most difficult situations for me because even though I knew Taisiya was protected, I wanted to be the one taking care of her.

I also know that she left the convent for Anastacia's wedding and for the birth of her nephew. Other than that, she remains detached from the world.

I am still on the hunt for Ayrtom's accomplice. The bastard has disappeared off the face of the Earth, took a leave of absence from work claiming health problems, but he won't be able to hide forever.

He's too well-known, and sooner or later, I'll catch him. It's just a matter of time.

I wonder if Ayrtom's disappearance made him flee. Probably, but didn't he think that by doing so, he was taking the blame for his relative's sins, making his involvement even more obvious?

"Now that the war with the Mexicans is over, our pact with the Russians is done," Cillian says, bringing me back to the present.

I put the phone down on the table, having just sent him a message, so I don't look like an idiot checking if she replied.

"It was a fucked-up surprise to find out that the one in charge was Isidoro, Morales' younger brother, and not that son of a bitch," Odhran says.

"You can't expect much from a family where the brothers kill each other. If they betray each other, they'd never be loyal to strangers. Their word and shit are the same thing," Kellan says, and everyone nods in agreement.

If you don't honor your own family, how can you respect others?

It sounds like a hypocritical speech when it comes to the mafia, but it's not. There has to be something sacred in your life, no matter how much of a bastard and bloodthirsty you are.

"I want you to talk to Brogan, Lorcan. With the current loss of our trusted men and after the shit that happened in Las Vegas," my older cousin says, referring to a battle between us and the Sicilians about a month ago, "it's better to bring the family over here."

"Did they get promoted to *family* because they are your wife's cousins?" Kellan asks, laughing, referring to Juno.

Juno, Cillian's now wife, spent most of her life in our homeland, Ireland, with her aunt and cousins. And they are the ones the boss wants me to bring to the United States.

"They've always been family," I snarl in response to my brother's mockery. "Six trusted men will help balance the contingent."

"Five, right?" I interject. "Glenn is still too young."

"And Knight doesn't want anything to do with the Syndicate."

"He has his reasons," I say, as few people know why the kid doesn't want to get involved with the mafia, whose whole family is in service. "I'll talk to Brogan. Are we done for now?"

Cillian nods, signaling yes, and I get up, ready to leave.

Before I reach the door, Kellan invites me to a party at one of our clubs.

"Not today," I say, as I plan to spend the evening with a bottle of whiskey.

It's Taisiya's birthday, and if I can't see her, I'll toast in her honor.

I reach the hallway and my phone announces a new message.

Finally.

T: *"I should thank you because I'm in a convent, I'm a novice, and I'm supposed to have a kind and loving heart, but I'm still hurt, so I don't accept your birthday wishes, Lorcan, let alone believe what you said."*

"Don't you believe I'm always with you?"

T: *"No, and stop writing to me. I don't need your pity. Feel free not to feel guilty just because today is my birthday. I don't even think about you anymore."*

"That's a lie. If it were true, you wouldn't still be angry."

T: *"I'm not going to reply to any more messages. If you think you're going to convince me with this story that you always think about me, or that I'm with you all the time, you must think I'm dumber than I really am. You didn't reach out for a year."*

Instead of arguing, I take a photo of my forearm and send it to her.

I know I shouldn't have done that. Neither the tattoo nor letting her know about it, but I also shouldn't be thinking about the girl who is now a novice, and that's all I do every damn free second.

I knew what would happen next, and when the phone rings, I don't hesitate to answer because the desire to hear her voice outweighs any fucking rational thought.

"You tattooed my name on your forearm. Why?"

"I told you that you're always with me, Taisiya."

"I don't understand."

"Answer me one thing: are you okay there in the convent? Is this really what you want?"

I've never considered myself an anxious person, but I feel my pulse quicken as I wait for her response. Depending on what she says, I'll be there in less than half an hour.

She stays silent before speaking:

"What does that have to do with your tattoo?"

"Answer."

She sighs.

"I'm fine in the convent. It's exactly what I want."

What did you expect, idiot? She went there by choice. No one forced her.

"Happy birthday, princess."

"Lorcan, I..."

"Live your dream, Taisiya. Live the life you've chosen. You deserve to have everything you want."

I hang up the phone and return to the meeting room.

"I changed my mind," I say to Kellan. "Let's go to the fucking party tonight."

Chapter 26

Taisiya

"I'm not going, Ana."

"What do you mean you're not coming? It's your eighteenth birthday!"

"It's just another day."

"Have you been seeing the therapist?"

"You know I have. Your husband keeps an eye on my life twenty-four hours a day."

"He doesn't mean any harm. Maxim is obsessed with security."

From what I've seen of my brother-in-law so far, whom I love by the way, just seeing how much he's crazy about my sister, Maxim is obsessed with everything, but I don't see why I should tell her that.

"Look, I'm going to be fine. Don't worry. I just don't feel like going out."

"You know it's impossible not to worry, right? I mean, you're my little sister, Taisiya. The one I thought I'd never see again. You're my miracle, and I'll always want to make sure you're happy."

"I need space to grow, Ana. Even here in the convent, you all don't allow that."

"And giving space means letting you spend your eighteenth birthday, your transition to adulthood, alone?"

"And what difference does it make, Anastacia, if I can't do what I want?"

"Try to tell me what you want."

"Alright, then for this party you've organized for me, can I invite Lorcan?"

"Lorcan? Where did that come from, Taisiya? I thought your friendship had ended."

"Ana, I love you, so don't disappoint me by lying to me and, more importantly, to yourself. Do you know what the beauty of therapy is? We learn to question everything, even what seems true only on the surface. I can't say I'm healed, especially since I don't remember that nightmare, but I can tell you that I'm stronger."

"I didn't say I wasn't." She sighs, sounding sad. "I'm sorry, Taisiya. I don't know what to say."

"There's nothing to say. I'll be fine."

"Don't hang up. You're sounding like you did in the early days when you went to the convent. Sad and depressed. Haven't you talked to him since?"

I'm torn between whether to tell her the truth or not, but I'm so tired of keeping everything inside.

"Not long ago, right after Grandpa Abramov called, I got a message from him wishing me a happy birthday."

"And what else?"

"I replied saying he didn't need to feel sorry for me. He said he really cared."

I keep the fact that he tattooed my name on his forearm to myself. I'm afraid it might start World War III.

"And what happened? Why do you sound sad? I thought talking to him after so long would make you happy."

"I called him instead of continuing to text, and I think we ended the call fighting. Can you believe that? I dreamed of hearing his voice for almost a year, and when it happened, he hung up as if... I don't know how to say it."

I don't even care how much I've revealed at this moment. I need to vent to someone to understand what made him end the call.

"What did you talk about?"

"Lorcan asked if I was okay in the convent and if this was really what I wanted."

"And what did you reply?"

"I said yes, although it's not true."

"It's not? You never told me anything about this, Taisiya."

"You have your own life to take care of, Ana. A husband who adores you and a little baby. I can handle my own craziness most of the time."

"Don't talk like that. You're not crazy. Now, tell me about this story of not being happy in the convent."

"I've been trying to find the faith I supposedly had once, Anastacia, but it hasn't happened yet. I just haven't asked to leave because I know what will be my fate if I do. Ruslan will want to find me a husband."

"Oh, my God, Taisiya."

I know she's crying. I am too. After a year of simmering, I feel like I'm about to explode.

"Do you know what's more ironic, Anastacia? We planned to free you from the prison of a convenience marriage, and now, who's trapped is me, between a faith that no longer exists or marrying someone I don't love."

"And who do you love? Lorcan?"

"How can I know? I never had the chance to find out! I came here thinking we'd continue our friendship and that, at some point, I'd realize I made the right decision coming to the convent. I was wrong both times."

"Why don't you want to be a nun anymore?"

"No, I don't want to."

"Why did you end up fighting on the phone?"

"When I said I was fine here at the convent, just to try to save a bit of my dignity since he had distanced himself from me without any explanation a year ago, he wished me a good life."

"Do you know why he ended your friendship? To protect you, Taisiya. You had just reconnected with me. He knew that if you continued to stay in touch, your life would become hell. I love my husband and also the big family we are part of, but they are extremely controlling. They would never even tolerate a friendship between you and Lorcan."

"Maybe that's the crux of the matter, Ana. I'm tired of living my life by other people's rules. I've never experienced anything. All I have to remember from my teenage years are scars from lashes on my back, so don't be surprised that I don't want to attend my own eighteenth birthday party. I have nothing to celebrate. Now, I need to hang up."

"Don't hang up yet, Taisiya. There has to be something I can do to make you feel better."

"There's nothing."

"What if I get permission for you to see him?"

"Lorcan?"

"Yes."

My heart is beating so hard I can feel it hardening inside my chest.

"Could you?"

"I don't know, but I can try."

"And if he doesn't want to?"

"I doubt it. If that were the case, he wouldn't have sent you a message earlier today. Stop overthinking. Let me talk to Maxim."

SHE TAKES A WHILE TO call back, and by this point, my brain is short-circuiting, with all possible doubts swirling in my mind; the biggest one being the fear of rejection.

He seemed almost indifferent when he hung up the phone.

When I finally hear the music I chose for my sister, I'm caught between the cowardice of answering and the need for an answer.

"I managed," she says as soon as I answer. "As long as you agree to have a female security escort. Actually, she's a soldier from the Organization."

"I don't care, but I think you're putting the cart before the horse. I still need to talk to him."

"One more thing: there's a curfew. Midnight. You'll come home and not to the convent afterward. Ruslan has already spoken with your Mother Superior. And finally, don't think this will become a habit, sister. It's a special concession for your birthday."

"Thank you, Ana. I need to hang up, but we might need to talk again today."

"Why?"

"If Lorcan wants to see me, I don't have decent clothes to wear. I don't want to look different from the other girls."

"Oh my God, I can't believe I suggested this craziness. Please be careful."

"He would never let anything happen to me."

I hang up the phone, trembling with anxiety, and search for his name in my contacts, just to buy some time since I already have it memorized.

When Lorcan answers with that voice that sounds more like a growl, I stop breathing for a few seconds.

Chapter 27

Lorcan

I can hardly believe it when I look at my phone screen.

"Taisiya?"

"I want to see you. It will be my birthday present. Anastacia managed to get a special permission from Maxim for me to leave the convent and be with you. I'm dying to see you."

She spills all of that out in a split second, and even through the phone, I can feel her nervousness.

Not just hers, because at this moment, my heartbeat is racing like hell too.

It's eleven in the morning. I was getting into the car to check a shipment before clearing the route to South America, but I signal to my bodyguards, Rourke and Keiron, to wait.

"What are you talking about?"

"I want to see you. I'm so embarrassed to take the initiative. You seemed angry when you hung up earlier today. I thought I was angry at you too. I'm a little bit, but not much, because I know you haven't forgotten me, or you wouldn't have gotten the tattoo."

I close my eyes, focusing on her voice. I don't even care what she's saying, as long as it's to me, for me.

"Where do you want to go?" I ask, without hesitation.

I know I'm going to have a hell of a fight with Cillian to make her wish come true, but at the moment, I couldn't care less.

"Anywhere. I don't mind. My sister told me to be happy today, and what will make me happy is spending the day with you. There's just one problem: Maxim said a Russian soldier will have to come with me."

"I figured. They don't trust me."

"But I trust you. Doesn't that count?"

"That's *all that matters*. Will the nuns let you go, or do I have to kidnap you out of there?"

"Would you do that?"

"Do you doubt it?"

"No. But you don't need to go that far. Your grandfather has already sorted everything out."

Of course, Ruslan had to be involved. He boasts about being omnipresent, and I swear to God it's true.

"I'll pick you up in an hour, is that okay?"

"No. I need more time. I'm going to ask Ana to help me choose what to wear. I don't want to look like a nun, at least today."

"Two hours then. At the front door of the convent. The soldier can come, but only her. I'll take care of you, not those damn Russian bodyguards."

I hang up the phone, trying to process what just happened, but my mind is far from its normal state. I'm a mess. However, I can see a straight line, and at the end of it is my prize: Taisiya.

I don't care if she's the bride of Christ for the rest of the days she's here on Earth. For today, she's mine, and I'm going to savor every damn second.

I go back into the Syndicate headquarters to talk to Cillian in person, but before I reach his office, my phone rings.

"I hope you know what you're doing," Ruslan says.

I don't even try to pretend I don't understand.

"The idea didn't come from me, but now, nothing is going to stop me from seeing her. I stayed away for Taisiya's benefit, but if what she wants is to be with me, if, as she herself said, I'm her birthday present, not even a fucking army will stop me from going to this meeting, grandfather."

"It was a special concession, Lorcan. Even Talassa, Yerik's wife, had to intervene. Ana was smart. She spoke to her before even talking to Maxim, and by the time she spoke with her husband, she had my granddaughter-in-law as an ally."

"I don't care about the path taken, only the result. For today, she's mine."

"And Cillian?"

"I'm going to talk to him now."

"NO WAY!" MY COUSIN shouts.

"I didn't come to ask for permission. I'm informing you out of respect, only."

"She's a Russian mafia princess, Lorcan."

"She's a novice. She couldn't be further from the Organization. She spent the last year locked up in that damn convent, and today is her birthday. Of all the things she could have asked for, she chose to see me, and there's nothing on this fucking planet that's going to stop me from fulfilling her wish."

"Damn, this can't be happening."

"What the hell are you talking about?"

"You've fallen for her."

"Are you crazy? Taisiya is just my ward."

"And for this ward, you tattooed your arm? Or do you think I didn't notice you marked your skin with her name?"

"I didn't bother to hide it, or I would have tattooed my ass."

"What the hell are you planning to do with a nun? Even if she weren't Russian, you're like oil and water."

"We're friends. She's mine. This is above the Syndicate and the Organization. It's a matter of loyalty."

"Love?"

"I'm not familiar with feelings beyond loyalty and duty."

"It's not just that, and we both know it. If it were only loyalty and duty that moved you, you would keep an eye on her from a distance, as I know you've been doing."

"I'm leaving. I didn't mean to do anything behind your back, but I'm not changing my mind."

He runs his hand through his hair.

"Does her Pakhan know about this meeting?"

"He's not her Pakhan. Taisiya's ultimate boss is God."

"Hell he isn't. The girl is Maxim's sister-in-law. She belongs to the Organization, no matter that she's wearing a black dress now."

"She belongs to herself," I retort, my anger getting the better of me. "This argument is pointless. Only if I'm dead will I stop seeing her today."

He stands up, looking ready for a fight. I don't back down.

After glaring at me angrily for over a minute, he finally says:

"I don't want to have to collect your body tomorrow. Does Yerik know about this meeting?" he asks again.

"Yes. Ruslan too. Don't worry."

"You're my blood, I can't help but worry. I don't trust those fucking Russians."

"But you trust me, and I know how to take care of myself."

Chapter 28

Lorcan

I know Cillian sent a team ahead to the convent to make sure it wasn't a trap. No matter how much I say that Ruslan would never allow the Russians to kill me, my cousin will never trust Yerik.

The moment I step out of the car, I notice peripherally that Rourke and Keiron have also gotten out, but I'm paying attention to nothing but her.

Taisiya walks toward me with her eyes locked on mine, and she seems as focused on studying me as I am on her.

Her hair has grown, her face is more angular, and what remained of her teenage look is gone for good.

My ward is no longer a girl. She's a beautiful woman.

"A nun," a voice warns. *"Or at least, a novice. Either way, unattainable."*

These are irrefutable truths, but they don't stop my eyes from falling to the gentle sway of her hips covered by jeans and the way her breasts push against the white silk shirt that even the heavy coat can't disguise.

I don't know what I expected. Maybe her to show up dressed as a nun, although she told me she wouldn't. The fact is, Taisiya in "normal" clothes makes her even more tempting.

I keep myself impassive, my hands in the back pockets of my pants to keep myself from rushing over and grabbing her by the hair, tilting her head back so I can look at that beautiful face for as long as I want.

She stops about a meter away, looking uncertain.

"You came."

"I came."

"Why did you want to?"

I glance at the blonde woman behind her, not much older than Taisiya, and she does the same, turning to speak with the Russian.

"Can you give us a moment, Tulia? Don't take it the wrong way. I know you were assigned to watch over me while I'm with Lorcan, but it's my birthday and I haven't seen him in a year. I want privacy."

I almost smile because only she could be so brutally honest and sweet at the same time.

With a grumble, the woman walks past me. I know she looks at me with a stance that's supposed to be a warning, but I ignore it.

"I once told you that I only do what I want."

"Even when you pulled away from me, then?" She shakes her head. "No, don't answer, or we'll end up fighting. Let me see your tattoo."

"Today you can have whatever you want, but let's get in the car."

I drape an arm over her shoulder, guiding her to the waiting vehicle. The blonde woman stops beside me, as if she thinks she's coming with us.

"You'll go with them." I nod toward Keiron and Rourke. Without giving her a chance to respond, I get in the car behind Taisiya.

"Show me," she asks as soon as the car door closes.

I take off my jacket and turn my arm so she can see. She moves her fingers over the place where her name will be permanently etched into my flesh.

It's a light touch, almost innocent, but it's the first time she's touched me since I admitted to myself that I desire her, and without my control, my body reacts as if I'm a damn kid.

I try to pull my arm away, but instead of letting go, she kneels on the seat, facing me, and hugs me.

I should push her away. Taisiya isn't aware of my arousal, but I am. I can't, though. I pull her into my lap and bury my head in the curve of her neck. She shivers and I wonder if she realizes that, nun or not, her body betrays that at this moment, she's responding to my touch.

"I shouldn't be holding you."

We're the only ones in the vehicle for now because when I entered, I asked the driver to wait.

"This can't be wrong. It feels so good. Besides, it's my birthday. Today, you said I could have anything, and what I want is to live. For one day, I want to live, Lorcan. It will be my gift, along with the tattoo you made for me."

Without letting go of the arm that I'm holding, I reach out with the other hand and grab the box I kept in the console.

"Another one," I say, handing it to her.

"Another what?" She takes the box, already smiling.

I shrug.

"Another gift. The tattoo was in your honor, but it belongs to me."

"You bought a gift for me? But how did you know you'd see me?"

"I didn't know, but if it weren't today, I'd find a way to see you."

"Because you missed me?"

"I'm a man. I don't miss people."

She gives me a well-deserved eye roll.

"Admit that you missed me."

"Open the box, Taisiya."

She takes out the platinum necklace and smiles when she sees the pendant.

"A grenade," she says, tracing her finger over the delicate piece, studded with diamonds. "It's you. I mean, your nickname in the ring, right? *The Irish Bomb.*"

I nod in agreement.

"I have you on my skin, so you'll have me with you. Seems like a fair trade from where I'm standing."

She smiles and, after handing me the necklace, holds up her hair, asking me to fasten it around her neck.

There must be an explanation for the satisfaction I feel seeing my gift on her. It's something almost primitive, territorial.

Taisiya smiles, her head lowered, examining the pendant. Then, suddenly, she lifts her face and moves closer to me. I wasn't expecting the movement. At that exact moment, I had stretched my body to place the empty box back in the console.

Without knowing what's happening, our lips meet. It's a light brush, and we both pull away as if we've been shocked by an electric current.

For whole seconds, we stare at each other, and then, without saying a word, I grab her by the neck and start my descent into hell.

As I seek her mouth, pressing it against mine with no delicacy, a million thoughts rush through my mind.

I know this is her first kiss and that I should pull away.

I'm aware that touching her this way is wrong because it will only worsen my desire.

I'm sure I'll be damned for eternity, because the girl in my arms is promised to someone with a rank much higher than mine—*God.*

And yet, despite every logical thought trying to infiltrate my brain, they all vanish when I feel the softness and warmth of her skin.

"Open your mouth," I command.

She does so slowly, and I don't wait to slip my tongue in and taste her. She doesn't push me away, allowing me in, but she doesn't mirror my movements, and I know it's due to inexperience.

I take control and, without caring about the consequences, lick and bite her mouth. I suck on her tongue until I hear her moan, pulling her against me, aligning her better over my cock; only when her body stiffens in my arms do I realize what I'm doing.

I force myself to return her to her seat, and I don't even know how to start apologizing.

Damn it! I acted like a pervert.

"Taisiya..."

"Was that part of the birthday present too?"

"No. And it shouldn't have happened."

"Why not?"

"We're friends, we shouldn't be kissing."

"I want it again."

Jesus Christ!

"You're a nun."

"*Novice.*"

"It's the same thing. Not for me. As I said before, it shouldn't have happened."

I open the car door and call the driver.

After he gets in, I make sure her seatbelt is fastened and turn to the window, trying to clear my mind.

I feel her eyes on me, but I choose to temporarily ignore her.

"Aren't you going to talk to me anymore? Do you want to cancel the plan?"

"No way. I'm just going to change my initial plan. I'm going to take you to meet someone."

"Who?"

"My aunt Orla."

I had planned to spend the day with her on a trip out of town, just the two of us, but after what just happened, I don't think it's safe for us to be alone.

Chapter 29

Taisiya

"So you're the famous Taisiya. I've heard a lot about you and was wondering when he would finally bring you here," his aunt, Mrs. Orla, asks about half an hour later, while I'm still trying to calm my racing heart.

It's not an easy task when my body is still tingling and I can remember the exact taste of Lorcan's mouth, how his tongue made me receive him, and how his strong arms pulled me close.

A few times, I dreamed that he kissed me. It wasn't just imagination; it was a dream, an unconscious act, so I won't even count it as a sin.

In the dream, he was affectionate and gentle. The kiss was good because it was with him, but perhaps because I'd never done it before, I had no idea what it meant to be kissed by Lorcan.

I don't even know if what we did can be considered a kiss. I felt overtaken by him, as if with his tongue, the touch on my hair, the firmness of his body against mine, he was telling me that I belonged to him.

I wasn't afraid of what we did; I was shocked by my own reaction, but I think Lorcan misunderstood.

It takes me a moment to respond to his aunt. Only when my heartbeat calms down a bit do I focus on what she said: *he talked about me?*

I search for the gaze of the man I no longer know how to label in my life and catch him looking at me, leaning against a counter, his huge arms crossed over his chest. My tattoo is on display for anyone to see, since he left his leather jacket on a chair.

I feel as if he belongs to me now because he has my mark, even though I know it's a silly thought.

For sure, based on his reaction in the car, he regretted kissing me. Or maybe he did it impulsively, just because I was on his lap.

He cares about me, I'm sure of that, but it doesn't mean there's something more behind it.

"Yes, my name is Taisiya," I say, giving a shy smile, because the woman seems like a whirlwind, almost as direct in speech as her nephew.

"I asked Juno to bring some cupcakes. If Lorcan had told me it was your birthday, I would have prepared a special menu with what you like for this late lunch."

"I'm not picky about food, besides, you mentioned cupcakes. I'm crazy about sweets."

"Really?" he speaks to me for the first time since we got out of the car.

"Yes."

His brow furrows as if he's filing away the information.

"Then you're in the right place. Cillian's wife supplies cupcakes for my restaurant. Juno is making a name for herself. She's opened several branches across the country. Her growth has been astonishing. It took just a year to dominate the market. She has more orders than she can handle at the moment."

She continues speaking, and from time to time, I interrupt her with a question or two, gradually feeling more comfortable and, to be honest, enjoying the family atmosphere.

I've only spent time with Grandpa Abramov for a long time, and Ana, on the occasions I stayed at her place, didn't seem very fond of household chores.

Lorcan's aunt excuses herself and steps away to go to the restaurant's office. Now, there are only a few staff members and the two of us in the industrial kitchen.

I cross my arms, mimicking his pose, watching her from a distance. I've never felt awkward in his presence, but that, of course, was before he gave me a kiss that shook the planet's rotation and then told me it should never have happened.

"What else do you want to do today?" he asks, and for a moment, the coward within me almost asks to be taken back to the convent as soon as lunch is over because I think he might have regretted agreeing to spend the day together.

I try to maintain a neutral expression to hide how embarrassed I am. I forced the situation. I practically coerced him into picking me up.

Oh my God, how embarrassing!

I glance at him, discreetly, through my lashes, because I can't help it. The man looks even more handsome this year we've been apart. His hair longer, his body stronger.

I don't know what he sees in my face, but he steps closer.

"Don't look at me like that, Taisiya."

"Like what?"

"Like you want me to kiss you again."

I open my mouth to deny, but I can't, because I'm not a liar. I want another kiss. Or a bunch of them, if I can choose.

I think he can sense it because his hand rises as if to touch me. I tremble in anticipation, but before it happens, a woman's voice says:

"Is this where we have a birthday girl?"

I turn around and come face to face with a very beautiful blonde. Since she's carrying a box decorated with sweets, I assume she's the boss's wife, Juno.

"If you're the owner of the sweets," I say to her, smiling, "I think you're going to become my best friend."

I THOUGHT IT WOULD be just us for lunch: Juno, Aunt Orla — she asked me to call her that — and Lorcan.

I quickly realized, however, that their family is quite close because Cillian's two younger brothers showed up and joined the table. Only the Boss, as they call him, didn't come.

I'm curious to meet him. I was introduced to Yerik at Ana's wedding, and he seemed extremely intimidating. I have no doubt that Lorcan's cousin is like that too.

The conversation was light during lunch. However, while the women in Lorcan's family did their best to make me feel at ease, his cousins spent a good portion of the meal watching me.

One of them is friendlier, I think he's the youngest, Odhran. He's also explosive. He says whatever he's thinking, like when he mentioned it was the first time he was sitting down with someone from the rival team — *me* — for a meal.

I thought Lorcan was going to kill him with the look he gave, but I didn't take it badly; after all, he didn't say something too far from the truth, though the idea of me being a mobster is so ridiculous I want to laugh.

The other one, Kellan, is a bit intimidating. He barely spoke to me, watching me in silence the whole time. So, when he called my name in the middle of dessert, I was startled.

"Eighteen?" he asks, and I nod. "What are you doing tonight?"

From a movement in my peripheral vision, I see Lorcan turn to look at his cousin. He doesn't say anything but has his fists clenched on the table.

"Going back to my sister's house," I say, dejected, because I don't want the day to end. "I have a curfew at midnight."

"Like Cinderella," Aunt Orla jokes.

"Yes, but she went to a ball."

"I don't have a gala night to offer, princess, but I can invite you to our nightclub."

"No, Kellan," Lorcan says, and his voice sounds icy.

"Why not? I'd love to check out a nightclub, although I don't know how to dance. The family dancer is Ana."

"You shouldn't go to a place like that."

"I don't see why. You told me today I could have whatever I wanted, and I've just decided that I want to see your nightclub."

"I'm going to kill you, Kellan," he says to his cousin, and at this moment, I know he'll give in.

"No death threats at the table, kids," Aunt Orla says.

"There's just one problem," I say, looking at Juno. The only one I believe can help me. "I have no idea how people dress for such a place."

"You look great like that," Lorcan replies, and his cousin's wife rolls her eyes.

"Don't worry, Taisiya. We'll find something suitable. You'll have your Cinderella night; after all, you only turn eighteen once."

Chapter 30

Taisiya

"**A**re you going to tell Maxim?" I ask Anastacia during a video call.

"*No need, he'll find out anyway. Don't fool yourself into thinking Tulia is the only bodyguard from the Organization watching you today, Taisiya. I'm sure there are many people keeping an eye on you, so think carefully about what you're going to do.*"

"The way you talk, it sounds like I'm about to commit a mortal sin."

"*Using your words, don't lie to yourself and especially, don't lie to me. You're in love with the Irishman, sister.*"

"I don't know anything about love between a man and a woman, but something happened between us today that I need to tell you about when I get to your house later. Can I send you a message when my Cinderella deadline is up? I'll be home before midnight. Twenty-three fifty-nine, to be precise, because I plan to enjoy every second."

"*Do you have any idea how hard it was to get Maxim, and then Yerik, to agree to this birthday plan?*"

"Yes, I imagine it was quite a struggle, but I'm so happy, Ana. I feel alive for the first time that I can remember."

"*And it's because of witnessing this joy in your voice that I'm willing to fight with my husband and the Pakhan if necessary.*"

"I don't want you to fight with Maxim on my account."

"*I'll fight with whoever it takes if it means your happiness, Taisiya.*"

"I'm happy among the Irish," I confess, and she groans.

"*Oh my God, why couldn't you fall for a nice Russian guy?*"

"Because it was the Irishman who woke my heart from its eternal slumber."

"*Wrong fairytale, sister. I thought you were Cinderella.*"

"I'm a bit of each... Ana, do you really think what I feel is love?"

"*No one can know but you, but what I can tell you is that you have all the symptoms.*"

"And if it is?"

"*I'm asking you: and if it is? Besides the fact that he's Irish, do you happen to know if he feels the same way?*"

"No. He likes me, but he once told me he'll never get married."

"*That's why I don't like him.*"

"Because he won't get married?"

"*Yes. It means he wants to stay loose, with multiple women.*"

"Do you really think so?"

"*I don't know. I have no experience in relationships outside of Maxim, but be careful with your heart. There are many more cons than pros when it comes to him, Taisiya.*" She pauses for a moment before continuing: "*What do you plan to do about the convent? Do you really want to leave?*"

"Not if it means marrying someone I don't love."

She sighs.

"*Let's do this: one thing at a time. Go live your dream night and please, be sensible.*"

"Juno helped me pick out a dress."

"*Who is Juno?*"

"The Boss's wife."

"*He's not your Boss.*"

"I didn't say he was. You're very nervous. I want to show you my dress. Tell me if I look ridiculous, please. It's my first night out ever."

I go in front of the full-length mirror so she can see the black dress that Juno had delivered, along with two others, to Aunt Orla's house. A red one and a white one. I liked this one the most because the others left the back exposed. I don't want anyone laughing at me. The scars are faint if you just look at them, but if someone touches me, they can feel them.

"Be honest. Is it too much?"

"*No. You look beautiful, Taisiya. So much so that now I'm even more worried. There's no way that hairy Irishman will see you and not fall in love.*"

"You're so silly." I almost tell her about the kiss but decide I'll do that when I get to her house later. "I have to go, Ana. I'll see you before I turn into a pumpkin, oops... before midnight."

She smiles, and I hang up. Less than a minute later, someone knocks on the door. When I say come in, Lorcan's aunt appears.

"You look beautiful, my dear. Happy birthday."

"Thank you for today, Aunt Orla. I loved everything and especially the time we spent at the restaurant."

"Lorcan told me you don't remember your past," she says, and it might sound rude if it were someone else saying it. However, she's just straightforward.

"Yes, I remember very little. I've forgotten the worst part. I think I'm too cowardly to recall, so maybe God is sparing me."

"Or maybe it's not the right time. He might be waiting for you to be stronger. And about God, how does being a novice fit with going to a nightclub tonight? Forgive me if I'm being nosy, but I'm old-fashioned and can't understand how these two choices can fit together."

"They don't fit. You're right. I've been thinking about leaving the Order. Not taking the vows," I say, and only God knows why I'm confessing this to someone who is practically a stranger.

"And what's stopping you from leaving?"

I hesitate about revealing that Ruslan wants to find a husband for me. Even though I hate the idea of being forced to marry, my loyalty is still to my family, and whether I like it or not, Lorcan's grandfather is one of the few people left to me.

"It's complicated," I say simply, and thank the Lord, she doesn't press further.

"You'd better go downstairs. It's time to leave or you won't enjoy the nightclub at all."

"Is Lorcan upset? I don't think he really wants to go."

"He doesn't like to be contradicted, first of all. He's temperamental, so his mood will change soon."

"And what else?"

"What do you mean?"

"You said 'first of all.' What's the other thing bothering him today?"

"My nephew doesn't know what to do with you, Taisiya. You're the most unlikely couple in the world."

"We're not a couple..."

She raises her hand, interrupting me before I can continue.

"Time will tell, my dear."

I go down the stairs of her house feeling shaky, and it has nothing to do with the high heels Juno helped me pick out from the *personal stylist* who came here. They're not too high and I don't feel like the ground is unstable under my feet like I did at Ana's wedding. I'm trembling with nerves because Aunt Lorcan's words keep spinning in my head.

Couple.

No, we're not one, but I don't think there's a name for us either.

I'm descending the stairs, paying attention to the thick carpet covering them, afraid of falling and making a scene when I get to the bottom, when I see him at the foot of the stairs.

He's changed from the white t-shirt he wore earlier under the leather jacket to a black dress shirt, and I have to control myself not to let my jaw drop as my eyes take in his body.

The black jeans cling to his thighs, highlighting the muscles, and I feel a flutter in my stomach as I continue to look up, especially when I pass over the large bulge between his legs. My body and face flush, and I quickly avert my gaze from that part, but when I look at him, I'm mortified because I think he noticed.

He climbs the stairs two at a time, and like the giant he is, he's soon in front of me.

He doesn't say anything but runs his finger over the choker he gave me.

"You're wearing it."

"I'll never take it off."

"Not even when you take your vows?"

I almost tell him I won't, but how can I say that before I have a plan *b* to get out of Ruslan's idea of marrying me?

"No, not even then."

"You look beautiful, Taisiya. I thought it was crazy to take you to a nightclub, but now that I've seen you, I've changed my mind."

He doesn't say anything more. He intertwines our fingers and starts to go down the stairs with me.

My heart is still racing when we get into the car, and I promise myself that I will enjoy tonight to the fullest.

I don't know *when* or *if* I'll have another chance.

Chapter 31

Taisiya

I try to hide a smile as we enter the Syndicate nightclub hand in hand. I had seen some places like this online but had no idea they were so cool.

The dim lighting, the glowing decorations, the light shows, and the loud music make me feel transported to an alternate reality.

I notice that people make way as we walk through the first floor. They watch me with curiosity, as if I were a rare species. Why? Did they guess I'm Russian? I don't think so.

Discreetly, I check my outfit to see if there's anything wrong, but soon conclude that I'm not standing out from the other girls present.

I squeeze Lorcan's hand to get him to lean down to speak to me.

"Why is everyone looking at me?"

"Aside from the fact that you're beautiful?" he replies, and I roll my eyes, but inside, I'm pleased.

"Go on, sir. This time, tell me the truth."

"Not here. Let's go to the VIP area."

He doesn't give me time to protest, walking away again, but now positioned behind me.

I feel his warmth and shiver. He stops walking, and I turn my head to look back. Lorcan is staring at me too, and for a crazy second, I think he's going to kiss me, but then he resumes walking, kind of forcing me to move along as well.

We enter an elevator, him still behind me, and I'm about to lose the strength in my legs. I don't know how to handle the things he makes me feel.

To avoid embarrassing myself by fainting from nerves, I focus on the elevator panel.

There are three floors marked "v," which I assume are the VIP areas. He presses the button for the top one.

His arm remains around my waist, and unable to control my anxiety any longer, I lean into his body. The heat of Lorcan's skin ignites me, and if I still had doubts that the convent isn't my final destination, they have just vanished. If I were truly called to this life, shouldn't I be bothered by his proximity? Instead, I want more.

The doors open, and now I understand why he brought me here. There are no more than twenty or twenty-five people gathered. I quickly recognize Kellan, who has a blonde woman sitting on his lap.

"Tell me why they were looking at me," I ask, as he leads us toward where his cousin is.

I really want to know and fear that I won't get another chance to discover why everyone seemed to be staring at me as if I were from another world.

He turns me to face him, his hands holding me by the hips.

The music isn't as loud as it was downstairs, so he could easily talk from a distance, but instead, he leans down and whispers in my ear:

"Because I've never come to the nightclub with someone. They're wondering if you're mine."

I swear on everything sacred that my legs just turned to jelly.

"And am I?"

"I have your mark, Taisiya. Some might say I'm the one who's yours."

I can't help but smile.

"I like how that sounds. It means you're off the market."

He doesn't respond further because Kellan approaches and, to my surprise, kisses me on the cheek.

"You look beautiful, birthday girl."

Then, Odhran appears as well.

"Ready to let loose?"

"What?"

"Dance, love. I'm talking about dancing, just that."

"Hmm... I think I have two left feet. It's not going to work."

Lorcan pulls me by the hand.

"I'll guide you. Come on. They're right. It's your day. Leave the good-novice fantasy behind for a few hours, Cinderella."

AN HOUR LATER, I DON'T know what's making me dizzy: the loud music, the fact that I've danced—yes, I danced, guided by Lorcan—several songs in a row, the flashing lights, or the most likely cause of all, seeing the man who makes my heart race moving his body so sexily that I need to hold back my drool.

"I never imagined someone your size could dance so well."

He gives one of his rare smiles.

"I do MMA," he says, as if that's explanation enough.

"And?"

"I also train in boxing," he continues, then moves his feet side to side in short steps, keeping his fists up.

"Seriously? Are you telling me that boxing makes you move your hips like that?"

I don't know much about men, but I don't need to be a flirting expert to notice that he just gave me a cheeky smile. The first one, as far as I remember.

Then, he whispers just for me:

"It can only be because of boxing. Or from practicing moving your hips."

I don't quite understand what he means, but I guess it has some sexual connotation. I pretend to understand, looking at him as if I hear that kind of thing every day, but I must be a terrible liar because Lorcan holds my face and presses our foreheads together.

"Sorry."

"Sorry for what?"

He takes my hand and leads me to a secluded corner away from the other guests. It's almost like a private room.

It's darker, more intimate, and I'd prefer to stay here alone with him than with the cousins and all those women outside.

"Because I forget how innocent you are."

I give up pretending to be mature.

"I didn't understand what you said about moving your hips."

I'm leaning against a wall, and he leans over me. I don't feel scared, but protected. I never want to leave his embrace.

"You don't know anything about sex?"

"The basics, because just as I remembered how to ride a bike, when I see a pregnant woman, I recall what I studied in school, in biology. But what does that have to do with you moving your hi— Oh!"

"Damn it, Taisiya." He closes his eyes.

"What's wrong?"

"I feel like a pervert because hearing you say that makes me want to..."

"Want to what?"

He looks at his watch before answering me:

"We'd better leave, baby."

"I have until almost midnight to stay here. Are you tired of me?"

"No, but if we keep dancing... If I stay by your side for another five minutes, watching you in that sexy dress, I'll end up doing something I'll regret later."

"Like kissing me again? Because if that's it, I want to," I say, not caring if I look foolish.

There must be some manual somewhere where girls are instructed not to be so direct.

He leans down again, this time his hands gripping my hips more firmly, his fingers digging into my flesh.

I gasp when a moan escapes me. I can't stop it.

"I don't just want to kiss you."

"I didn't understand."

Instead of answering, he presses his lips against mine.

Chapter 32

Lorcan

"**S**top", a voice warns. *"There's still time."*
But I know it's too late. It became too late the moment I kissed her in the car.

I don't just kiss her. I devour her.

This time, when my mouth descends on hers, Taisiya knows what to do. She parts her lips, inviting me. She wants my tongue tasting her.

My grip on her hips tightens and I lift her to my height, pinning her against the wall, exploring her mouth with my tongue and teeth.

The sexual tension dominates every cell of my body, and I need a lot of self-control not to wrap her thighs around my waist.

She had her first kiss today. Taisiya is too innocent, and I don't want to scare her.

That simple thought about her innocence should be enough to cool me down. Virgins have never piqued my interest. Yet, the connection with her has built up intensely, burning slowly, to the point where the desire I've repressed borders on insanity.

Her breathing is ragged, her hands no longer resting loosely at her sides as they did the first time I kissed her. Now they pull, grip, demand. Her teeth bite back, and her need is driving me crazy.

I trail my mouth to the curve of her neck, licking the soft flesh, and she moans, pushing against me.

"Does it feel good?"

"Don't stop. It's my birthday. I want more presents."

"Yes, it's your day. What do you want as a present, baby?"

She pulls back a little to look at me.

"More of you and this butterflies-in-my-stomach feeling."

"I want to make you come. I want more of those moans of pleasure."

I return my attack to her delicious mouth as I slide her down my thigh. Now, she's straddling my leg. Her dress has risen, and only the thin fabric of her panties protects her sex.

I want to touch her without the barrier of fabric. Feel her on my fingers, but I can't allow myself to forget for even a moment that Taisiya is not a one-night stand.

"I should stop, but it drives me crazy thinking that you're going to spend the rest of your life in that convent without having experienced anything."

"What are you going to do then?"

I bite her ear, pinning the warm flesh of the lobe between my teeth.

She moans softly.

"I want you to come for me."

The moans increase as my hand holds her by the neck, keeping her mouth still. The way I kiss her now is deliberately a simulation of the sexual act. I slide my tongue slowly, going in and out of her lips.

When her delicious body starts moving on my leg, desperate for friction, I feel like one lucky bastard.

I stop kissing her to watch her face completely consumed by passion.

Fucking gorgeous.

"Ask me to stop or I'll make you come for me, Taisiya. I'm obsessed with seeing you come."

Her hands come to my chest, caressing, one scratching me over my shirt and the other holding the fabric to keep me from pulling away.

"Please, Lorcan, I want more."

Fuck!

"Just for tonight. For one fucking night, I'll give you pleasure."

I grab her ass, controlling her hips, making her grind faster on my leg, and I can almost swear her panties are soaking my jeans.

"I'm not a prince, baby. I don't know how to say pretty words."

"I don't know any. Pretty or ugly. Give me what I need."

Jesus, how someone so sweet can drive me this wild, I'll never understand.

"Climb onto my thigh. Use my neck as leverage. Rub yourself against me."

This is my soft version because, if I had my way, I'd ask her to grind her pussy on my thigh until she came, screaming my name. Until my leg was soaked with her honey.

She obeys, and the movement makes one of her knees brush against my erection. I bite her lips to keep from moaning loudly, knowing I've never felt this much desire in my life.

Taisiya is lost in her own desire, uninhibited, eager, pursuing her pleasure.

"Say more."

"Fuck, you don't know what you're asking for."

"Just for today, I don't want to be a good girl. I want to be yours. Show me the real Lorcan."

I dig for willpower, but it's already vanished along with the awareness that I have a novice in my arms.

I lift her up and press her small body against the wall, fitting myself between her legs so that my cock, covered by jeans, reaches the apex, the exact point of her pussy.

"I was going to make you come on my thigh, but I want you to feel me. I want you to understand how hard I am."

"Do you desire me?"

"*Desire?* I want to live in your pussy, love."

She gasps but doesn't push me away.

She said she wants the real me, so this is me, no masks.

My hands are on her ass, even though it's over her dress, and I can feel the firm yet soft flesh at my fingertips.

"Please, make this agony stop."

"It's not agony. It's desire. Your little pussy wants to come."

We're in a private space. I know we're not at risk of being interrupted because when I move, wherever I am, my security follows and blocks the way. No one gets past Keiron and Rourke.

"Do people talk like this during sex?"

"I'm going easy, beautiful, being practically a prince."

"I won't have another day to experience this. Give me your worst."

She doesn't know what she's asking for. Taisiya might never be ready for my worst during sex.

But thinking about her words, I remember that, contrary to what I thought earlier, today won't be a first time. It will probably be the only time.

The kiss I give her now is hunger and farewell. Desperation and frustration. Desire and goodbye.

I push against her, rubbing the full length of my cock against her pussy. Soon, she's begging me.

I don't stop. I slide down a strap of her dress and lick the soft flesh of her shoulder. It's not enough, so I touch her hard nipple with my thumb.

"I want to suck you. Breasts and pussy. Drink when you come."

"Lorcan..."

She may be innocent, but she likes my dirty talk because as soon as she says my name, she trembles and comes.

She continues to move, and I kiss her neck and collarbone. Her chin, her mouth, the tip of her nose. I don't stop kissing her until her breathing returns to normal, and even after that, I don't let her go.

When she opens her eyes again, I finally come to my senses about what I've just done.

"This..."

"It shouldn't have happened?" she asks.

That's what I was going to say, but also to add that I don't regret anything.

Now that I've tasted a bit of her, I want more.

"Put me down, please."

She seems upset, and I do as she asks, unable to interpret her tone.

Is she scared? Does she think I'm a fucking monster?

"Where's the bathroom?"

"I'll take you there."

I guide her with my hand on the small of her back, but she seems emotionally distant, which causes me a fucked-up unease.

Not even when we pass Tulia and my security does she speak.

"I'll take her to the bathroom," I say to the Russian, who looks like she wants to kill me.

I know she's here for work, but I'm not in the mood to deal with other people's shit. She shouldn't have been allowed in the club in the first place. She should be on her knees thanking me.

When we reach the door, I say:

"I'll wait for you here."

She stops and looks at me as if she's going to say something. For a moment, I think she'll tell me what she's feeling, but then, as if she gives up, she goes in without looking back.

Chapter 33

Taisiya

As soon as I enter the bathroom, I look in the mirror, trying to see if anything has changed in my appearance after what just happened, but nothing has.

Aside from my flushed cheeks, a result of my first orgasm, I look the same Taisiya, yet I am not. Now, I know Ana was right. I'm in love with Lorcan.

I was still coming down from the cloud of pleasure, completely surrendered in his arms, when he came out with that talk about "this shouldn't have happened."

I couldn't hear that. Not after living the illusion for a few moments that my life isn't just a fucking void with several blank pages and some holes.

Now that I've taken a few breaths, though, I decide I won't run away from him and passively accept being sent away with a pat on the back. I'm going to tell him I'm leaving the convent, and if he still doesn't want anything to do with me, I'll move on.

I hear the sound of a few people entering the bathroom and my first reaction is to hide in one of the stalls.

Through the crack in the door, I see that it's two women who seem lively, laughing and chatting.

I need to pee, but I can't give away that I'm hiding, so I remain silent while they chatter.

Almost three minutes have passed, and the two are doing absolutely nothing, just looking at themselves in the mirror and talking non-stop, and I wonder how long it will take before Lorcan storms into the bathroom.

Despite still being upset about the end of my dream night, I smile because I imagine him doing exactly that: entering the women's bathroom to come after me.

I give up waiting and reach for the doorknob at the exact moment one of them says:

"Did you hear what he was saying to Kellan? He brought the poor thing out of pity. It's her birthday."

"Yes, I heard. Lorcan, despite being a bastard, is a nice guy. He felt sorry for the nun, but I'm sure he's dying to get rid of the brat."

"Uh-huh. I think so too. He told his cousin he's taking her home. Probably going to come back after me. He knows I can give him what he needs."

I feel my stomach churn and lean against the wall, closing my eyes tightly to avoid crying.

I want to go out and call them liars, because first and foremost, he's my friend and would never talk about me like that, but the problem is that what they're saying only echoes what he himself started to tell me earlier.

Jesus, how could I have been so stupid? Did I really think that blonde god would feel something for me beyond pity?

I hear the women leaving the bathroom and do the same, almost immediately.

When I step outside, he comes straight to me.

"You took your time. Is everything okay?"

"Nothing is okay with me. I want to go home. To be with my family. My dream night is over. You're free."

"I'll take you," he says, and despite being deeply hurt, I nod in agreement.

However, I walk towards Tulia and say:

"You're coming with us in the car."

Throughout the drive back, I feel his eyes on me, but he doesn't try to say anything more. I just want to get to Anastacia's house, lock myself in the bathroom, and cry where no one can hear me.

I sigh in relief when the driver parks. He walks around and opens my door. I know Lorcan can't do it because Ana explained it's the arrangement: he shouldn't even step onto their property.

Before I can get out of the vehicle, however, Lorcan grabs my arm.

"I didn't want to hurt you, Taisiya."

"And yet, you did. Goodbye, Lorcan."

I STAYED IN THE SHOWER as long as I could because even though I didn't send a message to my sister as we agreed, I know she's waiting for me. I heard the bedroom door open.

When I'm wrinkled and there's no way to keep the shower running without risking running out of water for the entire planet, I turn it off and put on a robe.

"I thought you went out to have fun," she says, and before I can reply, she hugs me. I know she notices my red eyes from crying, but she doesn't ask about it. "Happy birthday, little sister. I love you more than I could ever put into words."

"I love you too, Anastacia."

"Was the night not what you expected?"

"I don't know how to answer that."

"If you don't want to talk, that's fine."

"I don't. We have other things to discuss, but not today."

She steps back and nods.

"I've never seen you with that necklace."

"I got it today from Lorcan. It's his nickname in MMA: The Irish Bomb."

"Taisiya, this is getting serious."

"It's not. It's over."

"I don't believe it. You're in love."

"I am, but to him, I'm nothing but a pity case. End of story."

"That's okay. I don't want to make your night worse, we have so little time together. I have an idea. There's ice cream in the freezer and the birthday cake I ordered for the party you didn't come to," she says.

Only Ana could throw something like that in my face and still smile so I wouldn't feel guilty.

"What do you have in mind?"

"A sugar binge. We didn't drink alcohol, so let's indulge in our chosen poison."

"I'm in. But first, I want to check on my nephew. Every time I come here, he seems bigger."

Chapter 34

Lorcan

Three Weeks Later

"Are you trying to kill yourself?" Cillian asks from outside the ring.

I knew he was coming when I saw the gym empty quickly.

There are few fighters in the circuit who also work for the Syndicate, and those who aren't part of it are scared shitless of him.

"I don't know what you're talking about," I reply, continuing to punch the *sparring Bob*.

"What the hell is going on, Lorcan?"

I take off my gloves and throw them on the ground.

"Have I missed any of my Syndicate work?"

"You know perfectly well that's not what I'm talking about. It's not the work that's the problem. Or rather, maybe the problem is the *excess* of work. Is she the one driving you crazy like this?"

"Cillian, you're my cousin and the boss of our organization, but keep Taisiya out of this conversation. My..."

"Your what?"

"Protected, friend... I don't know. The title doesn't make a damn bit of difference. The fact is, her name isn't up for discussion. It's my personal life."

"Well, it's your personal life I'm talking about, hell. She's my right hand, but she's also my cousin. Blood, Lorcan. And if you're trying to kill yourself, I want to at least know why."

"Have you ever been ashamed of yourself?"

"More than once. I've been in the death business since I was a kid."

"I haven't. I've always taken pride in, despite what we do, trying to be fair. I've never killed an innocent. Never hurt someone weaker."

"What happened?"

"I hurt her."

Since the night at the club, I haven't tried to talk to her again, although I know it will have to happen at some point.

The time we're giving each other without speaking isn't just for her benefit, to be honest. It's necessary for me too. I can't look at myself in the mirror. I acted like an animal, abusing her trust. Hurting her so much she had to run away from me.

When we were together that night, despite all the differences—age, experience, even the damn organizations we belong to—I thought we were on the same wavelength. When she came out of the bathroom with a tearful face, I saw that I had read it all wrong.

I betrayed her trust. Seduced a novice, and now I need her forgiveness.

"Tell me what happened."

"No, I don't want to talk about it."

"Damn stubborn man!"

"Did you get the information I asked for?"

"Yes, of course. I don't think it should be resolved this way, but if that's how you want to do it..."

"Yes, it is. He's back. We'll wait. I'll make sure he feels comfortable. Safe. And then, when he believes he's untouchable, I'll take him out of his house in the middle of the night. I'll make him feel everything she went through—fear, pain, loneliness, hopelessness. Only then will I kill him."

"You don't just want to take him out of circulation."

"No, I want revenge. Maxim killed Ayrtom, but this bastard is mine."

I'M STANDING IN FRONT of one of Juno's stores. The first one she opened, actually, and I watch the bastard calmly walk in and place his order.

How fucking ironic can life be? I never would have guessed that son of a bitch was a regular customer of Cillian's wife.

By the way, from what I've researched, the entire law firm he's a partner in has become a frequent consumer of her products.

I get out of the car and walk slowly towards the store. I stop outside, pretending to look at the display window, because I don't know if I can go in there without killing him in cold blood.

He's charming the saleswoman. Like Ayrtom Stepanchikov, he's well-dressed, wealthy, and makes women melt—if the saleswoman's ear-to-ear grin is any indication.

A supposedly honorable man who, among other things, works *pro bono* to help underprivileged teens.

A sick bastard who had the chance to save a dirty, terrified, and injured girl, and instead joined her tormentor to destroy her soul.

I look at the card in my hand.

Lambertucci and Associates.

A famous firm, and he is one of the longest-standing partners.

He passes by me and smiles, wishing me a good day.

I nod in response.

Enjoy what little time you have left, you son of a bitch. Make the most of it, because your universe is running out of days.

I enter the store.

"Hi, Lorcan," the saleswoman says, smiling.

"Hi."

"The usual?"

"Yes. Don't forget the double chocolate topping."

I wait for her to prepare the box of sweets and as I'm leaving, I hear her say:

"I don't know who you're taking these cupcakes to every day, but she's a lucky girl."

I look back.

"You're mistaken. I'm the lucky one for having found her."

I get in the car and the driver doesn't ask any more questions. He heads straight to the convent.

This time, after waiting for him to deliver the sweets at the entrance, I wait half an hour and send a message:

"There isn't a single fucking day that I don't regret hurting you. I will never forgive myself for it."

Chapter 35

Taisiya

That Same Night

"**Y**ou took a long time to agree to a video call, Grandpa."

"I'm old, Taisiya. I don't like phones. I already use this damn device and we talk once a week. Why did you want to see me so much? I'm as ugly as sin!"

I laugh and can't deny it. He is indeed ugly, but he makes up for it with how much I love him.

I look at him, trying to memorize his image for the days when he won't be on this planet anymore, because something in my heart tells me it won't be for long.

Ruslan told me that, in addition to providing protection, he offered to arrange a residence for Grandpa Abramov in Moscow, but he refuses to leave Siberia.

"What? Aren't you going to deny that I'm ugly?" he says, joking.

"I can't. Lying is a sin."

His smile widens.

"I love you, dear. God knows how happy I was that you went away to be with your sister, but your face looks sad. What's wrong?"

"How can you tell that just by looking at me?"

"You're very expressive. Over the phone, I didn't notice anything, but now that I'm seeing you, it's obvious you're not okay. Is it just the convent issue?"

I told him about my dilemma: staying in the convent without a vocation to avoid a marriage of convenience or giving up the religious career and being forced to endure an "arranged" husband.

"Partly, yes. But there's something I haven't told you. In fact, I haven't told anyone."

"Has your memory returned?"

"No, it's about Lorcan."

"I'm listening."

Every time he asked me about Lorcan, I changed the subject, but today, maybe because we're seeing each other and I need to share this with someone, I tell him everything: from when we went to Boston together, the nearly year-long separation, and then, the night of my birthday.

Of course, I leave out the details that still make me blush, but which are also responsible for making my body feverish night after night.

"You're in love," he concludes the obvious.

"Yes, but he stayed with me out of pity."

"I don't believe that. I don't think pity is his style, dear."

"But those girls... they said..."

"Taisiya, my love, you've been away from the world for too long and maybe you don't know how envious and mean people can be. I wouldn't be surprised if they knew you were in the bathroom and did it on purpose."

"But why? They didn't even know me. I don't believe it!"

"Maybe because you had something they wanted: Lorcan."

Is it possible?

"He leaves me cupcakes every day."

"What?"

"His cousin's wife makes delicious cupcakes. I ate about three on my birthday, at Aunt Orla's house. I think he noticed. Since then, they always come with the same flavor and the double chocolate topping that I loved."

"And after that, you want to convince me that this guy doesn't care about you?"

"And if it's out of pity?"

"That would have passed, Taisiya. If there were any feeling other than pity, he would have forgotten you. From everything I know, a relationship between you two would be very complicated."

I nod in agreement.

"What should I do?"

"Only you can say, but if you want advice, give yourselves a chance, at least. Send a message."

"I said goodbye to you the last time we met."

"Out of pride?"

"No. Out of hurt."

"But you're suffering."

"Yes, I am."

"Examine your heart, and if you think it's the right thing to do, send him a message."

We talked for a few more minutes before hanging up, and before I lose my courage, I type quickly.

"You're going to give me cavities, Thor. I don't know if you hurt me on purpose, but I forgive you anyway, because I miss you terribly."

I barely have time to put down the phone when I receive one from him.

Thor: *"Not a damn day goes by that I don't regret hurting you. I'll never forgive myself for it."*

I check the time. We both texted each other at the same moment. If that's not a sign from the universe, I don't know what is.

"We texted at the same time?"

I send it, and to my surprise, the phone rings.

"I've never apologized to anyone, but I'm doing it now."

"I don't know exactly what you're apologizing for, and I'm not ready to talk about it, but I forgive you. I don't want to say goodbye forever, Lorcan."

"That sounds sad. Am I the cause?"

The lack I feel for you is the cause.

Loving you and knowing I'll never get that back is the cause.

Living in my voluntary prison knowing you're so close is the cause.

Of course, I don't say any of this because I don't want to upset him.

"Don't be conceited. I don't even like you that much."

"Oh, Taisiya, I would give anything to see you now."

"Video call?"

"No. I can't. Nothing has changed, baby. It would be risky for both of us."

"Then can we erase the rules of the past? I want to call you when I miss you."

That means I'll call you every day.

"Yes, no rules, just one. I'll always answer on the first ring. If I don't, don't insist. It will probably be dangerous."

A Week Later

IT'S FUNNY THAT NOW, when nightmares come, I'm aware that I'm dreaming.

They don't become any less frightening, though. It's like going to an amusement park, in those rooms where you have to open doors and know that behind some of them, or all of them, something truly terrifying will appear.

I'm conscious while dreaming. I know that a few weeks ago it was my eighteenth birthday and that I'm living in a convent.

Unlike what happened before, today, when the nightmare deepens, I let myself fall into the void of fear and then, I see everything.

And what I see is terrifying.

Chapter 36

Lorcan

My body feels like a cart has run over it. Probably the result of last night's binge—or is it the celebration of Saint Patrick's Day today?

Excess alcohol and women combined with little sleep are a shitty mix, even if, in my case, women are no longer on the agenda.

As a damn masochist, even though guilt for what happened completely overwhelms me, I can't forget her. I haven't been with anyone else.

It's been a long time since I've spiraled down so much. I usually take care of myself due to the fights, but I've been keeping myself numb since the last time we saw each other. Even now that phone contact has resumed, I still can't look at myself in the mirror without feeling like a bastard.

Fuck, I need to stop whatever is happening inside me, but no matter how hard I try, nothing changes.

I don't want to feel this. I can't desire her. I've already hurt her enough. I need to think of Taisiya now as someone untouchable.

She is sweet and innocent, and all she ever wanted from me was friendship. I will never abuse her trust again.

What did I expect? She went through hell and still wanted to continue her plan to become a nun, so she's obviously devoted.

"And if she wasn't, what would you do?" a voice mocks.

No, enough! I don't want to think about this. It feels wrong and very perverted to desire her after all she has suffered.

I have this conversation with myself every day.

It doesn't matter what my mind says, though, because my more primitive side keeps claiming her, screaming that she belongs to me.

No, Taisiya does not belong to you, according to what she herself stated, she belongs to the Creator.

Game over. I need to get it into my head that she will forever be only my protected one. I have to focus on living as I did before. No plans or commitments. Unattached, free, with no strings.

I step into the hot shower and much of the worry dissolves. At this moment, it feels better than an orgasm. I groan as the strong spray hits my back and promise myself that I'll get at least eight hours of sleep from today to tomorrow. Get back on track.

Five minutes later, I dry off and, as usual, lie face down on the mattress, feeling almost human.

The relaxation starts to spread through my body and my eyes grow heavy. I know I'll be out any moment.

I reach out to turn off the bedside lamp, and at that instant, in a fucking split second, my phone rings.

For a moment, I think I've fallen asleep, that it's not real. It's almost three in the morning.

If it were any other music, I would ignore it, but I will never stop answering her.

Given the time, something must have happened.

A nightmare? No, she wouldn't contact me for that. I'm sure that during the weeks we didn't speak, she had many of them and never reached out.

"Hey, little one."

"Lorcan, come get me, please. I'm in the middle of the street."

I sit up, fully awake.

"Taisiya, what are you talking about? In the street, where?"

By this point, I'm already halfway into my jeans.

"I remembered. I remembered everything. I need you."

"Everything?"

"Yes, I woke up in the middle of a nightmare and now, I know what happened from the night of the fire until Grandpa saved me. I couldn't stand staying at the convent. I was suffocating. I need you."

"I'm coming to get you, but you shouldn't have gone out into the street alone. It'll take me at least twenty minutes to get there."

"Maxim leaves bodyguards at the front gate. I went out the back. I don't want to go to my sister's house. I want you."

"I'm coming, Taisiya. Nothing will stop me from getting there, but you need to stay safe until then. Go back closer to the convent. Stay as close as possible to that back exit you mentioned, but try to hide so if any strange car passes by, they won't see you."

"There's no one here at this hour. Come quickly, please."

She isn't crying, but there's an emptiness in her voice.

In less than a minute, I'm already in the garage. I put on my helmet with the microphone on.

"Don't hang up. We'll talk all the way."

"The battery will die. Better save it."

Fuck me! I'm losing my mind. Thinking of her alone, vulnerable, in the middle of the street, is pushing me to the edge.

"Okay. Hide behind a car and if you hear any strange noise or see someone approaching, run. I'll find you."

I told her twenty minutes, but I arrive in fifteen, breaking all speed records. I'm sure I've aged ten years on the way, my mind not stopping for a second.

When I finally approach the old building, I call her. She answers on the first ring.

"Show yourself. I'm already on the street."

I walk only a few meters before seeing her, still dressed in the novice's attire.

Fuck, she must be freezing!

I turn off the bike and jump down. As I approach, Taisiya leaps into my arms.

Weeks without having her with me, and she still seems to fit so well as always.

"Because she belongs to you," the fucking voice screams.

I try to silence it, but inside me, a certainty takes hold.

She is mine.

"Lorcan," she says my name and tightens her hold in my embrace. "I didn't want to see anyone else. Just you."

"I'm here, baby. I'm not going anywhere."

I pick her up, and at that moment, I regret not coming by car because I want to comfort her, but we can't stay in the middle of the street.

I have many enemies, and if someone has followed me, I would be putting her life at risk as well.

"I'll get you out of here and then we'll talk, okay?"

"Where are we going?"

I close my eyes for a moment, knowing that the decision I make will change our lives forever.

"My place."

Chapter 37

Lorcan

She remains clinging to me. It's as if she thinks I'm going to disappear at any moment.

This isn't what I expected. After what happened, even though she said she forgave me for almost seducing her at the club that night, I thought Taisiya wouldn't want me to touch her again, and for the first time in my adult life, I'm completely fucking confused.

"We can't stay here."

"It's okay. Just take me with you. I can wait to tell you everything."

I try to focus on the practical aspect, although it really messes with me seeing her eyes looking like a stormy sea. Stormy and empty.

"Have you ever ridden a motorcycle?"

"No."

"I'll have to tie your dress, okay?"

"It's called a habit. And yes, that's fine. You can tie it."

I kneel and arrange the large amount of fabric as best as I can. Then, I pick her up again and sit her on my Harley.

"When I settle in front of you, you'll have to hold on to me. Hold on tight, and when I move my body, lean in the same direction. Our balance will depend on that."

The chance of her causing any damage if she doesn't follow the instructions is minimal because Taisiya weighs as much as a feather, but I don't want to take any unnecessary risks.

I put my helmet on her and adjust it. In the rush, I didn't bring another one, and besides, I never take anyone as a passenger.

"Is everything okay?" I ask before getting on in front of her.

She nods, and I position myself in front.

I bring my hands that are wrapped around her waist to my lips and kiss them.

"We'll be home soon, and we'll talk. You'll tell me everything. You're not alone in this."

I drive calmly this time, as much as I can anyway, because my whole body is fucking agitated.

Twenty minutes later, we enter my garage. I jump off and don't let her walk, picking her up and carrying her up the stairs. The entire floor is mine, and the building, except for my apartment, belongs to Cillian, but it's empty. I could have taken the elevator, but I need to move. Being trapped in a metal box for minutes would only make me more restless.

When we arrive, I enter the code to open the door and set her down on her feet, already inside the apartment.

"Can I take a shower?" she asks.

"What?"

"You said we'd talk, and I really want that, but I'd like a shower first. I can't stay in this dress. I will never wear it again."

I think she sees the confusion on my face. Just a few weeks ago, on her birthday morning, Taisiya told me she was in the place she wanted to be—the convent.

That night, I was sure it was the fault of coming in my arms that made her pull away from me, and now she tells me she hates her nun's dress?

"I can put it in the wash. Maybe tomorrow you..."

"No. If you can lend me something of yours, I'd appreciate it. As for this dress, burn it. I will never go back there. I'll tell you everything I remembered, and then I'll leave forever. No one will ever force me to do what I don't want again."

"I THINK I DIDN'T HEAR that right," my grandfather says over the phone.

I took Taisiya to one of the suites in my apartment, which, by the way, have never been used.

After lending her a T-shirt and boxer briefs, which will probably swallow her, I went out so she could take a shower.

She seemed desperate to get rid of that outfit, and to be honest, I didn't want to see her in it either.

When I looked at her in the dress—or rather, habit, as she corrected me—I felt even more of a sinner than I already am.

The girl who makes my blood boil is a sweet, innocent angel.

A novice.

Jesus!

"You heard me," I reply, forcing myself back to reality. "Taisiya is with me."

"You brought her to your apartment? A nun? Worse, a nun who belongs to the Russian Organization?"

"She doesn't belong to any Organization. Don't talk like that, Grandpa. We're in the twenty-first century. I understand her connection with Maxim and that this arrangement of her staying with me isn't very usual, but Taisiya was, in the past, a mafia princess. She's a novice now. If she belongs to anyone, it's to God. Anyway, I didn't call to explain. I called to let Anastacia know she will stay here as long as she wants, so consider this call a mere courtesy."

"Courtesy my ass, Lorcan! Christ, I don't even know where to begin analyzing this mess, but let's start with the obvious: how and why did she escape from the convent?"

"She escaped in the middle of the night. Evaded the bodyguards by leaving through the back door."

"And why the hell would she do something so stupid?"

I take a deep breath to avoid sending him to hell considering his age and that he's also my grandfather.

"She woke up from a nightmare. She remembers everything now. Every detail, she told me."

"Everything?"

"Yes. We haven't talked yet, but I believe her memory has fully returned. When I picked her up, she was desperate."

"Holy shit!"

"She asked me to come get her because she didn't want to stay with her sister."

"And you, of course, went."

"What do you think? I told you once that Taisiya was mine to care for and protect, whether we stay together or not."

"Have you stopped to think that you just turned on the inferno switch?"

I ignore his anger. No one is going to take her away from here unless she wants to leave.

"The only thing I thought was that she wanted me close. She's taking a shower now."

"What? Are you out of your mind? Do you know what will happen when Yerik finds out? He and Cillian will go to war."

"I get along with my cousin. As for Yerik, he's not my problem. I owe no respect to the Pakhan."

"Lorcan, I don't want to see either of you dead. You're both my blood."

"Death is certain for everyone."

"Don't say such bullshit."

"I'm not sending her away. Taisiya will stay as long as she wants. No one will forcibly remove her from here."

"Hell, why the hell get into a dispute over a girl like her? Unless you're in love, which I doubt, Taisiya isn't right for you. She's too innocent and broken. An explosive package."

My explosive package.

"I'm not going to discuss my relationship with Taisiya, but just so you know, even if I wanted her, it would never happen. She told me a few weeks ago that she is devoted. She's confused now that she's remembered everything, but I think once she gets her head straight, she'll go back to the convent. End of discussion. But until then, she stays here. Talk to Anastacia."

"The truce between Yerik and Cillian is over, son. Do you know what that means? If neither of them backs down on this, there could be a bloodbath."

"She's not leaving here, Grandpa. It's not up for discussion."

"And what am I supposed to tell Maxim? How do you expect me to explain that his virgin sister-in-law is staying at my grandson's place, an Irishman, indefinitely?"

"Maybe you shouldn't talk to him then. Talk to Anastacia. I'm sure she'll be concerned about Taisiya and not the Organization's distorted sense of ownership. She's not an object, Ruslan. She's young and broken as you said, but I won't let them force her to do what she doesn't want."

Chapter 38

Taisiya

As the water runs over my body, I try to focus on the task of cleaning myself instead of thinking about the actions that brought me here.

I acted on impulse—or desperation—but I don't regret fleeing.

I'm not afraid of the consequences. Maybe if this had happened a year ago, I would have been terrified for various reasons: for the horror movie I lived through while still so young, for challenging the Organization by escaping the convent, for seeking refuge in the arms of the man who sees me as a duty.

Three hundred sixty-five days of therapy didn't fix me, but it did stitch together many of my shattered pieces, and all I can think about is what Aunt Orla said: that I didn't remember before because I wasn't ready.

Not that I feel ready now. How could I? Who can prepare for what I've lived through?

I'm confused, with a lot of anger inside me, but despite that, I don't feel like a victim.

I feel strong and... protected.

Yes. He always manages to do that.

Being near Lorcan gives me the sensation of being guarded by a fortress, and I will need his strength to do what I'm planning.

I'm going to tell him everything I remember, then ask him to arrange a meeting with my sister and then leave.

I meant it when I said I wouldn't go back to the convent. There's nothing for me there anymore.

If I weren't so fearful, I would have left months ago, but instead, I stayed hoping that something would change in my heart.

It didn't happen. Now, after my memory has returned, I know that the chance of that happening is nil. I wasn't born to be a nun. There's no vocation in me, only a will to live.

I want what was taken from me, and although I know some of the losses I've suffered are irreversible because you can't go back in time, I won't bow my head and passively accept that others decide my fate for me.

I hear two knocks on the door and then Lorcan asks:

"Is everything okay?"

"I'm coming out."

I dress at record speed because I'm eager to talk to him.

In fact, I think anxiety isn't the right word, but rather urgency. The need for everything: to face my fears, to vent about my nightmare, to know once and for all if there's a name for what's between us.

In less than two minutes, I leave the bathroom and am not entirely surprised to find him in the middle of the room instead of waiting for me in the living room, as social norms would dictate.

He looks at me, and I wish I were more experienced to interpret his face, but I have no idea what he's thinking.

Since the day we started talking again, Lorcan has been treading lightly with me. There's no more naturalness in our exchanges, and even when I tease him on the phone, he doesn't take the bait.

My mind is a mess. Thoughts colliding. The urge to fight the whole world, but among all these needs, there's one that weighs most at the moment.

I need something concrete, real. I won't ignore the questions that haunt my mind out of fear of the answers.

"Did you stay with me that day out of pity?" I blurt out before I can stop myself.

"What? Why are we talking about this now? That wasn't the reason you called me."

"No, it was because of the nightmare and the memories, but then, after I got here, I decided to put you ahead of everything else, you know why?"

"No."

"Because you are my present, one I'm not afraid of. I'm tired of fearing the past, and whenever I'm with you, you manage to drive away my anxieties."

"Taisiya, you're confused. We need to talk about what happened that night at the club, but not today. The priority is to share your bad memories with me."

"And I will, at some point, but don't you think I have the right to choose what to face one thing at a time?"

He doesn't respond, and I continue:

"I choose to face both of us first."

"Why?"

"Because I don't want you to change how you see me. I want you to continue looking at me the way you do: without pity, as if I were just a normal person."

"You *are* a normal person. No matter what they did to you, you're here, whole."

I close my eyes, absorbing his words.

"That's why, for telling me things like that, you're unique in my life, Lorcan. I love my sister above all else, but Ana isn't ready to accept what I've become. Her guilt makes her see me as a victim, and I don't want to be one. I'm young, broken, full of scars, but I refuse to be a victim."

"Come here, Taisiya."

"Why should I come over there? You never expected me to get close before, and it's one of the things I like most about you. You don't ask for permission. You take, you possess, you claim."

"That was before I hurt you. I don't want to make you suffer ever again."

"You didn't answer whether you stayed with me out of pity."

"Pity?"

I nod in agreement.

"On my birthday night, when I went to the bathroom, I heard two women talking. They said you had taken me to the club out of pity. They knew I had no memory and that I was a novice."

He takes a step closer, his face hardening. I've seen this expression before: anger.

"What exactly are you talking about?"

"When we were at the club, and shortly afterward you started telling me that 'that shouldn't have happened,' I needed to step away because I couldn't bear to hear, just moments after touching the sky in your arms, that you were regretful. I went to the bathroom to think, and two women came in. They didn't see me because I was in a stall, but they mentioned hearing you tell Kellan that you only took me there because you felt sorry for me and that you'd probably go home and spend the night with one of them. Is that true?"

"I came here after I dropped you off at your sister's house. How could I be with someone after having you?"

"Didn't you regret it?"

He runs his hands through his hair.

"I only regret betraying your trust."

"Betraying my trust?"

"Yes. I acted like an animal. I let my desire for you overshadow your faith in me."

"You didn't betray my trust. When I said you hurt me, it was because I thought you were with me out of pity. I don't regret anything we experienced. Being with you was what I wanted most in life."

I'm the one moving closer now, trying to untangle the confusion we've both caused due to a lack of a simple conversation.

"I'm not what you want most in life. You want to be a nun. That's what you told me that morning: that you were in the right place, that the convent was where you wanted to stay."

"I had no choice. It was stay there or be forced to marry someone Ruslan chose. What did you want me to say? There was nothing you could have done if I had told you the truth. You cut me out of your life for an entire year. So, what was I supposed to do? When we first spoke, should I have begged to be saved from your grandfather's plans to find me a husband?"

"I would never allow him to force you into marriage."

"Yes, maybe you would have stopped him, but here's a secret: I'm tired of needing to be saved. I'm not made of porcelain. Want to know what I remembered? I won't give you the details now, but I can give you a preview: I was beaten and tortured by two adult men. I heard that miserable man, who was my mother's cousin and thus my relative too, talk about all the cruelty he wanted to inflict on the most important person in my life, Ana."

"Damn it!" he roars, and I can see the pain on his face.

I don't want that. I want the man I love, not the protector.

Chapter 39

Taisiya

"I want to hear everything."

"And I'll tell you, but not now."

"No, Taisiya, it has to be now. I don't want my anger to fade."

"Fade in relation to whom?"

"To the son of a bitch who hurt you. Do you remember everything?"

I nod in agreement.

"So you know there were two of them."

"Yes."

"I'm going to kill him, Taisiya."

"Just one?" I ask carefully. "Or is one of them no longer a threat?"

Although I've never directly touched on the subject of my abduction, I know enough about Lorcan and Ana's husband now to understand that they wouldn't let it go unpunished.

"Did they kill one of them already? Who? Ayrtom or his accomplice?"

"Ayrtom will never harm you again. To anyone, actually," he answers succinctly.

"Did he suffer?"

"Not as much as he deserved, because nothing we did would have been enough."

I never thought I would wish this on someone, but at this moment, I genuinely hope Lorcan hurt him badly.

"I don't feel pity."

"You shouldn't. He was a son of a bitch." He looks at me before continuing: "And what about me?"

"What?"

"What do you feel about me knowing that I'm a killer?"

"I remember everything, Lorcan. I grew up in that world. It's no different from what my father did. Ana and I might not have had details on how Dad made a living, but we were raised as mafia princesses. We knew, even if implicitly, what our father's job was."

He looks at me, and his expression softens a bit.

Somehow, what I said seems to calm him. My acceptance of what he does brings us closer.

"Talk about the past. Tell me everything."

"Not now. You'll see me differently afterward."

"No, I'll see you as always: beautiful, incredibly strong, and mine."

"Mine?"

"Yes, you are mine. I've controlled myself up to this point. I spent weeks in hell, submerged in guilt, because I thought I had hurt you, betrayed your trust. But now that I see it was all just a misunderstanding, there's nothing that will stop me from taking what I want."

"And what you want is me?"

He comes closer, and I feel a shiver in my stomach.

"Don't tease me, Taisiya. You're my innocent girl, but not to the point where you don't know how much I desire you. The day I made you come, you felt how you drive me crazy. You came with my hard cock pushing against your pussy. I'm hanging by a thread. Only a thin layer of ice, a remnant of civility, is stopping me from touching you, because I think you need, above all, to talk. But I'm human and I have my limits."

His words awaken desire in me and drive me crazy at the same time, because while I'm feeling a flutter of arrhythmia hearing him admit that he wants me, I'm also frustrated that he thinks he can see inside me, that he presumes to know me better than I do.

"You don't know what I need!" I say, pulling away. "No one does. Or rather, no one is concerned with knowing. You, like everyone else, treat me like a crystal that will shatter into a thousand pieces at any moment!"

I know I'm shouting, but I'm exhausted from being the pathetic and predictable victim; from continuing to wear the guise of the suffering girl. For once, I need Lorcan to see me as an equal.

"What do you want from me?"

He comes very close, leaving only a small space between our bodies.

"Everything. I want everything. Afterward, we can talk, and you can go back to seeing me as the girl who needs to be surrounded by a protective shell, but for tonight, just once, give me everything."

"You don't know what my *everything* is."

"Test me."

"You want to be tested? You want me to treat you the way I'm used to? Because the truth is, I don't know what to do with you. You're too precious and delicate. And yet, in my filthy mind, I imagine fucking you in every possible way. I don't want there to be a single part of you that I don't possess."

I should be shocked, but I'm not. Instead, a warm, wet desire spreads at the apex of my thighs.

"Did you desire me even when you thought I was going to be a nun?"

"Even then. Even knowing that my rival was more powerful, because I don't know a single person who has won a contest against God, I wanted to take you *from Him.*

"And do what?"

"Taisiya..."

"Tell me, I want to hear what kind of affection you would give me. I liked it when you said those things at the club."

"*Affection?* I don't want to just give you affection; I want to fuck you hard."

I feel my heart pounding in my chest, and it's not because of the harshness of his words, but because I know I'm managing to pull him out of his armor. I think he's finally going to let me see him not as my hero, my knight in shining armor, but as my man, my love.

"Do you think I'm going to run away?"

I don't even know how I had the courage to say something like that, but maybe it's pure desperation. I know that after what happens tonight and then, when I tell him the truth about my past, I'll have to run away.

I'm not going back to the convent, and I'm not marrying someone chosen for me.

Nor can I stay with the Irish. Ana explained what would happen — a bloodbath — if Cillian and Yerik went to war over my relationship with Lorcan.

With the clock *ticking* in my brain, I don't have much time, and I'll take what I can. Balancing the bad memories with the moments I'll spend with him.

"Kiss me again," I ask, moving closer. "Make me feel like I did that night."

He breathes heavily, his eyes locked on mine.

I feel his tension, and maybe, in a different situation, I would be afraid, but it's not just Lorcan who has reached his limit. I have too.

"I'm not the right kind of man for you," he says, grabbing a handful of my hair with enough force to make me tilt my head back, "but the running is over, Taisiya. You're mine. Want to be free? Living with me is a prison. Not just because of my lifestyle, but because I won't let you go anymore."

I close my eyes, wishing it were true, but I know I can't put his life at risk. The Organization will want to kill him if they know I'm here.

"I'm your what?"

"My wife."

I feel my face heat up and my skin tingle with the desire to be touched.

"I'm not a woman yet. I'm a girl."

"Not for long," he says, and the next thing I know, he lifts me off my feet, his mouth devouring mine with an urgency that sends shivers down my spine like little electric shocks.

Chapter 40

Lorcan

Taisiya is pure fire against the palms of my hands. Wherever I touch her, her heat calls to me.

I'm not the kind of guy who fucks without kissing. I never understood this bullshit from some people saying that kissing on the mouth is too intimate. What could be more intimate than shoving your cock into a partner?

I like kisses. On the mouth, on the pussy, on the ass. I don't impose restrictions, but taking Taisiya's lips is different from anything I've experienced before.

She's responsive, despite her inexperience. She gives herself up, passionate and tempting in my arms, letting me do whatever I want, biting my mouth, running her delicious tongue over my lip. Moaning every time I brush my thumb over her hard nipples.

Knowing that everything is new to her, like a learning experience, elevates my arousal to the moon.

I bite her lower lip, sucking, and she moans, scratching my biceps.

I want more. I want her hands on me. Skin against skin, so I take a step back and remove my shirt.

"Please, don't go away."

"I'm not going anywhere. Never again. And neither are you."

It's a promise and a threat. An oath and a request. A pact, but also, my surrender.

I don't care if I have to go to war with the whole damn world. She's mine.

When I pull her into my arms again, she opens her mouth, bringing her warm tongue to mine. I suck her as I will with her clit, and crazy with this thought, I run my fingers down her abdomen, touching her pussy with my open hand through the thin fabric of the boxer shorts I lent her.

I lose myself in the softness of her mouth, devouring her with hunger and demand.

She rubs her bare breasts against me, her nipples like little stones against my flesh.

I want to take her to bed, strip her naked and lick her all over, but I need to remember that it's her first time, so instead of risking rushing things, I pick her up and sit in the armchair near the full-length mirror, with her straddling me.

"Open your eyes," I command.

She complies.

"What's wrong?"

"Do you know what's going to happen?"

"You're going to make love to me."

"I'm going to do *everything* with you. Taste every piece."

"I'm yours. You were right when you said that. I was born to be yours, Lorcan. I'm not afraid."

She's surrendered and passionate, and her trust does me a world of good. After what she's been through, Taisiya's faith in me is something I will honor for the rest of my days.

"I want you out of that shirt."

Her eyes widen, and then she lowers her head.

"I'm embarrassed. Not just because I've never been naked in front of a man, but because of the scars... they..."

"Shhh..." I hold her jaw, lifting her face and forcing her to look at me. "There's nothing that will make me see you as less beautiful, baby."

I turn her around, so she's now against my chest, her pussy over my cock.

I push her hair to the side and bite her delicate neck.

She moans, shivering.

I don't stop licking and nibbling, and when she's lost in arousal, grinding on my lap, I put my hands inside her shirt.

She stiffens.

"I want to feel you, love. Never be ashamed of me. I'm crazy about you, Taisiya, and to me, you're beautiful. Entirely beautiful. Every little bit."

I drag my hands down her abdomen, slowly climbing until I reach her breasts. I place them over the two firm, round mounds and bite her neck.

"Grind on my cock, angel. I want to feel that virgin pussy on me."

She starts slowly, moving timidly, but when I pinch both nipples at the same time, she screams and gives herself up.

She plants her hands on my thighs and rides me, whimpering.

"Faster, Taisiya. I want to feel you dripping through the jeans."

I'm not gentle when pulling on her nipples because my arousal is already on the edge, flirting with losing control.

When she starts trembling, moaning my name, giving me the first orgasm of many I plan to give her today, I don't wait for her to recover. While she's still in the throes of passion, I pull her shirt off.

I grab her long hair in my fist, and for a moment, I need to control my rage when I see the scars. They're clear but deep. I knew, from feeling them with my fingers once, that they were there, but seeing the depravity of those bastards makes me decide something.

Tomorrow will be Levy Goldberg's last day on Earth.

"Lorcan?" she calls, sounding insecure.

"I'm here with you, baby."

She's tense again, but before she can try to get off my lap —which I guess is her intention —, I start kissing her back.

"No."

"Yes. You're all mine. There's no part of you that I don't desire."

She still can't relax, so I fit my hand between her legs.

The contact was meant to help her overcome her shame, but the moment I feel the soaked fabric, undeniable proof that she came, I lose my mind.

I gently bite the skin of her back, alternating with kisses, and slip a hand inside the boxer shorts. Her clit is hard, swollen, and when I start flicking it, she forgets her shame and starts moaning again.

I'm like a damn addict to her reactions. Hungry for her sounds, juices, and breaths.

I pull her closer to me and with my legs, I spread hers wide, massaging her clit, until she starts moving her hips, seeking more from my hand.

I release her hair and grab a breast, pulling the nipple between my thumb and forefinger.

I need more, though, and still holding her, I stand up, reversing our positions, and sit her in the armchair.

I kneel in front of her, and she tries to cover her breasts.

"No."

"I'm embarrassed."

"Do you want this?"

"Yes."

"Then give in, love."

I hold both arms, pushing them away, and I need to take a deep breath when I see her bare breasts for the first time.

"I can't believe you're mine, Taisiya. There's no woman more beautiful in the world."

She gives me a shy smile, and when I reach out to grab one of the soft globes of flesh, she no longer tries to hide.

I pull her by the neck and knead one of her breasts, squeezing it in my hand. She moans loudly, and hungry, I lower myself and take one in my mouth, sucking and rolling my tongue around the nipple.

"I think I'm going to die..."

"No. You're going to come many times. Just pleasure. No pain, baby."

I increase the pressure with which I suck her breast and at the same time, I pull down her boxer shorts, completely removing them.

"Spread your legs for me."

She spreads them, but I want more.

So, I lift both legs, placing them over the arms of the armchair.

She closes her eyes.

"No, look. I'm going to eat your pussy and I want you to see my tongue licking you for the first time."

The skin of her thighs is goosebumpy and she shivers, I think from shyness and desire, but she does as I asked and, bravely, meets my gaze.

I return to focusing on her breasts but touch her pussy, massaging her clit with my thumb and using my middle finger to gently fuck her untouched channel.

When I feel her on the tip of my finger for the first time, my cock is about to explode in my jeans.

It takes a lot of effort to control myself. Her pleasure is my priority.

Soon, she surrenders again, and every little thing I do with her is like breaking down barriers. It's delicious and new to me. I've never had to be gentle because I've never had inexperienced partners, but every time I see a reaction from Taisiya, I'm driven wild with desire.

As good as it is to suck on her breasts, I want to taste the pink pussy with short hair.

The position I've put her in is unabashed, and Taisiya looks like a sex goddess, innocent and wicked at the same time.

I slide my thumb to her opening and she bites her lower lip, I believe to stifle a scream.

I do it again, but this time, I press our lips together.

"Scream into my mouth. For me. Inside me. I want everything from you."

I push my thumb inside her, but not too much, and even so, she almost lifts off the couch, her body more than sensitive, eager for pleasure.

Wild desire makes my muscles contract, hardened by lust.

I kiss her mouth, growing hungrier for her taste.

The contact is ravenous, lewd, our tongues clashing, demanding her surrender.

One of my hands continues to caress her nipple while the other lifts her by the ass, further onto the edge of the couch.

I look down and see the lips of her pussy glistening with desire.

Taisiya moans loudly, grinding, taking what she wants.

I trail my lips from her mouth to her chin, neck, and hard breasts.

I run my tongue over her abdomen, and her breathing quickens as I approach her sex.

She gasps, trembling, as she feels my mouth on her flesh.

She can't hide her need. She doesn't know what she wants, but she knows that she wants it.

I part her pussy lips with both hands, and when I lower myself, even before tasting her, I get a bit drunk on her delicious female scent.

I lick her whole pussy, and she screams, almost lifting off the couch.

I can't wait any longer, and driven mad with desire, I feast on her honey, thrusting my tongue into her virgin channel.

I can barely hear her moans now because I can't focus on anything but the sweet pussy oozing pleasure onto my lips.

Her legs tremble, in uncontrolled spasms, warning me that she's close to an orgasm and this time, it's going to be in my mouth.

I don't slow down, sucking and licking, stimulating her clit with my thumb.

Her taste dominates my tongue, her scent, my sense of smell, her skin, my flesh. I have all of Taisiya in me.

I bury my face between her thighs, as if it were my last meal. She comes, but I don't stop, savoring every inch of the sweet, hot flesh, sucking the bundle of nerves while my middle finger starts a slow in-and-out motion at her entrance.

She wraps around it, and when I add a second finger to prepare her for me, because she's so tight, I have the sensation of touching warm silk.

She's tight, and I need to get her ready, or she'll feel a lot of pain.

I let my fingers delve deeper into the velvety walls, increasing the rhythm and force, but not pushing too hard.

She sighs, breathing ragged, her hand moving to my hair, signaling that she wants to come.

She needs more. She doesn't want me to stop, and satisfaction spreads through my blood as she begins to show herself to me.

I suck her clit harder, and with a loud moan, a cry of pleasure that's the fucking sweetest sound in the world, she comes in my mouth, pulsing on my fingers and tongue.

I don't stop fucking her, the thrusts stretching her more and more for my cock.

Her shame has given way to raw desire, and now she's coming toward my face.

When she comes again, surrendering to pleasure, she screams my name and then says something that will change our lives forever:

"I love you, Lorcan."

Chapter 41

Lorcan

Body and mind, which were already on the brink of breaking, lose the battle completely, and my true nature comes to the forefront.

I lift her in my arms, the insane need to possess her, to mark her as mine definitively, overtaking reason.

I sit her down in the middle of the bed and step back to undress.

"Rest on your elbows while I get naked, Taisiya. I want those beautiful eyes on me all the time."

She tries to close her thighs, but I return to where she is and spread them apart.

"In our bed, there will be no room for shame. Here, you won't be the good girl, the innocent novice, the mafia princess raised to be sweet and obedient. You will be my woman: naughty, shameless, screaming loudly, moaning my name every time my cock is buried inside you."

She no longer looks away from my eyes as I pull down my jeans and boxer, and even when my thick, erect cock bounces against my stomach, she doesn't stop looking at me.

I stretch out my hand and bring her to the edge of the bed. I lower myself, forcing her face backward. I don't kiss her, just tease her lips with mine. She grows impatient, and that's what I wanted.

No shame. Desire in its purest form is what I intend to draw from her.

When she holds my face, taking the initiative to kiss me for the first time, I growl with satisfaction.

"Suck my tongue," I command.

She does so timidly.

"Not like that. Suck, Taisiya. You're going to learn to take my cock in that beautiful mouth. This is the first lesson."

She surprises me when she starts to loosen up, sucking eagerly, and in the blink of an eye, the spell turns against the sorcerer.

Needing more, I hold her hand around my shaft. She panics and tries to pull away. I grip tighter.

"Feel me, baby. I'm crazy for you."

The words seem to work because she lets me guide her, while she goes back to sucking my tongue as I commanded.

Her free hand starts to slide intuitively up my thigh, lightly scratching, sending a jolt of pleasure up my spine.

I rise, and my cock is at the level of her face. I caress her chin, and when she looks at me, her cheeks flushed with desire, her beautiful mouth slightly open, wet from my kisses, I know what I want.

"Bring my cock to your lips."

She was still masturbating me, even after I removed my hand, but for after what I say.

"You're trembling, Taisiya. Are you scared?"

"No. I just don't want to do anything wrong."

"Nothing involving your mouth and my cock can go wrong, sweetie."

I lower my hands, gripping both nipples simultaneously. She softens, surrendering, her eyes shining with pure lust.

I don't move. I want her to take me, this first time, on her own initiative.

"Masturbate my cock while you lick the head."

I go crazy when I see her pink tongue coming out and softly tasting me, but when she repeats the motion, this time looking up, I lose myself completely.

The determination to wait for her to take the initiative will be saved for another day. I need to see her sucking me off.

"Open that hot mouth for me, I want to feel you around me." When she obeys and takes a small portion of my shaft between her lips, I groan with pleasure. "Use your tongue."

She starts slowly, gently sucking, licking, while simultaneously caressing my length. Still inexperienced and hesitant, when she begins to moan with me in her mouth, my desire makes a load of pre-cum spread across her lips.

"Lick it all. I want you to swallow."

Seeing her sucking my rigid flesh, taking my cock as I slide in and out of her mouth, is like the fucking dirtiest erotic fantasy.

Taisiya stirs a complex array of feelings in me that I can't process.

She is the sacred and the profane. My angel wrapped in a provocative body. My ward, my wife.

My love.

I want to close my eyes and enjoy the delicious touch of her tongue, but I also want to keep them open and relish the sight, to memorize her transition from girl to woman.

I can't continue, however. I'm too aroused and I'm not going to wait to make her mine.

Pulling away, I nearly go insane when I see her resist before letting my cock slip out of her mouth.

I push her body so she lies on the bed, and still standing, I pull her legs up. Now, only her shoulders are on the mattress.

I don't give her time to prepare, I lower myself and suck her clit, working my fingers into her tight sex.

She tenses at first, but then loses control, grinding against my face.

She stiffens, and I know she's about to come, but this time, it's going to be on my cock.

I lay her back on the bed and kiss her mouth. I position her body in the center and step back to put on a condom.

When I return to her, I slide, not breaking our gaze, two fingers into her wet pussy, penetrating her deeply but stopping at the proof of her innocence so she doesn't feel pain.

When she moans and spreads her thighs, I know she's ready. Aligning myself between her legs, I brush the thick head of my cock against her opening.

"Tell me if it hurts."

"I want this."

"I know, love, but I can go slowly."

Even if it kills me.

I push just enough to part her slick lips, and she holds her breath.

As I push in further, making the head widen her tight channel, she squirms, restless and anxious.

"You have to trust me, baby. If you try to move, it will hurt more."

I know she's very wet, but the difference between our bodies is too great.

I pull out and push in a few times, trying to make her adjust, and when the head passes all the way through, we both moan.

It's a slow, controlled thrust, and even though it feels like it's going to give me a stroke, I go as slowly as possible.

I grip her thighs and test a harder thrust. She stiffens but doesn't ask me to stop, so I don't pull back. I enter and exit again, going deeper and deeper.

She moves instinctively, and I have to stifle a groan because her tight passage is squeezing me, stimulating every nerve ending in my cock.

"I want you, Taisiya. So much that if I had to stop now, I'd die."

"But would you stop?"

"Yes, because I will never do anything that could hurt you. I want to be the cure, not the pain."

"You are my everything, Lorcan. Friend and lover. Be my lover too."

We look at each other in silence, and I lower myself to kiss her. Mouth to mouth, I whisper on her lips:

"You are my love."

I don't wait for her response and enter fully, stopping at the deepest part of her body, possessing her completely.

She screams in shock and her pussy tightens around me.

I grit my teeth because her spasms are driving me crazy; the pressure of her tight sex almost makes me come.

She cries without complaint, and I lower my face to kiss her forehead.

I pull out slowly and start a slow rhythm, caressing her nipple.

Gradually, the crying stops.

I fuck her with steady strokes, feeling her flesh stretching around my shaft.

I lift her thighs, bringing them to my waist, and thrust deeply inside her.

The moan of crying turns into pleasure, and she starts to rise to meet me.

"Move your hips. It will feel better for both of us."

She obeys, and as I fuck harder and faster, her lips part in surprise, and then she begins to beg for more.

I fuck hard now, and her pussy receives me, gripping me with contractions every time I pull out, as if trying to trap me.

I pump into her, fascinated by the pleasure I see on her beautiful face.

At this moment, Taisiya transforms from my ward to my queen. Every drop of blood running through my body belongs to her.

Being inside her is like finding the perfect place I didn't even know I was searching for. My private paradise. Home and refuge.

Our bodies collide incessantly. Sweat and flesh mingled.

When she digs her nails into my chest, uncontrolled and demanding, I know I can let my desire fully emerge.

I grip her ass cheeks and fuck without mercy, thrusting into her slick interior.

I position my hand between our bodies, reaching her clit, and she roars like a wildcat, coming shamelessly, squeezing me with rhythmic contractions.

I wait for her to come, and only when her breathing calms, do I pull out, turn her onto her stomach, and enter her pussy again.

I kiss her back, and once more, she tenses.

"There's no need to feel ashamed. I'm going to show you how beautiful you are, Taisiya. All beautiful, perfect, and mine."

In this position, I can go deeper. I pump my hips with a hard rhythm, and less than a minute later, she's with me, forgetting her shyness, focused on our pleasure.

Gradually, the sweetness with which I started to fuck her is replaced by a brutal rhythm, and when she arches her ass, pushing her pussy into me, I turn her face to kiss her.

"I'm going to come like this. Your tongue on mine, my cock buried in you."

"Take it all. I'm yours."

"Oh, yes, you are," I groan, not stopping my thrusting.

I finger her pleasure button because I know I need to make her come. I'm very close.

"I want to fill you with my semen, Taisiya. I can't wait to see my cum dripping from that delicious pussy."

The words seem to drive her crazy because, screaming my name, she gives in, soaking my hand.

"I want to mark you," I say, continuing to fuck her.

"How?"

"Come in your ass."

She nods, I think she's too embarrassed, but I've long past the point of chivalry, and after fucking her for another minute, I pull out, kneel, and remove the condom.

Instead of doing what I said, however, I turn her to face me.

Looking into her eyes, I masturbate and when my sperm explodes from the head of my cock, I direct the jets to her stomach.

I lie beside her, kissing her, while spreading my semen with my fingers over her breasts and belly.

"Mine."

"Yes, I am. I love you, Lorcan, and that will never change."

Chapter 42

Lorcan

"I have to leave. Yerik will send someone after me," she says, leaning against me in the bathtub.

"You're not going anywhere," I reply. "Now, I want to hear about your memories."

I lift her hair and kiss the marks from the lashes. For the rest of my life, whenever I see them, I'll feel the urge to kill Ayrtom again.

"I can't do it like this."

"Like what?"

"So close to you. I'd feel like I was tainting you with my memories."

She doesn't give me a chance to respond, moving away and pressing her back against the opposite side of the tub. Even her feet don't touch me now, and although everything in my mind screams to bring her back, I feel she needs space.

"You know Ana was promised to that wretch, right?"

I nod in agreement.

"To understand my crazy plan to take her to the convent, you have to first understand how my mother was cruel to her. Anastacia has a sweet temperament. She always has, since we were little. She smiled a lot, and so, I nicknamed her 'smiling girl.' Her mother died when she was still a baby, and Dad remarried very quickly. That's why there's such a small age difference between us."

"Was he good to you?"

"He was, yes. We thought he was the best father in the world, within the possibilities."

I notice the "thought" but don't interrupt her.

"Within the possibilities because of the Organization, you mean?"

"Yes. We grew up knowing we had obligations. Among them, accepting a husband who would take care of us. We wouldn't choose him, and the house we'd move into with him would be an extension of the one we grew up in: we would continue to be obedient and well-behaved."

"I can't picture you like that. I don't know your sister, but as for you, I can't imagine you accepting everything."

"I had no choice, Lorcan. Now, after my memory returned, I think I unconsciously decided to go to the convent out of rebellion. Of the two of us, Ana was the compliant one. I didn't want to feel obliged to live with a stranger, to be obedient just because someone said I should."

"But wasn't it like that with your father?"

"Yes, but he, as much as possible, was flexible with both of us. We learned other languages, were encouraged to read books, and he even set up a ballet room for Ana. I think that permissiveness from our father is what made my mother angry with me and my sister."

"I knew she didn't like Ana, but I had no idea it extended to you as well. Wasn't she your biological mother?"

"Yes, she was, but Anastacia was always my world. I ended up resenting my mother for the way she treated her, and later, when I heard her talking to Ayrtom... planning the marriage. I was only fourteen and Ana was fifteen at the time, Lorcan. How could she even consider offering my sister to someone so old?"

"But your father agreed, right?"

I try to hide my contempt, but I can't.

To hell with political alliances, I would never give my girl to a bastard old enough to be her grandfather, and beyond that, I would turn his life upside down, researching every background before allowing him to even breathe the same air as my daughter.

"Yes, he agreed. You know what's strange? Before my memory came back, I didn't understand how I didn't miss either of them. I knew there was a father and a mother who died in that fire, so why, I wondered, didn't I even subconsciously mourn their loss?"

"And why do you think that was?"

"I believe deep down I always knew my mother was worthless. When I had the conversation with Ana where I convinced her to go to the convent, I had just heard her talking to her cousin. At the time, I didn't understand it well, but now I do."

"What did you hear?"

"She knew the cousin was a bad man, because I heard her say: *he'll be able to punish her at will when he owns her.* They were talking about my sister."

"Damn it, Taisiya!"

"I know I shouldn't feel ashamed of others' sins, but I do anyway. I despise her, Lorcan. Even though I know she had a horrible death, being burned alive, I despise her because she put us in that situation."

I can't deny it, so I just listen to her pour out her bitterness.

"And your father?"

"My heart is torn about him. I remember all the good things he did for me and how we loved it when he came back from trips, but now I wonder if it was because we had to choose between the bad and the less bad. I don't know if, in my fantasy world, in my bubble, I saw him as better than he really was. In what world would a father, in the name of interests that did not concern us, give his eldest daughter, whom he claimed to adore, in marriage to an old and, beyond that, cruel man?"

"If you're expecting me to contradict you, it's not going to happen. To me, he was as guilty as your mother, Taisiya."

"I'm not. That's what broke me when I finally remembered everything. I thought that when my memory came back, I would see my perfect home falling apart in detail."

"But that's not what happened?"

"No. Despite mourning the loss of two human lives, I don't mourn their deaths as a loving daughter. Does that make me a bad person?"

"No, it makes you honest. Most people feel obliged to mourn. As if, after death, everyone becomes saints, which is not true. The son of a bitch in life remains a son of a bitch after death. God is the one who has to absolve him, not you."

"I like the way you see things."

"I'm a brute, Taisiya, and that's just one more thing we don't match on."

"What do you mean?"

"You seem very cultured for someone who didn't finish high school, or whatever they call it in Russia."

"I didn't do formal schooling, but I read a lot with Grandpa Abramov. He was a scholar. A former priest."

"Did he tell you about that?"

"Yes, but he didn't give me details about the past, and I never asked. We didn't force each other to confess anything."

"Go on."

"He taught me the subjects I would study in a regular school and also encouraged me to read a lot. We had a TV that we never used. Even now, I don't care about television programs. I rarely access the internet."

"I understand now."

"What?"

"Since the first time we talked, back at the cabin in Siberia, I found you innocent, but very intelligent too. You spoke clearly, with organized ideas, despite everything. I think when I got there, I expected to find a girl out of touch with reality."

"Why?"

"I didn't know what to expect, Taisiya. I arrived ready to kill Abramov if he was the one still hurting you."

"He was nothing but wonderful to me, Lorcan."

"I know that now, but you need to understand that in my world, good people are the exceptions. I always expect the worst from everyone."

"Why?"

"Because I have no faith in humanity."

"You never talk about your family."

"I have nothing good to say about them."

"But I'd like to hear about them."

"Maybe, one day. Today isn't about me, it's about you. Continue your story."

Chapter 43

Taisiya

I don't think I would have the courage to open up like this to anyone else.

Certainly not to Ana.

After my memory came back, I know my sister would be tormented forever if I told her how that man hurt me to get revenge on her.

"I don't remember much of the fire. When I woke up, I was already suffocating."

"Your nightmares were from that day, then? You always talked about the smell of smoke and heat."

I nod in agreement.

"Somehow, I was aware that I needed to try to save myself, but I wanted to save my parents too. At that time, I didn't know everything."

"Everything what, Taisiya?"

"I'll get to that. As I was saying, I woke up frightened, and when I felt someone picking me up, I thought it was a firefighter."

"Was it Ayrtom?" he asks, his jaw tightening, showing all the tension.

"Yes. When I asked him to save my parents, he said I deserved to be left to burn and that I should be grateful he was saving me. I recognized his voice immediately, and even terrified, I connected the dots when he said he was angry with us both because of my plan to take Ana to the convent. I screamed, partly in desperation knowing he was leaving my parents behind, but also out of fear for myself. He put something over my mouth, and the next time I woke up, I was in that house, in Siberia."

"We can't do this here," he says.

"Do what?"

"Have this conversation. I need to hold you, Taisiya. Even now, with that son of a bitch dead, I still need to have my arms around you to make sure you're safe."

He gets up, completely at ease with his gorgeous body, but when he reaches out to me, I hesitate.

"Come here, baby. What did I tell you about not being embarrassed?"

I rise slowly, and when his eyes roam with desire over my body, I feel a bit braver.

He embraces me, and after giving me a kiss on the forehead, he gets out of the bathtub and wraps a towel around his waist. Then, he grabs a robe for me. He helps me out of the water and covers me with the towel-wrapped robe.

This time, I'm the one who takes the initiative to hug him.

"If this is a dream, don't wake me up, Lorcan."

"Life with me is far from a dream, love."

I don't respond because it would lead to a conversation I'm not ready to have yet, like the need to leave to ensure he isn't killed because of me.

He picks me up and walks to the bed. We're no longer in the room he gave me when I first arrived here, but in the master suite, his.

Lorcan reclines with me in his arms.

"Much better this way," he says.

"The memories should hurt more."

"Don't they?"

"Yes, but maybe not for the right reasons."

"I don't know if I understand."

"After we got to that house... I won't detail the first day because I still can't believe that it happened to me, but suffice it to say that he beat me so badly I lost consciousness."

"Fuck me!" he roars.

"He kept repeating what he was going to do to Ana, that I would see her suffer and regret proposing the convent idea."

"He never tried..."

"No. I was terrified he would because he described in detail the horrible things he would do to my sister. In a way, I got *lucky* being related to him, I guess."

"How so?"

"He told me he was Catholic and that incest was forbidden in his religion. Can you believe that? He killed my family, kidnapped me, beat me, wanted to rape my sister, but still hoped his soul would be saved just because he didn't practice incest."

"Crazy as hell, but his madness was your salvation, baby."

"Yes, it was. He was only with me a few times. I don't know exactly, I lost track of time a bit. One day, when someone gave me water, I thought I was dreaming. I thought I had been rescued."

"Was he the accomplice?"

"Yes. Do you know who he is?"

"You don't need to hear this, Taisiya. Just understand that I'll take care of this matter."

I look at him in silence because I think that the *taking care* he refers to directly means *killing*.

"I think I'm losing my mind, Lorcan. Or I'm empty of feelings."

"What? Why do you think that?"

"I can't mourn my parents' deaths. I told you Ayrtom was with me only a few times, right? But the sessions were intense, and he talked all the time."

"He talked about what?"

"Besides confirming that it was my mother who orchestrated everything because she hated Anastacia, he told me that what made my father agree to the 'sale' of Ana, as he called it, was a huge amount of money he would receive for her."

"Your father wouldn't marry her off for a position within the Organization, but for money?"

"Yes. It had nothing to do with political alliances but with material gain."

"Ruslan has no idea about this."

"I don't think so. Now I remember that he and Dad were friends."

"My grandfather had no idea that your father sold your sister, Taisiya, I'm sure of that. Ruslan is stubborn and has some outdated opinions, but it's always in the name of family and the Organization. Those two entities for him are intertwined. However, I'm certain that if he knew your father was motivated by money, he would never have allowed Anastacia to be used as a bargaining chip."

"I don't know, Lorcan. I have few certainties these days."

"Continue."

"I think that during the time I was memory-less, I somehow knew my parents had betrayed us because I never, not even in my dreams or after moving to Boston, missed them."

"How could you, Taisiya? Because of your father's selfishness and greed and your mother's cruelty, you lived in hell."

I hide my face in his chest.

"I don't know what to do. I don't know if I should tell Ana who he really was."

"Don't think about that now; you'll have time to decide. But if you want my advice, tell the truth. It would be unfair to your sister to let her believe a lie, thinking her father was loving."

"Ana is a good soul. In her place, even without knowing about the financial gain, I would never forgive him for not having investigated who Ayrtom really was." I pause, my heart racing. "Do you think he knew?"

"We'll never be sure, but I can't believe that. It's one thing to be greedy enough to sell a daughter, but to know he was selling her to a sadist... that seems too much even for me, and I'm not one to trust humanity."

"I'm not finished with the story yet."

"Yes, I know. You haven't talked about the despicable accomplice."

"Exactly. Ayrtom's plan wasn't just to marry Ana, Lorcan. After a while, when he got tired of her, he would hand her over to this accomplice."

"Fuck! Damn sickos."

"There's more. This man didn't beat me as much, but he tortured me psychologically. He said he was on vacation in Russia and promised his cousin by affinity, Ayrtom, that he would take care of his pet, me."

"Son of a bitch!"

He pulls me tighter in his arms.

"Continue."

"Their pact was... to use us both... in front of each other... they..."

"I get it, baby."

"He told me he promised Ayrtom he wouldn't violate me, but he couldn't wait... Oh, my God!"

I stand up, horrified.

"Taisiya, what happened?"

"You can't do anything about him until you find out, Lorcan."

"Find out what?"

"He said he was going to take me to an island. This man, I don't know his name, said he owns an island in the Caribbean where he keeps several pets. They are girls, Lorcan, I'm sure of it. This monster has a private island where he keeps girls as prisoners!"

Chapter 44

Lorcan

I don't want to leave her side because I still can't believe she's finally mine, but there are several matters to address, especially now that Taisiya has remembered this crucial detail — that son of a bitch Levy keeps sex slaves, girls, on an island.

Apparently, the truth serum that Maxim administered to Ayrtom wasn't that effective, as there are several gaps in the story that the bastard told Yerik's trusted man.

The main one being that Ayrtom never intended to rape Taisiya, since, as she herself recounted, he considered incest a sin. This means that the omission of Levy's name was deliberate. Stepanchikov knew he was going to die and took the name of the relative with him to the grave, perhaps hoping, in his twisted mind, that the bastard would continue the same atrocities he could no longer commit, subjugating innocent girls.

I open the fridge and grab a bottle of water, drinking it in one gulp. Then, I place my hands on the table, trying to think about the next step.

I start to walk towards the office to get my notebook when the doorbell rings.

I shake my head, pissed off, because I'm sure who it is. No one — not even my bodyguards, Odhran or Kellan — knows the entry code.

Just to be sure, I check the hallway camera on my watch and am surprised to see not only the Boss but also Ruslan.

Fuck me! Family meeting in the middle of the night.

I should be tense, supposedly, because I know why they've come: they want to make me give her up.

However, I don't even feel agitated because it's not going to happen.

There's not a living soul in this world that can make me give up my wife.

"Why am I not surprised?" I ask as I open the door.

"Maybe because you're a fucking suicidal?" my cousin replies angrily.

Ruslan steps forward.

"Yerik already knows, Lorcan, and he wants her back."

"No."

"This is not a choice, my son. We've already talked about this."

"I'm not going to repeat what I said, Ruslan. Taisiya is mine now, in every sense. Not just protected, but a wife."

"Fuck!" Cillian roars. "Do you have any idea what you've done? We'll have to go to war with the Russians to keep them from killing you, Lorcan!"

"No one is going to kill him, Cillian. Yerik knows that Lorcan is my blood too. Where is she?"

"Sleeping in my bed," I say, closing the door.

"You can't keep her like this, Lorcan," my grandfather says. "Regardless of whether I convince Yerik not to start a war against you, if he agrees, he will demand that you marry her."

"No," Cillian responds. "A marriage between them would create an eternal bond between the organizations. I don't want that. I don't trust your grandson. Before we knew about Lorcan, we never made any kind of pact. The one with the Mexicans only happened out of necessity."

Ruslan ignores my cousin, looking at me.

In turn, I look at Cillian.

"You're my blood, and I love you as if we were born of the same mother. I also love the Syndicate and have proven my loyalty to it. I've been stabbed several times, shot, and survived a bombing attempt. I would die for you, my cousin, but I will not give up the woman of my life, the one who is, and from now on will always be, the only one for me, in the name of the Syndicate."

He takes a step back as if I had assaulted him. His face shows not disappointment but disbelief.

"It's not a phase," he says finally.

"No. I just didn't go after her before because I was sure she wanted to become a nun. Now I know that Taisiya loves me too, and I won't allow anything to separate us."

"You have to marry her then. It's the only way to avoid a tragedy," my grandfather says.

"That's what I intended to do. I just hadn't gotten my thoughts in order yet because so much happened today."

"What happened?" my cousin asks, still as tense as before.

I know that if Ruslan weren't here, he would have already started planning retaliations against possible attacks from Yerik or maybe even taken the first step himself.

"As I told my grandfather earlier, Taisiya remembered everything, and her nightmare didn't end with Ayrtom's death."

I quickly share with Ruslan what I had previously only discussed with my cousin, and give him the name of Ayrtom's accomplice.

"That son of a bitch is famous," my grandfather says.

"Yes, he is. A respected lawyer."

"And what's he still doing breathing?"

"You can't kill him, sir," I hear Taisiya's voice say. "You need to save them."

"Save them who?" Cillian addresses her, and I see her shiver.

I go to where she is, covered with my robe, looking small and frightened.

That angers me. I don't want her to feel afraid ever again.

I pull her into my arms, indifferent to the other men in the room.

"That man, Ayrtom's accomplice," she says, turning to answer my cousin, "he has an island. There are many girls there. They need to be saved."

Chapter 45

Lorcan

"**Y**ou shouldn't have left the convent," my grandfather says, after kissing my wife's forehead. "Regardless of the... conflict between the two organizations, you have connections with both, Taisiya, both because of my Irish grandson and because you are Ana's sister. God knows we have many enemies. Anyone could be lurking to take you."

She tries to hide a shiver.

"Even that man..."

"Yes, even Levy Goldberg."

"That's his name?"

"Yes," I reply.

"Did you always know Ayrtom had an accomplice, even before I told you?" she asks.

"Yes, I knew, and since he returned, I've kept him under surveillance."

"Returned from where?"

"After Ayrtom... um... disappeared," I say carefully, "Levy vanished from the planet for a while."

She hides her face in her hands.

"Oh, my God, he was probably on the island!"

I won't lie to calm her. Now that I know about the place, I think he was indeed there.

"Tell me about this island, Taisiya," Cillian requests, and she looks at me as if asking what to do.

I nod and watch her take a deep breath before beginning to narrate.

She doesn't mention the night of the fire but talks about what she went through at Ayrtom's hands and also about her father selling Ana.

I see Ruslan's eyes widen in surprise and get confirmation of what I suspected: he didn't know that his friend, the father of the girls, had made the deal with Ayrtom.

Taisiya continues narrating but doesn't give as many details as she did when she told me.

She speaks quickly, and I know her well enough to recognize it as a sign of nervousness.

She only touches on a few facts she considers important, like how Ayrtom didn't assault her because they were relatives. She finally reaches the part about Levy.

When she finishes, Cillian looks at me.

"What do you want to do?" he asks.

We exchange glances between us and with Ruslan as well, but we don't say anything, in a silent communication. We never involve our women in wars, because if we were to be captured, they could be accused of being accomplices.

But Taisiya isn't naive and realizes this.

She stands up, looking upset.

"I need to leave," she says. "I know why you two are here. My sister explained to me what would happen if I stayed with Lorcan. Yerik would kill him," she says, looking accusingly at my grandfather.

"Sit down, girl," Ruslan says, without losing his calm. "We have a lot to discuss."

"I don't want to be a nun, but I won't marry for an alliance. It's Lorcan I love."

She's challenging my grandfather, and my admiration for her only grows, because few people on this planet would have the courage to defy him face to face.

"Sit down, Taisiya," he repeats, and this time his voice is cold.

She obeys but stays glued to me.

When I turn to face her, her eyes are anguished.

"What's going to happen?" she asks me.

"We're going to get married," I say calmly.

"What? No! Yerik will kill you anyway! I can't live with that, Lorcan."

"No one will kill him, Taisiya. If Yerik makes any move against my cousin, the war will be declared."

"That may be, but if Lorcan is dead, I don't care much about the war between you. Besides, on the other side is my sister. It's a battle where I'll lose either way."

I pull her into my arms, thinking about the chaos we're involved in.

The need to save the girls on an island whose location we have no idea about.

An impending war between the organizations.

Taisiya hides her face on my chest, and I remain silent, trying to find a solution. I see only one.

"We're leaving."

My grandfather leans back in the leather chair.

"No, I have a better idea."

THREE HOURS LATER, as soon as they leave, she runs into my arms.

"This is crazy. I'm going to have to lie to Ana."

"Just for a while. We can't fight on two fronts at the same time, baby."

At the moment Ruslan spoke, the proposal seemed absurd, but the more I think about it, the more it makes sense.

Taisiya will return to the convent, as if everything that happened between us was a friendship: a friend taking in another friend in a time of crisis.

No, the situation doesn't please me, but it will be temporary and I only agreed because Ruslan committed to making an arrangement with Yerik so that she can continue seeing me, with Tulia by her side, claiming that I would be part of the "cure" for her troubled heart with the return of her memory.

Meanwhile, we gain precious time to try to save the girls and—she doesn't know this part—to eliminate Levy afterward.

"I'm scared," she says, standing up and moving away.

"Don't be. It will be alright."

"And afterward? We'll be in this secret relationship, with poor Tulia as our babysitter? Okay. You rescue the girls, if God wills it, but that doesn't change the situation with Yerik."

She walks to the window and looks at the cloudy day.

It's already eleven o'clock, and to stick to our plan, I'll need to hand her over to my grandfather in just over an hour.

"Afterwards, I'll buy you a white dress and a ring. I'll make you my wife."

She still doesn't turn to face me and I hold her from behind.

"You don't want to get married."

I untie the robe and slide it down her shoulders.

"I want to marry you," I say.

She shakes her head, and I press her naked body against the window.

I run my fingers over her sex, which is already wet.

"You want me."

"I do. I've already told you, I want to live inside this pussy."

She moans as I spread the cheeks of her ass with one hand. I use the other to unzip her jeans.

"This isn't love. A marriage based on desire will never work."

I brush the swollen head of my cock against her entrance.

"It's always been love," I say, before driving in fully.

She screams, but doesn't pull away. She presses her hands against the glass.

"First, I loved you because you were my princess, my angel. Then you became my temptation, my sin. But it's always been love, baby."

I make her almost double over and grip her hair in a tight hold, while I steady my hand on her hip, thrusting forcefully.

I look down and see my cock stretching her small, pink pussy like a flower.

"I will never give up on you or stop loving you, Taisiya. I will protect you and fill your womb with our children. There is no goodbye for us, baby. It's forever."

Chapter 46

Taisiya

On the Same Day

"Sister, I'm so sorry!" Ana says, crying, as soon as I enter her house.

Rarely, when I come here, I meet my brother-in-law, but this time, he's at the entrance, arms crossed, watching me.

"You should have called me, Taisiya."

"I needed him, Ana. I was so distressed and wanted someone to whom I could confide without getting hurt."

"I'm your older sister. I need to be ready for anything."

"Yes, but you're also a mother and have your family to care for."

The guilt of having to lie to her makes me nauseous.

It's one thing to omit what I went through in the house of horrors, as I've started calling it in my head, to protect her from feeling guilty. It's another to lie consciously.

My God, I feel like I've aged ten years in a day.

"We're family, Taisiya. I can handle anything for you."

"The arrangement Ruslan made with Yerik for your benefit has to be temporary, Taisiya," Maxim speaks for the first time, and if I didn't know him, I'd say he's commenting on the weather, his voice is so monotone.

However, I know he's angry. I can see it in the way he looks at me.

I nod in agreement.

"Thank you for that," I say.

"Don't thank me. He was against it," my sister says, wrinkling her nose and looking upset. The feeling of guilt increases.

I'm disrupting their relationship.

My God!

"The only reason Yerik hasn't declared war on the Irish, Taisiya, is that you had the good sense to come back. Don't make that mistake again," my brother-in-law continues. "If you need help, to vent, or even if you have a damn ingrown toenail, you should turn to family."

"Maxim," Ana says, and for a moment, they stare at each other like two opponents in a ring. "Taisiya went through hell. She didn't plan for her memory to come back. It happened, and she sought help from whom she thought was best able to assist her."

I feel like crying. I've been a firsthand witness to how crazy they are about each other, and now, my relationship with Lorcan is causing friction between them.

He turns his back without saying goodbye, and I know it's time to leave.

"I can't stay long," I say. "I need to return to the convent. I left without informing the sister, and I feel like a horrible human being for it."

The lies keep piling up, and my place in hell is surely secured.

"You just arrived."

I sigh, deciding to tell at least part of the truth.

"I'm not okay, Ana. I came here knowing you'd be worried and want to see me in person, but my mind is a mess. You said I was in love with Lorcan. It's not infatuation, sister. It's love. I'm madly in love with him. When I hear your husband talking about war, I can't stop the bleeding in my heart. I can't choose between you. I'll die if I have to do that."

She hugs me, and I feel the tears running down my cheeks. I'm so tired of lies, losses, pain.

I just want to live a little.

"Are you going to talk to the psychologist about it?"

"No. Even though she only sees women from the Russian Organization, I can't bring Lorcan into the discussion. It would be treacherous to him and very risky as well. Her loyalty is only to us Russians. Who's to say she wouldn't spill our story to the enemies?"

"If she opened her mouth, Maxim would kill her," she says, and at that moment, I realize how much she's changed. In fact, we both have. From girls raised in a bubble, we've become women who talk about death as if it were commonplace.

"I don't want to carry that guilt. No more deaths."

"Alright, but promise me you'll call if you need to talk?"

"I promise. Take care, Ana. Don't fight with your husband because of me."

"We're not fighting. It was a misunderstanding."

"He's the one you owe loyalty to."

"Just as you owe it to Lorcan?"

I don't answer. I kiss her cheek and turn to leave.

Three Days Later

"YOU HAVE TO KEEP BOTH phones on, baby."

"I know."

"But you can only talk to me on this device," he continues, referring to the "secure" cell phone he gave me.

It's almost the same speech Maxim gave me when he gave me the Organization's phone.

"I understand, sir. I won't forget."

"I hate this shit, Taisiya."

"Which one are you talking about?"

"Did you implicitly swear?"

"No. I made an allusion to your statement. I don't curse."

"And yet, you're going to marry a sinner."

I feel a flutter in my stomach upon hearing that.

The idea of marrying Lorcan, the love of my life, my forbidden Irishman, makes my legs weak.

"Are we really going to do this?"

"Yes, I've already claimed you, little one. You're mine."

"I'm scared."

"Nothing will stop me from being with you. Not even death."

"Don't say that."

"Hey, I don't want to hear sadness in that beautiful voice. I have a surprise for Saturday."

"What kind?"

"I'm going to take you to the gym where I train. I have a fight next week. So, your schedule will be to watch my training, and then I'm going to fuck you in the locker room."

"You can't say these things over the phone."

"I've said much worse to you in person. Do you have any idea how hard it is for me to accept this crazy plan of you being stuck in a convent?"

"If I hadn't come here, Ruslan's plan wouldn't have worked."

"You could have stayed with your sister."

"No. I prefer it here."

I didn't tell him about Maxim's reaction the day I was there. God knows I don't need to fuel the anger between them.

"What aren't you telling me?"

"Nothing. I'm just worried and miss you a lot."

"Three more days, baby, and I'll have you with me."

"And what about that issue?" I ask, referring to the island.

He sighs, sounding irritated.

"Nothing yet, but we're working on it."

"Lorcan?"

"Yes?"

"I love you. Don't get hurt because of me. I'd rather our paths separate than see you get hurt by Yerik's men."

"It won't happen, love. Nothing will separate us."

Chapter 47

Lorcan

"There is a solution," my grandfather says.

"I don't want help from Yerik's friend."

"He's not Yerik's friend; he's Grigori's."

"Oh, right. So it's not the Russian Pakhan's friend but the Advisor's. Much better," I say with irony.

"They are not just that, Pakhan and Advisor; they're also your cousins."

I give him a sardonic smile.

"I respect your sense of family, Ruslan, but we both know that neither of them thinks that way."

"It doesn't matter what they think; we're all relatives. You can't escape the power of blood."

"I am the greatest proof that this isn't true. After all, I killed my own brother."

Fuck, I didn't mean to say that. I don't like digging into the past.

I get up from his apartment chair and start walking toward the door.

"You didn't kill your brother; you killed a rapist and murderer, Lorcan."

"Your grandson. My blood. As I said before, family doesn't always mean anything."

"My son..."

I raise my hand.

"Stop. You know I never talk about this, Grandfather. It was a lapse. You brought up the topic, and I wanted to show you that family is blood, but it's also a choice."

"I won't insist, but don't leave yet. We haven't talked about Taisiya."

"Everything that needed to be said about her has already been decided. Taisiya is mine, and we're getting married. End of discussion."

"I'm not going to try to dissuade you from the idea. I feel at peace now that you've finally found your home. You'll have your own family."

"I have you and Cillian. Kellan and Odhran. Aunt Orla. And now, I also have my wife."

"Yes, now you have your wife. And as much as I want to say that you're making a mistake by choosing to be together, I can't. Do you know why?"

I don't answer, and he continues:

"Because I've never seen you at peace. Of all my grandchildren, you are the most tormented. The storm always looming in your eyes. Now, what I see makes me certain that you should be together."

"And what do you see?"

"You're home, son. Taisiya is your home."

He comes closer and embraces me. I let myself stay.

"What you did to rid the world of your brother... I would have done the same, Lorcan. He didn't deserve to live."

I listen attentively to what he says. Ruslan is all about unity and never says anything to ease another's burden. He truly believes I acted correctly. Part of me agrees, but it doesn't change the fact that I destroyed my relationship with my parents.

"I have to go."

"Let me talk to Odin. It's not about the Syndicate or the Organization, but about saving those children."

"Do it, but don't involve the Organization. Don't associate my name with theirs. Just you and Odin. Cillian's name must not be mentioned either."

"I'VE HAD MEN WATCHING him twenty-four hours a day, and so far, nothing," Cillian says at the table where my three cousins and I are sitting, referring to Levy.

My relationship with Kellan is still pretty fucked up because I confronted him about the mess with Taisiya and the two women at the club, and he admitted he had mentioned to Odhran something about my wife being a hot nun, but he doesn't remember saying anything about memory loss. It must have been him since he was incredibly drunk that night.

"If I hadn't gotten Ayrtom's confession myself, I'd also doubt it. That bastard Levy seems beyond suspicion."

"Why can't we just blow his head off? Or better yet: give me five minutes in a room with him and some knives. I'll make him spill the location of even Santa Claus," Odhran says.

"It's not that simple," Kellan says. "He's smart, meticulous. He's probably been at this for some time, maybe forever, and nothing has ever come to light. Lorcan only discovered because he 'talked' to

Ayrtom. Even Taisiya didn't know his name. If we catch him without finding the girls, they could all end up dead."

"So what are we going to do, then? Sit and wait?"

Cillian exchanges a look with me. I told him about Odin, and despite his reluctance, he agreed.

"No," my oldest cousin says. "We have a backup plan."

"YOU TOOK A WHILE TO answer."

"I was getting out of the shower," she says, and my cock, which was already half-hard just from hearing her voice, wakes up fully, pressing against the zipper of my jeans.

"Send a picture."

"Once, you said you couldn't. It was risky."

"And it is. I was testing you to see how much you're feeling horny."

"I'm not..."

"Liar. Of course you are. It's been fucking six days since I've had you, baby. I'm sure your pussy is throbbing right now just from hearing my voice."

"We're going to hell. I'm in a convent."

"But you're not a nun. You're there as a guest."

"Yeah, I can't deny that. I even think Ruslan said something like that to the Mother Superior because she doesn't even try to scold me anymore."

"If you wanted to cool me off, you succeeded. Bringing the image of a grumpy penguin into my fantasy is the most deflating thing you could have said."

She laughs, and I end up smiling too.

"I'd die just to hear you laugh, Taisiya."

The laughter stops.

"That's why it will never pass, Lorcan."

"What won't pass, angel?"

"My love for you. You manage to be everything I want in a muscle package. You're handsome, grumpy, protective, kind even when you're rough, and..."

"And what?"

"Delicious."

"Am I?"

"I miss you," she says, her voice growing husky, turning me on again.

"I want to get you out of there right now."

"There's nothing I want more, but I won't risk your life. We have to follow your grandfather's plan. I love you. Good night."

Chapter 48

Ruslan

New York

The man is an eagle.

That's my first thought as I face my grandson Grigori's best friend, outside the family.

I can almost hear Odin's mental gears turning as he observes me from behind his desk, not from the headquarters of *Lykaios Systems*, but from the office he uses for personal matters, outside the city.

"You seem surprised," he says, a few minutes after I've sat down.

We've been studying each other, and I quickly conclude that he is a trustworthy man.

He looks into my eyes without hesitation. Not for a second does he look away.

I'm sure he knows who I am, and for such a famous businessman, even the remote possibility of being linked to me could bring him trouble; after all, to the world, he is beyond suspicion.

I, however, see further.

Anyone connected to one of my children or grandchildren receives the privilege of my attention. Odin is not just a powerful Greek, a family man, and a successful magnate. There's a wild light in the depths of his eyes, a strength that even with all his coldness, he can't conceal. I have no doubt that I am facing a man who would do anything for those he loves, even if it means sending some souls to the Creator, or His Competitor, before their time.

And in that, we are alike. And it is the reason I know he will find the damn island.

"Yes, I was surprised you agreed to meet me. I wasn't sure you'd want to be seen with me."

"We are not being *seen*. Don't you know I am invisible, Ruslan?"

"Greek arrogance."

"Almost as much as Russian arrogance?" He raises an eyebrow, and I can see, from a contraction in his jaw, something akin to a smile. "Why didn't you contact me through Grigori?"

"Because what I came to discuss here is not directly related to the Organization."

"It's about your Irish grandson?"

"You seem to be unfamiliar with the word subtlety, my young man."

"We are both busy men, *Pakhan*."

"I am no longer the Pakhan, my son. I am just an old man trying to protect his family."

"Once a Pakhan, always a Pakhan, Ruslan. How can I help you?"

As he said himself, neither of us can afford to waste time, so I explain in detail the whole story of Taisiya, her connection to Lorcan, and finally, reveal about the damned island.

"What do you want to do?"

"Rescue the girls, if possible."

"You don't usually involve yourself in matters that are not your business," he says, making it clear that just as I have watched him over the years, he's returning the favor.

"You're right, but I'll make an exception for Taisiya. Somehow, she feels guilty for forgetting this information for so long."

"I don't need to tell you that the chance of them still being alive is minimal. It's been over three years and the bastard revealed secrets to a kidnapped girl — Taisiya — who managed to escape his clutches."

"I know, but it's worth a try, at least."

"And then?"

"Your work will be done, son. All I need is to know where this place is."

I stand up, and he mirrors the movement.

I extend my hand in greeting, and he accepts it.

"I'll owe you a favor forever, Odin."

"Does that bother you?"

"No. For now, it's a means to an end. I gave my word to Taisiya, and I never go back on it."

Chapter 49

Lorcan

Two Weeks Later

My pulse quickens as I watch her enter the gym. It was hellish work to keep pretending to focus on the workout when, in reality, all I wanted was to go to the car, pick up my wife, and lock us in my apartment for days.

As she walks towards me, escorted by the Russian soldier, I notice that all the assholes present in the gym turn their heads to look at her.

"Get out!" I shout to whoever needs to hear it, and immediately, I see my trainer gesturing for them to leave.

The place empties in a split second, but despite being pleased with the privacy, my focus is now entirely on her.

Taisiya looks gorgeous in her *casual wear*, as she calls everything that isn't her novice habit.

Her softly rounded hips, secured in tight jeans. She's wearing one of my leather jackets, which, although it swallows her whole, makes me feel like a Neanderthal wanting to beat my chest and shout: *mine...* And finally, her hair is pulled into a ponytail that I plan to tangle my hand in a few minutes while I fuck her from behind.

"Hi, little one."

"Lorcan." She breathes out my name.

I raise my eyes to the blonde behind her. It's already the third or fourth time Tulia has accompanied Taisiya to our meetings, and each time, the ritual repeats: I always tell her to keep her distance, and she insists her role is to stay around my wife.

Taisiya intervenes, with her passive-aggressive manner, winning the battle much faster than I could.

"Go take a walk," I tell her and see the resentment in her gaze.

"My role..."

"How long are you going to keep this up? You know you'll have to go. I want to be with Taisiya, not with you. Move away."

"Lorcan, calm down," Taisiya says and looks back. "Tulia, he's right. I'm not eleven. I came to meet him and there's no way I'm letting you stay to overhear our conversation. Have you had the sandwich from the gym's snack bar? It's delicious. Or you can go take a walk outside too."

The blonde's frown deepens.

"It's freezing cold outside, Taisiya."

I don't think that's the issue; rather, she'll have my two bodyguards for company. I might be overthinking it, but I'm almost sure there's some kind of energy between the three of them.

There are some rumors about Rourke and Keiron's preferences, and although both are straight, they enjoy sharing women. It's none of my business, but maybe that's what's making the blonde grumpy and uncomfortable.

I look back and speak so only they can hear, especially Keiron:

"Behave yourselves; she's the enemy."

He raises both hands.

"We're just killing time, as always, boss. We'll be outside."

The woman huffs and, after giving one last irritated look at Taisiya, who remains unfazed and waves goodbye, she stomps out.

As soon as the door slams, I advance on her and pull her into my lap.

Our mouths devour each other hungrily. Each week, the desperation for contact increases.

I start walking her towards the locker room. Even though I'm a bit pissed for not giving her the queen treatment she deserves right now, the desire to be inside her is greater than the anger at the situation.

"I thought you were going to watch your workout," the provocateur says.

"Later. I need to taste you."

"Oh my God, Lorcan," she replies, melting, and attacks my mouth, licking and nibbling my lips.

"I want to take you home, Taisiya. I need you naked in my bed," I say as I take off her jacket, "on top of the kitchen counter," I kneel and quickly remove her boots, jeans, and panties, and she tosses the flannel shirt she was wearing haphazardly on the floor, as needy as I am "I want you on all fours on the living room rug..."

I lift her thigh over my shoulder and, separating the lips of her pussy with my fingers, lick the honey I know is already soaking her sweet folds.

The first taste of her is always my undoing.

I eat her out, sucking, fucking her with my tongue, and she stands on her tiptoes, trying to take in as much of the pleasure I'm giving her as she can.

Her hands come to my hair, and when I look up and see her watching me with her lips parted, I know I'll never see a more beautiful sight in my life.

"I want you to come in my mouth."

"I need you inside me, love," she pleads, breaking the rest of my control.

With a growl, I lift her into my arms and bite her neck.

Her small hands come to my shorts, but the position makes action impossible, so she pushes them down with her feet, along my legs.

"Tell me you want me to fuck you."

"I would never have the courage to ask for that."

"But that's what you want," I provoke, rubbing the tip of my erection against her opening. "Confess you can't wait to feel my cock filling this hot pussy."

"Oh! Please."

"Please, let me fuck you hard?"

"Yes."

Even knowing she's drenched, I test her sex once more, fucking her with my fingers.

"You're always ready. It's like you've been touching yourself so that when you got here, you'd drive me crazy with that delicious scent and that honey dripping. My favorite food in the world. I'm going to make you come hard and fast because a week of dreaming about this beautiful face watching me while you moan my name is too long, angel. Then I'll taste you completely, slowly, but I need this first time strong."

I dig my hands into her ass with brutal force, keeping her sex stretched to the limit, and enter deeply.

She contracts around my shaft, her body trembling from the greed with which I fuck her.

I pull out and push back in without mercy, leaving just the head in and then thrusting again with voracity.

"See how perfect you are for me? See how this little pussy fits me, stretches to swallow me?"

The way her sex grips me is almost painful, and combined with the spasms of her excitement, it quickly drives us to climax.

I thrust my hips, fucking her with rough movements, muffling her moans of pleasure with my tongue in her mouth.

Taisiya comes without warning, digging her nails into my neck, wild and fucking beautiful.

I thrust half a dozen times and feel myself swelling, my cock thickening even more between her walls, until finally, I spill inside her.

"I love you, Taisiya. I don't know how you managed to... break through the ice around my heart, but I love you."

WE LEAVE MY PRIVATE training space after hours of fucking and then lying on the couch, talking.

She never complains about having to leave, but I notice her sigh when I open the door to meet our security.

Every time we part, it's like this.

She asks me how much longer we'll have to go through this, and I don't have an answer to give.

Odin hasn't located the island yet.

As for me, I'm reaching my limit. My nickname, Irish Bomb, fits perfectly, as I feel like I'm about to explode. I know I won't be able to handle this arrangement for much longer.

When we arrive at the main warehouse, where several people are gathered, the sour and awkward bodyguard, sitting between Rourke and Keiron on a couch, heads towards us at lightning speed.

I don't hate Tulia. At first, I resented her presence more, but now I understand she's trying to do her job as best as she can.

The problem is she's fucking bitter, always complaining, and that irritates Taisiya, which ends up pissing me off.

I watch my wife approach her.

"Lorcan will take us today," she says.

"Why?"

I hold back the urge to respond. I need to let Taisiya fight her own battles.

I see her shrug.

"I want to talk a bit more with my *protector.*"

There's irony in the statement, but I don't think the blonde notices, as she's too concerned with strictly following protocol.

"You shouldn't talk like that. Your protector is your brother-in-law. Maxim would go crazy if he heard that," she says, supposedly quietly, so only Taisiya can hear.

"Don't be petty, Tulia. I only leave the convent once a week."

I know she feels bad about lying. More than once she's asked me if I think God will forgive her for it.

"Tired of it?" the soldier asks. "Why don't you ask to leave permanently?" she says, seeming to pity her.

"I'll only do that when I remember everything from the past. Living in the dark is frightening," Taisiya responds, awkward with yet another falsehood.

To consolidate Yerik's consent for Taisiya to come see me, Ruslan's plan — which Anastacia already knows about, because Taisiya couldn't hide the truth from her sister — was to tell the Pakhan that there are still some gaps in her memory.

"Alright," the woman finally relents, "I'll go with you."

"Um... no. Actually, I want to talk privately with Lorcan. Go with the guys," Taisiya says, pointing to my bodyguards. "They'll take you to the convent and you can check if I arrived safely."

She looks back, and when she turns back to face my wife, she's sulking.

"Go, Tulia. They won't harm you. They're under Lorcan's orders."

She doesn't seem willing to give up easily.

"They've announced a snowstorm, Taisiya. We have to leave quickly."

"We're big girls. We'll be fine. See you at the convent in half an hour."

The woman gives her a tight-lipped smile and finally leaves.

Taisiya looks at me as if she's uncertain.

"Do you think she'll be okay?"

"What do you mean?"

"She doesn't seem to like the two of them much, I think."

"I think the problem is quite the opposite."

"I don't understand."

God, she's so innocent. Anyone with a bit of experience would realize that the sexual energy between the three of them is palpable.

"It's nothing, baby. Let's go, I'll get you safely to your *home*."

Chapter 50

Lorcan

"**O**h my God!" she moans beside me.

"Calm down, baby. Everything will be alright."

"We'll never get to the convent with the streets like this. There's so much snow! I shouldn't have gone out. Poor Tulia!"

It's been snowing heavily for several days, and it's one of the things I hate about Boston—we can have snow even well into spring.

When she came to meet me earlier, the streets were already covered in ice. Despite the maintenance from the transportation department, traffic becomes a mess.

I knew a snowstorm was expected for tonight, but I didn't think it would be something out of an apocalypse movie. You can't see anything.

"Grab the phone, Taisiya. Let Tulia know that we're heading to my apartment. Yerik can go fuck himself if he wants, but I'm not putting her life at risk."

"I need to call Ana too."

"Do that. I'll drive as carefully as possible. We'll get there safely."

"I'm not scared, I have you. I'm just worried about Tulia."

"Rourke and Keiron will take care of her."

She hesitates before doing as I asked.

"I don't think she'll be happy about being with them."

"There's no option. It would be too risky for all three to try and get to the convent. Besides, what will she do there without you? Do this: call your sister first. That way, when you talk to Tulia, she'll have to accept the separation because Anastacia will already be aware of this new arrangement."

I see her tap the screen of the phone she uses to talk to her family and soon after say:

"Hey, Ana."

"Taisiya, where are you?" I hear her sister reply, and only then do I realize she's put the phone on speaker.

"With Lorcan. We'll have to go to his apartment. It's impossible to drive."

She's silent for a few seconds before sighing.

"Are you sure about this?"

"Ana, he's listening."

Another sigh before she says, surprising me:

"Hi, Lorcan."

I've never spoken with one of the Russian wives, so I'm unsure how to respond, but a look from my wife tells me I need to act.

"Anastacia, how are you?"

"I'm fine and I hope my sister is too. Will you take care of her?"

"Always."

"Alright," she responds, as if she had any other option.

The weather is deteriorating rapidly, and not even if God himself descended to Earth would stop me from taking Taisiya with me.

Taking the road now would be suicide.

"We're close to my place, Anastacia," I continue. "She'll be safe."

"Let me know as soon as you arrive, sister," she says. "Keep me updated."

"I'll be safe, Ana. With him, I'm always protected."

"I love you, Taisiya."

"I love you too."

She hangs up, and seconds later, calls back. This time, however, I only hear part of the conversation, and it doesn't seem pleasant.

Tulia must be very displeased with the change of plans, and to avoid creating an even bigger problem, as soon as Taisiya ends the call, I tap the car panel and call Rourke.

"Yes, boss."

"Leave her wherever she wants, Rourke."

"There's no option for that anymore, Lorcan. All the streets are closed."

"Alright. Then bring her to my building. There are several vacant apartments."

It's not what I want. If the irritable blonde stays with us, she'll interfere with my time with Taisiya, but I also don't want to be responsible for her freezing to death.

"Um... boss..." now it's Keiron speaking, so I know they're on speaker "we won't be able to reach your building."

"So what do you plan to do?"

"Go to my apartment."

I see Taisiya turn her face to look at me, seeming shocked.

"Are you okay with this, Tulia?" she asks.

"I have no choice, 'boss'" she mocks, imitating my men. "Between freezing to death and staying with the enemy, I'd choose the first option, but I'm not ready to say goodbye to this world just yet."

"Alright, take care, kids" I say and hang up, because listening to complaints or sharing other people's drama isn't my idea of fun.

Almost twenty minutes later, I arrive home with difficulty.

"Is this destiny?" she asks as I go around to open the car door and help her out. "I'm talking about the snowstorm."

"I don't know, baby, but whoever planned this must be rooting for both of us. For the next few days, you're mine."

WE'VE BEEN STUCK IN the apartment for two days, and without a doubt, they've been the best of my life.

The snowstorm shows no signs of letting up, and according to the forecast, we'll have at least another forty-eight hours — which isn't nearly enough to satisfy my hunger for her.

"I don't know if I'll be able to let you go," I say after we've fucked for hours.

It's not just because the sex is the best of my life or the desire Taisiya stirs in me, it's her entire being.

I'm addicted.

I stay awake, watching her sleep.

She has this habit of gripping my right thumb between both her hands. If I try to free it, she whines.

She smiles at the stupid videos she watches on TikTok and gets emotional when she talks about her nephew.

She likes soda at room temperature and iced coffee.

I'm filing away every detail, every second, because I don't know when we'll have this time together again.

"I don't want to go."

"There will come a time when you won't have to leave anymore. You'll be my lady."

She rolls her eyes.

"That sounds like something out of the eighteenth century," she says, laughing.

"You're tied to me forever, Taisiya," I say seriously. "Doesn't that scare you?"

"Many things have caused me fear and some still do, Lorcan. Your love doesn't," she says, kissing my chest. Moments later, she lifts her head as if wanting to ask me something.

"What's wrong?"

"Will your family come to our wedding?"

"I don't have family."

She frowns until realization dawns on her.

"Your parents died?"

"Yes. Both of them, five years ago, but I lost them long before that."

"I didn't understand."

I twirl a strand of her hair around my finger.

"It's not a pretty story. My family's, I mean."

"And is mine? I'm eighteen on paper, Lorcan, but my soul is much older." She looks down. "So is my body."

I run my fingers over her scars.

"You don't know how important it is to me that you don't look at me with pity or..."

"Or what?"

"Disgust for the marks on my back."

"You're perfect, Taisiya. I'll repeat this until my last breath on Earth: nothing that was done to you changes the fact that, to me, you're the most beautiful woman in the world."

"I wouldn't believe it if it were anyone else telling me this, but I see it in your eyes."

"See what?"

"Your love, that you truly find me beautiful. It helps my self-esteem."

"Are you ashamed of your back?" I ask, and just the thought that that bastard not only marked her on her skin but also destroyed her self-worth drives me insane.

"I am. I don't think I'll ever have the courage to wear a bikini."

"I have a tattoo artist friend. The best there is: Linus King. My whole body was designed by him. If you want, I can schedule an appointment."

"Seriously?"

I hold her face.

"I don't mind, baby. For me, it stays as it is because it doesn't change anything. The only thing it causes me is hatred knowing that you were hurt. But if it will free you, make you feel better, we can choose a design to cover them."

"I want to. I've always loved swimming, but if it's in front of anyone other than you, I'll die of embarrassment because of my back."

"As soon as we're married, I'll book a session so he can talk to you."

"You talk about our wedding so naturally."

"It's become natural because it's with you."

"You once told me you'd never get married."

"I never found anyone who made me want to take a definitive step."

"Tell me about your family. If we're going to live our *forever*, I want to share everything, not just the nice things."

"Not that there's much of that in my life."

"Tell me."

"I killed my younger brother."

She widens her eyes, and I can see what's going through her mind. Taisiya is comparing what I just said to her relationship with Anastacia. The next question is already expected.

"Why?"

"He was a rapist."

She sits up on the bed with a start, and I see a range of emotions passing across her face.

None of them, however, are fear or contempt for me.

On the contrary, as if she knew how hard it was to talk about it, she positions herself at the edge of the bed and pulls my head into her lap.

"I want to hear. Was he part of the Syndicate too?"

"No. He was a college football player. The golden boy of my parents. None of us lived with them anymore, but we always went home for holidays. At a Thanksgiving party, the maid's daughter, a sixteen-year-old girl, told me that he had seduced her when she was only thirteen and that they continued to be together whenever she went home since then. There is no seduction with a thirteen-year-old girl. He raped her, but maybe she couldn't understand that."

"Was he already an adult?"

"He was of legal age when he had sex with her. There were no excuses. Besides, she wasn't sure what happened the first time they were together."

"What do you mean?"

"She didn't remember much, just that they were watching a movie in his room and the next day, she woke up bleeding and in pain."

"Oh my God!"

"I never had faith in humanity. The first thing I thought was: why is she only telling me this so long after? I asked her that."

"And what did she say?"

"She said she was pregnant and that my brother didn't react well to the news she gave him over the phone. She said he refused to take responsibility. He threatened to accuse her of theft and evict her family, who lived in a caretaker's house on my parents' property. But again, I don't believe everything I'm told. People lie, and my parents always said that the girl was always hovering around my brother, giving him loving looks."

"Was he there when she told you this?"

"No. He called and said he would be late, I don't remember the reason. — I close my eyes. — I intended to clear the story up, of course, but I couldn't believe it. He was my younger brother. A football prospect. A guy who never caused trouble."

"What did you say to her?"

"I told her to leave and gave her my word that I would check into what she told me, but I don't think she believed me."

"Why not?"

"She came from a poor and humble family, we were her employers. Anyway, I decided to wait to talk to Ronin and confront him. The next day, he arrived. Denied everything, said it was absurd, and that the girl had always wanted him, but to him, she was just a child. He left the house upset, and the guilt hit me hard."

"I can imagine. Did you follow him?"

"No. I did what I do best. I investigated. I went into his room and searched through everything. I spent over an hour there, and when I was about to give up, thinking I was acting like a traitor, doubting my brother, I found an old cell phone."

Her hand wanders through my hair in a rhythmic caress, and it calms me enough to finish the story.

"I waited for almost half an hour for it to charge a bit, because it was very old. And then, I found many videos and photos. Records of girls clearly drugged and being abused, but there was a special file named Cibele, the daughter of our maid. She was telling the truth, my brother filmed himself taking her virginity and also recorded several non-consensual sexual acts between them, as it was obvious in the videos that she was unconscious."

"Oh, Lorcan..." she says, crying.

"I left the house like a madman, determined to punish him. I would find a way to turn him over to the authorities."

"Not to the Syndicate?"

"No. I knew what they would do to him if I handed him over to Cillian. The treatment we give to rapists is inhumane, and despite everything, he was my brother. I promised myself, though, that I would make sure he stayed imprisoned for the rest of his life."

"I don't understand..."

"I hunted him down in the city. It was small, with just over fifteen thousand inhabitants. I kept tracking his cell phone because even though he wasn't part of the Syndicate, he was my brother, and someone might want to get back at me by getting him. It didn't take me long to find him, but by the time I got there, it was too late."

"Too late for what?"

"He went after the girl, Cibele, and killed her. She was a witness to his crimes and could destroy his life forever. When he saw me, he panicked. I could see the terror on his face. He tried to explain himself. I wouldn't let him. I killed him with my own hands. I saw the life drain out of him, Taisiya."

She moves from behind me, straddles me, and cries while holding me for a long time.

Despite feeling sorry for her pain, remembering his death doesn't affect me because there is no regret about it.

"Do you blame yourself?"

"Yes, but not for killing him. I would do it again. I blame myself for not protecting Cibele."

"Oh my God! I don't know what to say."

"There's nothing to say about it, except that you need to know who you're joining."

"An honorable man?"

"I'm not a hero, Taisiya. I killed my own flesh and blood."

"You took a rapist out of the world when others, in your place, would have looked the other way because he was a relative. He killed the girl he raped and used for years. He got her pregnant and then killed his own child when he killed the mother. Your brother was a monster."

"Aren't you disgusted with me?"

"No. I won't lie. The story is horrible, but after what I've been through, I can understand why you did it." She pauses and gives me a kiss on the chest. "Is that why your parents stopped talking to you?"

"Yes. I told them the truth, but to them, the life of the dead son was above all those he harmed. They blamed me."

"Good Lord Jesus! And what about Ruslan in this story?"

"My parents disowned me. Ruslan disowned them. My grandfather stood by me, and after that, never left my side. From then on, my family consisted only of Aunt Orla, my grandfather, and cousins."

Chapter 51

Taisiya

One Week Later

"**D**id you manage okay during the snowstorm? You didn't say anything about the days you had to spend in the company of the *enemies*, as you called them."

For the first time since we met, I see her blush.

Tulia surprised me by visiting me at the convent today. There was no reason for her to be here since it's not my day of the week to see Lorcan.

We're walking in the courtyard, and the day is beautiful, sunny, with the temperature finally beginning to feel like spring.

"They're not as bad as I thought."

I stop walking and look at her.

"I'll have to disagree. They're quite bad, indeed. After all, they're mobsters, just like you."

She crosses her arms in front of her chest, which, by the way, is quite generous, God bless her. If I had half of that, I'd be happier.

"You're a pretty strange nun."

"Maybe because I'm not a nun yet," I say carefully.

Tulia has been spending a lot of time with me, and if I'm not careful, I might end up revealing more than I intend to.

"Something tells me you'll never become one."

"I don't know what you're talking about."

"I'm not stupid, Taisiya," she says challengingly.

I look at her without hesitation.

"If you're not as stupid as you claim, don't stick your nose where it doesn't belong, because it could be bad for you. Next time, you might be sent to Siberia."

"Are you threatening me?"

"Me? Far from it. I'm just a mere novice."

"You're quite clever, that's for sure."

"Oh, I can't deny that. Unlike you, who earned the eternal hatred of Leonid's wife. Anastacia told me that Sierra can't even hear your name."

"I was on a mission, following orders."

"How unlucky, then, that your *mission* turned into the wife of one of Pakhan's trusted men."

I don't want to hurt her, but I won't accept being threatened by anyone.

To my surprise, she laughs.

"Yes, I'm the most unlucky newbie in the world. Did you know that Sierra was my first job in the Organization?"

"Uh-huh. If someone looked up the word unlucky in the dictionary, I'm sure your photo would be there."

She starts walking again, and I follow her.

"I like you, Taisiya. I don't know what your life has been like up to now, because no one talks in detail about how you ended up in the United States, but from what I know, I really like you, and that's why I'm going to give you a piece of advice: I hope you know what you're doing."

"And I'll return with another: watch what you say, Tulia. I don't want to involve you in my problems. I might get into trouble, but I will always be Ana's sister. Maxim would never let anything bad happen to me, but if they find out you're turning a blind eye to my actions or..."

"Or what?"

"Somehow, you got involved with the Irish guys..."

I hope she will deny it, but instead, she replies:

"I know," she says, seeming disarmed and rubbing both hands over her face.

"Do you want to talk about it?"

"No, thank you. I don't even know why I came here."

"Maybe you needed to talk."

"Yes, maybe, but you're right about one thing: we can't talk about the present. It would be dangerous for both of us."

"And the past?" I ask, because something tells me that, like me, she also has hidden monsters in the closet. Maybe not the same kind, but still, monsters.

"No, I don't want to talk about the past."

"Alright. Can you answer basic questions, then? We seem like two secret agents talking."

"I suppose we're almost that. Ask your question."

"Were you born here in Boston?"

"No. In the central United States. My parents, however, are Russian."

"And where are they?" I continue, because you don't need to be a genius to guess that she is very alone.

"Together."

"Far from you? Don't you see them?"

She shakes her head, indicating no.

"Do you have siblings?"

"A married sister."

"I'm sorry if I'm being intrusive, but..." A strong dizziness hits me before I finish the sentence, and I need to hold onto her arm to avoid falling.

"Taisiya, are you okay?"

I feel my heart race. For days I've been having strange symptoms and I looked them up online.

Just the possibility of what I'm suspecting coming true makes me tremble.

"No, I'm not okay. Take me to my sister's house, but please, for all that is holy, don't report this to Maxim."

She pulls me into an embrace.

"Report what? I don't know what you're talking about. As far as I'm concerned, you missed Anastacia. That's all."

"OH MY GOD, I KNEW THIS would happen!" Ana exclaims, pale. "You're pregnant."

"Shhh... There's no way to be sure yet. If I am, it's very early."

"I need to take you to a doctor."

"Are you crazy? Yerik will find out!"

"Taisiya, this is..."

"For God's sake, the last thing I need right now is to hear you say this will turn into a war. I'm already nervous enough."

"I'm sorry, I'm even nauseated at the thought of a war between the organizations with you in the middle of it. How did they let this happen?"

"How did you get pregnant by Maxim, Ana?"

Her cheeks turn red.

"It's different. He was my husband."

I step back, shocked.

"I can't believe you said that, Anastacia. If I still have to hide to see the man I love, to marry him, it's because of that damned Organization your husband is part of. I'm tired of apologizing for falling in love with Lorcan. I won't renounce him. And not my child."

"Taisiya, calm down. I will always stand by your side."

"Against Yerik?"

"Against God, if necessary. It's us two. It will always be us two against the world."

Chapter 52

Lorcan

"We made it," I say as soon as she answers the phone.
"What did you make?"

"Wait, now that I think about the time, won't it hurt if I'm calling you so late?"

"I'm not at the convent."

"Why not? I mean, not that there's anything wrong with visiting your sister, but you told me you didn't feel very comfortable with Maxim's looks since you and I started our arrangement."

"And I really don't, but I decided that I'm not going back to the convent. It doesn't make sense. Ruslan won't force me to marry another man anymore."

An alarm bell goes off in my mind.

"What aren't you telling me, Taisiya?"

"Nothing. I just want to stay here. We'll see each other on Saturday, right?"

"I'm not in the United States. That's why I called. We found the island. I'm going to try to save them..."

"Lorcan, that's wonderful!"

I take a moment to respond because even though I don't want to hurt her, she needs to be aware of the reality.

"You have to understand that they might not be alive anymore, baby."

It's her turn to be silent for a while.

"Taisiya?"

"Yes, I know, but I have hope. Promise me you'll be careful?"

"I'll be fine. I'm used to raids."

For the first time since we started talking, she laughs.

"Our world is so crazy, isn't it? I wanted to be a nun when I was younger, but I knew the names of all the weapons from 'a' to 'z' because even though my father never taught us to shoot—something I only learned from Grandpa Abramov—he cleaned them in front of us and explained everything about how they worked. Today, you tell me you're used to raids, as if you're saying you know how to play tennis."

"It's our reality, Taisiya. Not pretty, not close to a fairy tale, but it's what we are."

"Lorcan?"

"Yes?"

"When you come back, are we going to sort out our life?"

"Baby, I didn't bring you to stay with me yet because I knew at some point I would have to leave the country to check out the island. I didn't want to leave you alone in the United States in case the organizations went to war while I was out rescuing the girls, but when I come back, nothing will stop us from being together. We'll sort this out once and for all."

"I love you."

Something in the melancholy way she says it doesn't sit well with me.

"When you come to meet me, I won't give you back, Taisiya. Don't you dare doubt us. From our next kiss, it will be a "forever.""

"YOU SHOULDN'T HAVE gone. It's not a job for the elite, it's for soldiers."

"I made a promise to her, Grandpa, and I'm going to keep it. Thank Odin. I owe him one."

"No, that debt is mine. As much as I respect the Greek, he's not someone I want my descendants to owe favors to. Will you let me know as soon as you get there?"

"You're talking as if I've never taken a bullet in my life, Ruslan."

"I'm old. My losses are felt more now. You were an unexpected grandson, my child, because I never imagined having an Irish descendant, but that doesn't make me consider you any less than Yerik or Grigori."

"Ruslan, everything is under control. Cillian already sent men to get Levy. They took him to one of our warehouses. As soon as I return from the island, I'll deal with the son of a bitch."

"I could send your cousins..."

"No, I don't need favors from them. My cousins, the ones who really count, aside from Cillian, will be with me. Now stop worrying and take care of Taisiya for me. When I return, I'll come for her, Ruslan. Permanently."

AS WE APPROACH THE island in four rowboats, I observe some of the men sent ahead, for reconnaissance, crawling along the sand.

I know Odin is monitoring everything via satellite. He provided my grandfather with communicators attached to the watches we carry with us, so any abnormal movement can be detected.

I have no hope of finding them alive. Too much time has passed since Levy revealed the existence of this place to Taisiya. Someone so meticulous, who has remained in the shadows practically like a king of this legacy of pain, wouldn't take such a big risk.

Although Odin didn't find anything linking the lawyer to the island. The owner only exists on paper, and tracing him was convoluted. In the end, we came across the name of a dead person.

"Our men are already inside the main house," Rourke informs, shaking the intercom he's holding. "There's nothing there but bodies, Lorcan."

Even though I expected that, I still feel like I've failed Taisiya.

"When did they kill them?"

He seems to listen to what one of my men is telling him and then looks back at me.

"You'd better see for yourself."

We land on the beach and some soldiers move ahead while my cousins, Kellan and Odhran, stay by my sides.

The distance between the sand and the headquarters is not very large, but the building is really strange. It doesn't fit with an island. It looks more like something medieval with wide stones and high walls.

A fortress? No.

The likelihood that someone would come here is very remote. This is a prison. They had no way to leave the house, not even to the beach.

With the warning that the perimeter is clear of threats, we go to meet the reconnaissance team. For this mission, the training I received while I was a federal agent has been very useful, as it helped in organizing the raid.

"There doesn't seem to be a soul here."

Rourke looks at me and I realize he knows more than we do. And then, when we reach the main corridor, the bodies start to appear.

Young people of all ages, I would say the youngest around fifteen, up to about twenty-one, wearing nightgowns, the dried blood sticking their clothes to their bodies.

I've seen a lot of shit in my life, I've been through hell a few times, but I've never encountered so many innocents dead all at once.

"Jesus Christ!" Keiron says. "They didn't leave any alive."

"It was recent," my cousin Kellan points out. "No more than twenty-four hours. They knew we were coming."

Almost at the same time, we think the obvious: it's a trap.

And at that moment, I don't need to turn around to know that I'm in someone's sights.

I feel him before the others realize.

Chapter 53

Taisiya

Hours Earlier

"**D**o you want me to come there and be with you?" Grandpa Abramov asks through the video call.

"Would you do that?"

"Don't you know that I live for your happiness, my daughter? When you came into my life, I had practically given up on everything. Taking care of you was what kept me strong enough to get up every day."

I feel my eyes well up. I know his health is getting worse and how much he hates leaving the cabin. This offer means a lot to me.

"Even though my selfish side wants to say yes, Grandpa, I would feel very guilty if you came all this way feeling pain."

"Just say the word and I'll come. I don't like imagining you in the middle of a war. Especially now, with a great-grandson on the way."

"Everything will be fine, God willing."

"I don't know, daughter. An excess of testosterone gathered in one place can go very wrong."

"I have my sister with me. Anastacia would never stop supporting me."

"Even if it means going against her husband?"

I open and close my mouth, not knowing what to respond. Perhaps because there is no answer to that.

When seconds pass and I don't say anything, he continues:

"Let me rephrase the question: will you feel good if your sister's marriage is at risk because of your problems?"

I cover my face with both hands and shake my head from side to side, crying.

"I didn't say that to hurt you, Taisiya, but to say that at some point, you'll have to take a stand instead of letting others decide your life. I don't want to see you cry, but I feel like you're a bit lost."

"I am *completely* lost. I don't want to hurt my sister or interfere with her life, but I can't give up on Lorcan."

"And you shouldn't, daughter. No one can decide your happiness. Remember, there's a baby inside you."

I'm talking to him on the phone Lorcan left with me, the Syndicate's secure line, not the one Maxim gave me, because honestly, I don't trust they would respect my privacy and not eavesdrop on the conversation.

"What do you want to do, Taisiya?"

"Leave. I want to stay with his family until he comes back from his trip. I know I will always be welcome at my sister's house, but I also know that my child, half Irish, won't be."

"Do what your heart is telling you, then."

"And if it makes everything worse?"

"Worse how, Taisiya? You're pregnant and distressed. You don't deserve to go through this. Both your sister's husband and Lorcan, as well as their respective bosses, are adults and can handle their own problems. Take care of yourself and, most importantly, of your baby's well-being."

"Thank you. I needed to hear that. I love my sister, but she still thinks I'm incapable of deciding for myself. Our conversation cleared the clouds from my mind. Now I know what I want to do."

ANA SHAKES HER HEAD in disbelief, and I can see from her expression that she is also suffering, but I doubt it's even a third of how I feel.

"I'm terrified, sister."

"I'll be fine, Ana. I'm scared too, but I can't keep hiding behind other people's decisions."

"What do you want to do?"

"I called Aunt Orla. I'm going to stay with her until Lorcan returns."

She pulls me into a hug.

"I'm going to have to lie to Maxim if I want to get you out of here. And to Tulia as well. I'll feel safer if she accompanies you at least to your man's aunt's house."

"That's fine, but don't tell her the truth. Just say you need to take me there. Tulia already has her own problems to deal with, and there might come a time when she'll need your help, Ana."

"Help her how?"

"I can't say. It's more of a gut feeling than a certainty, but I think she has many secrets, and some, if discovered, could become dangerous for her life. I'm just asking you that if anything bad comes to light, try to support her. Talk to Talassa and the girls. If they all come together, they'll be able to protect her."

"Sierra hasn't forgiven her yet."

"Yes, I know. And I also know that Leonid resents Tulia by association, because anything that bothers Sierra becomes the target of his hatred. But Tulia wasn't doing anything but fulfilling a mission. It's not fair for her to be punished for being obedient to Pakhan's orders."

"You're too kind, Taisiya. Your life is in chaos and you still manage to think about others."

"I'm not kind. I'm realistic, I suppose. No one is a saint, Anastacia, even though some people like to see themselves that way. We all sin and make a lot of mistakes. Judging others without looking at our own sins is, at the very least, a hypocritical act."

"You've matured. I still struggle to see the woman in place of the girl I kept in my memory when we lived in Russia."

"Pain matures you. When you feel alone and hopeless like I did during my captivity, there's no choice, no matter how old you are: either you face your fears or you give up entirely. I would never give those miserable bastards the satisfaction."

Suddenly, I stop talking as a strange sensation spreads through my chest.

It's like a wave of anguish, growing and growing, but I can't guess the reason.

I examine the last sentence I said to her.

"I would never give those miserable bastards the satisfaction."

In that moment, I know what's wrong and need to lean on my sister as the room starts spinning.

"There are two."

"What? Taisiya, are you okay?"

Ana knows about Lorcan's mission. I told her he was going after the second man who tortured me while I was held captive at

Ayrtom's house, and she swore she wouldn't tell her husband because Maxim would want to handle it alone.

"They're twins. Lorcan said the so-called lawyer who was related by affinity to Ayrtom was named Levy. He has a twin brother. Now I remember perfectly. His name is Lott. They used to mess with my head sometimes, taking turns torturing and scaring me. But I'm sure there are two of them. I need to warn Cillian."

Chapter 54

Lorcan

Explosion of gunshots, simultaneous with the sound of a body hitting the ground.

All of this happens in a split second as I turn to face my opponent—or death.

I'm ready for either.

I feel a sting in my shoulder and realize I've been grazed.

Around us, it feels like the apocalypse has begun.

The room is dark, and although I'm sure the person who tried to kill me was shot as well, I check the surroundings, weapon in hand, unsure if there are more enemies. Someone touches my ankle, and when I look down, Rourke has his hand on my arm.

"Damn it!"

I crouch down and see he's losing blood.

"It's just the arm, boss. I'll be fine."

"There's no one else!" Kellan shouts. "It was just one," he says, pointing to a woman lying on the ground.

"Open the windows," I command when I see Keiron approaching to assess Rourke's wound.

"He'll be fine," Keiron concludes, and my attention shifts to the bitch on the ground.

Odhran has a gun pointed at her head, which is resting face down, appearing unconscious.

"Did you shoot her?" I ask my cousin.

"Yes. She was aiming at your head. There was no time; I had to act quickly, which is why she still managed to hit you and Rourke."

"How did you see her in this damn darkness?"

"Despite the sweep our men did, I found it odd that there wasn't a single enemy left on the island."

"And then you saw her?"

"No, but I was more alert than you, I think. When I saw someone getting up, I hesitated a bit because, even though she was facing away from me, from the dress, I realized it was a woman. I thought she might be a survivor until just before she aimed at your head."

"Why didn't you shoot to kill?"

"I'm curious. I wanted to interrogate her and find out why the hell she specifically wanted you."

He nods and gestures for one of the men to turn the woman over so we can get a look at her.

At that exact moment, the windows are opened, and when I focus on her face, I'm certain I've woken up in a parallel reality.

The one who shot me wasn't a woman; it was Levy Goldberg.

"What the hell is this? It's the fucking lawyer dressed as a woman!" Odhran says.

"No, it's his twin," Kellan says, pointing to a message on his watch. "My brother was trying to tell us that Taisiya remembered there were two of them. They're twins."

"Taisiya..." The bastard starts to regain consciousness and repeats her name, laughing and spitting blood. "The only one who got away."

The violence I've been holding back for so long while forcing myself to take one step at a time in this hellish puzzle to try to protect the girls, who are now all dead, finally emerges with ferocity.

I crouch down and dig my finger into the bullet wound; satisfaction spreads through my system when I hear him scream.

"You're already dead, motherfucker, but it will take you many days to realize it. How could you be so stupid and stay on the island even after you killed them? Even if you had hit me, you'd never leave here alive."

The false smile he gave me earlier fades, letting me see all the madness he carries inside.

"They took my twin brother. There was no reason to live anymore. I just wanted you, the bastard who caused all this."

It's my turn to smile.

"You have me, though I'm sure you won't be able to handle it. If you were looking for me, you know who I am. The girl you tortured is now my wife. You have no idea what your next days and your brother's will be like. What you did to those girls, stealing their lives, abusing and torturing... You will pay for every second."

I stand up, still looking him in the eyes, and crush his cock and balls with a stomp.

"Taisiya told me everything she remembered about the time you spent together, but do you know what stuck with me? When you or your fucking brother, at the time she didn't remember there were two of you, kept asking over and over if she knew what it was like to beg for death... I'll assume you know how to do it. You'll need to."

"DAMN IT, YOU THREE trying to give me a heart attack?" Cillian asks when we finally speak.

"Everything worked out in the end."

"Barely, Lorcan. That was the last mission you're going on. You're above this. I can't lose any of you."

"Because Aunt Orla would kill you," I joke, knowing deep down that after his parents were killed by our enemies, protecting us is crucial to him.

"Go back. You've done what you needed to do there."

"I'll wait for the cleanup crew to finish up. We can't leave any traces, and I need these girls to have their names back, even if only after death. There must be families looking for them."

"How do you plan to proceed?"

"Once we've erased all our traces and have that bastard Lott far away from here, I'll find a way to let the FBI know what happened. I don't know their nationalities, but there may be some Americans."

"How many are there?"

"About a dozen."

"Damn it."

"I should be back in two days at the most."

"There's something you need to know."

"What is it?"

"Taisiya left her sister's house. She's with Aunt Orla and under my protection now."

"Something happened. She would never make such a move on impulse. I need to talk to her."

"Talk to her, but while you're there, don't worry. No one will take her from us."

I hang up and then touch my wife's name on the screen.

"Is it over?" she asks, without even greeting me.

I can feel the fear in her voice, and it hits me hard.

I decide that no way, without knowing what made her leave her relatives' house, am I going to give her the news over the phone that the mission failed.

"It's over. Why are you at Aunt Orla's house, Taisiya?" I ask, then realize how that might have sounded to her. "Don't get me wrong. I prefer that you stay there. Your place is with me, and you'll be safe with Cillian protecting you, but the last time we spoke, you didn't mention any intention of moving."

"Can we talk in person?"

"No" the voice inside me screams, because just the thought that something might be wrong with her drives me insane.

"Please, Lorcan. I prefer face to face."

"Alright. But promise me you won't leave the house before I return. It's risky."

"I won't. You have my word. I love you."

Chapter 55

Lorcan

I hang up the phone, determined to do exactly what I told Cillian: erase all traces as quickly as possible so we can leave.

Knowing that Taisiya is with my aunt relieves me, although I have no doubt that hell will break loose as soon as I return to the United States.

I'm preparing to leave the room when I hear a cry so faint, almost inaudible.

At first, I think it's my imagination, but when it repeats a few seconds later, I start looking around, certain I'm going to find an injured animal.

I listen closely and then, finally, I realize it's coming from a heavy wardrobe near the window.

I approach with my gun ready and carefully open the door, even though it's impossible for an adult to be hiding there.

I find a little girl sitting and crying. Next to her is a note:

"Take care of her for me, whoever you are. He will kill us all."

I quickly understand what has happened.

The baby's mother, probably a victim of that hell, must have found the strength and presence of mind to protect the child from the same fate she would have had.

She can't be a year old yet, and her cheeks are wet with tears.

I've never dealt with little ones before, so I do my best not to scare her.

I put the gun away and then extend my arms. To my surprise, she doesn't hesitate, making an effort to come to me. The moment I hold her against my chest, the crying stops, and she clings to my neck, still sobbing.

"Shhhh... I'm here with you, baby. Everything will be alright now."

"IT'S YOUR FAULT, YOU bastard! All your fault!" I hear Levy shouting at his twin.

I haven't started working on them yet. Maybe it's my "agent" side that drives me to want answers.

It always works.

Want the truth? Put accomplices in a room after a round of individual beatings and wait.

When it's your own ass at stake, alliances dissolve in the blink of an eye. Not even blood can override the urgent need for survival.

We arrived in the United States about four hours ago, heading straight to the property we keep for more "extended" work.

I told Cillian that I would remain here until I'm satisfied with the two bastards.

Partly because I intend to have my time with them. I will make them regret every damn sin they've committed on this Earth; the other reason is that there are gaps only they can fill.

Both have undergone a brutal beating session, but from what I've heard so far, Levy, the lawyer living a double life, is much less resilient than his brother, whom we know only met as an adult.

I'll give them another half hour before I go in, and then the three of us will truly start to "interact."

"You knew we were at risk when you got into this," Lott says.

"I never should have joined your rotten world. There was a reason you were a nobody while I am rich and successful. You're nothing but a psychopath, you bastard."

"And what do you think you are? Some kind of saint? When we got close and I showed you how I enjoyed myself, you had time to denounce me and run. What did you do? Let your true nature show. Took off that false guise of a good guy. We're the same."

"We're not the same. I made a mistake. I'm an upstanding citizen!"

"Upstanding citizen? Was that what you told yourself every time you fucked our slaves? Was that the explanation you used to justify your actions when you beat the Russian mafia princess's bitch? You and that idiot Stepanchikov got obsessed with the Russian sisters. The plan was to grab unknown girls. Poor souls no one would miss. It was that Taisiya who fucked everything up."

"It was you who fucked everything up," Levy accuses.

"I even tried to avenge you, you bastard. I went there and eliminated the witnesses to what we were doing. I tried to kill the Irishman. I should have left and left everything behind."

I open the door and look at the two men, who look more like bloody pieces of meat than humans.

"No point..." Lott, right? I ask, looking at the man hanging to the right of the warehouse. "Naked, toothless, and beaten, I don't see much difference between the noble and the scum. But back to what I was saying. It wouldn't have done you any good to run. Taisiya, my wife, remembered that they were twins. I was never going to stop hunting you." I start walking toward the knife table and pick out my favorite. "And speaking of hunting..." I continue, smiling as I show a Buck 113, specially designed for hunting and my favorite for separating skin from bones.

"You're crazy, fuck!" The lawyer breaks down long before his brother.

"That's an amazing conclusion, doctor, coming from a man who bought an island to take underage girls and turn them into sex slaves. However, yes, I have to agree with you that I'm not normal. Who is these days? I think it has more to do with the mix of my blood. You picked the worst kind to have as your pursuer: me. I'm half Russian and half Irish, to your misfortune, two peoples who value family and never forgive an enemy."

I go to Lott and open his abdomen with a single blow. It's not the first time I've given this treatment to a prisoner, and I know he'll take at least twelve hours to die. I've cut the flesh but made sure not to hit any vital organs.

Levy's scream tells me I made the right choice. I spent a lot of time thinking about which of the two I should torture first. I concluded that the wealthy lawyer would suffer much more if he saw his brother being sliced up.

"Fuck! Fuck!" The man who is a partner in one of the most respected law firms in the country yells.

"Not yet. But we'll get there. You're a lawyer, right? So I suppose you like explanations. I'll tell you the schedule for the next few hours... or *days*. Haven't decided yet. There will be pain on the menu, of course. Lots of it. Cuts with mutilations. Shocks. More mutilations, and in between, someone fucking those skinny asses during the break."

"Shit!" Levy screams again, but Lott just shrugs.

"I've been to jail before," he says, as if that's a sufficient explanation.

I smile.

"Where's your imagination? Who mentioned love here? Did I say you'd be fucked by a cock?"

For the first time, Lott seems to understand that he isn't going to hell when I end his life. He's already in it.

"Well, boys, I'm ready for action. I hope you are too."

Chapter 56

Lorcan

I instructed Cillian to have Taisiya wait for me at home.

After everything that happened, I didn't want to be with anyone other than her.

The hunger and need I'm feeling for my wife right now are nearly uncontrollable. She might be shocked to see me for the first time in the state I'm in right after committing murder, but I will never hide my true nature from her.

I punch in the apartment code impatiently, and under any other circumstance, I would be irritated with myself for such a loss of control.

Not today. Not after spending more than twenty-four hours extracting the truth about everything they did to her, how those sadistic sons of bitches made her suffer, both physically and psychologically.

When the door opens and I finally see her, without saying a word, I scoop her up and carry her to our bedroom, laying her on the bed.

The sense of urgency persists, but now that I have her in my arms again, I want this reunion to last so that Taisiya will never doubt that, no matter what hell we face, we belong to each other.

Apparently, I'm not the only one who needs to be inside her. Taisiya sits up again and pulls the dress she's wearing over her head, showing me that she's not wearing anything underneath.

As I strip off my clothes, I'm mesmerized watching her stand and kneel in front of me.

"I want to pleasure you first."

"No. I'm starving and I can't go without," she says, looking up and touching my cock, starting a light masturbation, hiding a smile.

Despite the arousal, I want to understand what she's hiding from me.

"Have I ever left you wanting?" I ask, as if I have control in the palm of my hand, when in reality my legs are nearly buckling at the feel of her warm tongue on the swollen head of my cock.

"Not that I remember," she says, opening her mouth again and shyly running her tongue along my entire length.

It drives me crazy to know she's aroused enough to take the initiative because Taisiya's nature is always to let me lead.

"But..." she continues, now taking me all the way into her mouth and looking up at me, completely filled with my cock.

I grip her face with my hands and push my hips forward.

"But what, baby?" I taunt.

I start to fuck her slowly, gradually picking up speed, but soon she seems impatient, greedy for more. She sucks me and moans around my shaft.

"Fuck, Taisiya!"

She smiles and pulls me completely out of her mouth.

"But... I'm pregnant now. They say it's not good to leave us wanting."

For a moment, I think I didn't hear right, but when she continues to look at me and smiles, my heart races in my chest.

I lower myself and pick her up, carrying her to the bed. I spread her thighs and position myself between them.

I slide a finger between her wet folds to make sure she's ready, and when she opens up like a flower, begging, I enter her completely.

"Are we having a baby?"

She whimpers like a kitten, pulling me inside her as I push deeply into her body.

"Answer me: did I make a baby in you, my wife?"

"Yes, I'm going to have your baby," she says, between moans.

Her hands grip my ass, pulling me, and as I thrust in and out of her, her gaze is locked on mine.

I pull back and plunge into her repeatedly, but I need more, so I grab her by the hips, angling her to go even deeper.

"We're a family now. Me, you, our child," she says.

I thrust hard, repeatedly traversing the hot walls of her sex.

I caress her clitoris and feel her little spasms around my cock.

"Yes, and no one will separate us," I warn.

I spin her around, positioning her on all fours; I grab her hair as I enter her again. Impatient, Taisiya rocks her hips and pushes her body back, making me bury myself completely in her sex.

The sensation is so intense I feel a jolt in my balls.

I pull her up, forcing her to ride me backward. With one hand caressing her clitoris and the other on the belly where my child resides, I have her completely under my control.

"I'm happier than I could ever show, Taisiya, but with or without a baby, no one would take you away from me. You're mine. You always were."

The declaration of possession seems to excite her, as she raises her arms back and begins to ride me deliciously, using my neck to leverage herself.

Seeing her so needy makes my arousal explode, and I begin to fuck her voraciously, taking her pussy to its limits.

I lick her neck, bite her shoulder and ear, not decreasing the intensity with which I fuck her sex or attack her hard clitoris, and when she starts moaning loudly, begging for release, I reposition her on all fours again and pound into her relentlessly.

Taisiya moans loudly and rocks. The contractions come strong, and then she orgasms, collapsing like a rag doll on the bed. I still hold her hips and continue thrusting. Seconds later, my orgasm comes with the force of an earthquake, and after one last thrust, I cum, filling her with my hot sperm.

"My wife. My child," I assert, lying on my back and pulling her up onto me.

"We are yours."

Hours Later

I HEAR THE SOUND OF my phone vibrating and look at the nightstand with the urge to throw it against the wall. It's four in the morning, and she's just fallen asleep after hours of being awake, fucking.

I didn't want to stop. I wasn't satisfied yet, but I'm not going to act like an animal, no matter how much my body craves being inside her. Taisiya is pregnant, and I intend to let her rest for a few hours.

I look at the screen.

Ruslan.

Fuck, I love my grandfather, but couldn't he have waited until tomorrow?

"I heard you've taken care of those fuckers. Maxim is pissed off because you didn't tell him Ayrtom had an accomplice," he says when I answer.

"Maxim's issue was with Stepanchikov. He wanted Anastacia. The twins tortured *my* wife, which made them my problem."

"He doesn't see it that way. Hell is breaking loose, Lorcan, and this time, even I can't keep the temperature down."

"With all due respect, grandfather, I want Maxim, Yerik, and all the other members of the Organization, except you, to go fuck themselves. Taisiya is pregnant, and no one is taking her away from me."

"What?"

"She's carrying my child, and if any of them think they're going to take her from me, they should know that war will be declared."

"She's pregnant? The situation is completely different now. I'll arrange a meeting with Yerik and Cillian."

"For when?"

"There's no time to wait. As soon as possible."

Chapter 57

Lorcan

"**Y**ou know you've abused the power given to you during the deal," Yerik accuses me.

One thing to be said about the men gathered here is that despite our hatred for each other, no one raises their voice. Anger and contempt lie just beneath the surface, but they are still under control, for now.

I don't doubt that Ruslan is the one responsible for keeping things at a level where no one has drawn their weapons.

With him present, no one wants to be the first to start the bloodshed. Disrespecting my grandfather is a death sentence.

I look at the table around which we're gathered.

On our side, the Boss, myself, Kellan, and Odhran.

On the Russian side, Yerik, Maxim, Leonid, Dmitri, and Grigori.

The meeting is taking place in a warehouse owned by my grandfather, in the center of the country, in neutral territory where neither we nor the Russians have control.

"Meeting" is a mild way to describe an unarmed battle, of course. Emotions on both sides are volatile at the moment. After just ten minutes, mutual accusations have begun.

"The deal was for Lorcan to locate Taisiya. He fulfilled it," Cillian says, surprising me with how he manages to keep his voice steady.

We Irish aren't as cold as the Russians. Our anger is visible.

"You understood perfectly what I said," Yerik continues. "He should never have touched Maxim's sister-in-law."

"My grandson didn't touch Taisiya while she was a minor," Ruslan intervenes for the first time.

"No, he didn't. He touched her a few months later," Maxim retorts.

"How old was Anastacia when she married you, again?" I ask.

He remains unfazed.

"It's different. I only slept with her after she became my wife."

"Because if you had done it before, my grandfather would have ripped your balls off," I say.

No one responds because they know I'm speaking the truth. A man who slept with Ruslan's goddaughter without marrying her wouldn't live to see the sun rise the next day.

"But if what's bothering you is the fact that Taisiya and I aren't married," I continue, "the issue will be resolved soon. I'll apply for the marriage license tomorrow."

"Fuck you're not," Yerik says, standing up. "The girl is ours."

"No, she's not." My grandfather steps in before I have a chance to respond. "Taisiya is pregnant with my great-grandson. The son of Lorcan. She belongs to him now. And the baby that will be born is my descendant. There will be no war *for* or *against* him. I forbid anyone from touching the child or its parents for any reason, and this will be respected even after my death."

A grave silence falls over the room because no one except me and my grandfather knew about the pregnancy.

I can see the shock on the faces of my two cousins, the Pakhan and the Boss, because now, whether they like it or not, Ruslan's words have undoubtedly secured a peace alliance.

There's an exchange of glances between the members of both organizations, but before either of the two leaders can speak, the warehouse door explodes with the entry of the men we left on watch.

"We're being attacked, fuck! The Sicilians are coming!" someone shouts, and everyone reacts immediately, drawing their weapons, ready for whatever comes.

"Stay behind me," I tell my grandfather.

"No way. I'm old, not dead."

I see our men and the Russians retreating into the warehouse while hearing gunfire behind me.

When I turn around, Cillian and Yerik have their guns drawn. One has killed the attacker who was behind the other.

In another scenario, it would be an ironic situation—enemies who've just mutually saved each other—but all I can think about is that I can't die today.

I only see Taisiya's face in front of me. I won't leave my wife alone and unprotected in this fucked-up world. I want to see my child when he's born and hold him in my arms.

The gunfight lasts about fifteen minutes, and we have two casualties among our own and three more among the Russians, but in the end, we manage to turn the chaos to our favor.

And then, amid the silence that follows, as we are all still recovering from the shock of the surprise attack, a single shot breaks the silence.

We all turn toward the back entrance of the warehouse. There's a man there, apparently pointing a gun at Dmitri.

"Don't shoot!" the Pakhan's underboss shouts. "He saved me!"

"What the hell is this?" Leonid approaches the two, but Dmitri seems focused on the stranger in front of him.

"Drop the gun, Damien," he says. "I didn't spend over ten years without you just to see you die now."

"ARE YOU TELLING ME that man was a brother Dmitri thought had been dead for over a decade?" I ask my grandfather as we fly back to Boston in his private jet.

Cleanup teams from both organizations stayed at the farm to dispose of the bodies, but a meeting has been scheduled between Cillian and Yerik.

The two leaders want to devise a strategy for how they will retaliate against the Sicilians.

Until now, the Cosa Nostra's problem was primarily with my grandfather due to a past dispute, and with us regarding the Knight issue.

Now, they were stupid enough to declare war on two powerful organizations simultaneously, and they'll have to face the consequences.

"Yes, it seems to be him, Damien."

"Sounds like a fucked-up fiction story."

"I want to know in detail how he stayed hidden for so long, but right now, what interests me is paying those sons of bitches who attacked us back in the same coin." Seconds after saying this, he shakes his head, laughing. "Nothing like a good war to seal the peace. They did us a favor. By attacking Yerik and Cillian at the same time, they created an alliance between the two, stronger than I could ever have managed."

"I think that word, *alliance*, is unreal. Cillian will fight those sons of bitches and, if necessary, create strategies side by side with Yerik, but I doubt they'll ever be friends."

"Who cares? As long as my new great-grandson has the protection of both organizations, I'm fine with it."

"I CAN'T BELIEVE THIS is really happening," Taisiya says, hiding her face in her hands and crying in the backseat of the car.

After we woke up the day after I arrived from the island, I told her everything that had happened there, leaving out no details, including the baby rescue.

She cried in my arms for many hours, feeling guilty for the death of the girls, which, of course, made no sense. The only ones responsible for that outcome were those damned bastards.

In the following weeks, she needed to see her therapist every three days because she told me she was struggling to cope.

Slowly, she improved, and then, in a conversation about our future, she asked me to adopt the child I had saved.

In secret, she had visited the girl a few times with Anastacia.

Shortly after the rescue, I used my influence to bring the girl to Boston. The social workers and the FBI identified only the mother's nationality. They knew she was American, but if she had relatives, it was never discovered.

At first, upon hearing Taisiya's request, I was concerned and spoke with her new psychologist, now someone who works with the women of the Syndicate.

I needed to know if it would be harmful for Taisiya's emotional state to have a constant reminder of her past nearby.

Through meetings with the therapist and conversations with my wife, I realized that the little girl would be a catharsis, a cure, and not a reminder of pain.

I pursued the possibility of adoption.

I used all means and employees on the Syndicate's payroll to expedite the process. Even so, with lawyers charging four digits an hour and my generosity *incentivizing* the professionals involved, it took months to bring her to be with us.

Taisiya is now just under two months from the end of her pregnancy, and our wedding will be in fifteen days, but starting today, the girl we will call Nikita will finally be ours. We are going to get her.

"It's happening, baby. We'll be three, and soon, four."

"How many more?"

"Babies?"

"Yes. How many can we have?"

"I'm Irish and Catholic, beautiful. Fill the house. The more, the better."

Epilogue 1

Taisiya

Taisiya and Lorcan's Wedding Day

Anastacia said she thinks Ruslan is jealous because he is a father, grandfather, and great-grandfather to someone somewhere in the world, and she's sure he would have liked to walk me down the aisle.

I have learned to love him and respect him as the grandfather of my future husband and great-grandfather to my children, but if it weren't for Abramov, I wouldn't be here, and he's the one who will have that role today.

The man who considers himself a sinner — he told me about the priest he killed when he was young and the reason he did it — was my salvation. Had he not been merciful and, above all, courageous, my fate would have been the same as those poor girls on the island.

I look at the chairs set up on the beach — Russians on one side, Irish on the other — and I'm certain this is the first and most likely the last time they will be gathered like this.

The island we're on, of course, belongs to Ruslan. After the declaration he made at the organizational meeting about who my unborn child belongs to, neither Cillian nor Yerik would dare challenge him.

"Are you ready?" Grandpa Abramov asks, and I nod my head in agreement.

I know we can't delay because he can no longer stand for long.

I take a deep breath, thinking about the man who should be by my side today and the woman who gave birth to me.

I still can't forgive them.

Mom, because your resentment against Ana got us entangled in a plot that brought tragedy into our lives.

My father, because he allowed greed, the thirst for money, to overshadow his love for us.

I will cover my scars with a beautiful tattoo that will be done by Linus King: a winged horse, flying free and unreachable, but those are just the physical ones. The emotional ones might be hidden too, but never completely healed.

One step at a time, I approach my destiny. Going to meet and into the arms of the man I love, refusing to let the past ruin my big day.

When I look ahead, Lorcan is attentive to my face and, as always, understands what no one else can.

He sees me inside out. With fears, flaws, and weaknesses.

The pain and anguish that always come over me when memories return.

He knows the exact moment he needs to be my lover, my sex god, or my healer.

He steps away from the altar and starts walking toward me, but first, he stops and takes Nikita from Juno's arms, and when she smiles at her father, the oppression immediately disappears from my chest.

My past has lost. They are my future.

"I can take over from here, Abramov," he says to Grandpa, who kisses each of my hands, then my forehead, and extends his arms to take our girl.

Nikita smiles at me and him because my daughter, my miracle, is the happiest little girl in the world.

When they leave, Lorcan, indifferent to the guests and the officiant, places one hand on my belly and with the other, holds my face.

"I know what you're doing, Irishman."

"What am I doing, my wife?"

"Being my prince. Erasing the darkness and pain. Making sure today I only feel joy."

"I'll be whatever it takes, Taisiya, if it means seeing you smile. I love you, my temptation. First, I crossed seas to find you, then I fought against myself because I didn't think I deserved your love, and then I realized there was only one path for us both and that in any case, we'd end up like this."

"You challenged adversaries on Earth and in the sky."

"I'd challenge death to try to separate me from you. I will love you forever in this life and beyond."

Epilogue 2

Lorcan

Donovan's Birth

I learned many things from Taisiya in the months leading up to the birth of our son.

The main one is that loving is not weakness. Admitting that someone is the air you breathe and that you would die for them without a second thought is, on the contrary, strength.

When you are certain that the woman you love is the center of your world and that nothing and no one can separate you, you become invincible, no matter how much shit comes your way.

Our relationship has been a rollercoaster.

I rescued her, and at first, I loved her as my protégé; I watched her go from girl to woman, and from then on, I loved her with my desire. I made her mine, and then she became the owner of my soul.

And today, as I see my wife in the hospital bed with our son in her arms and Nikita sitting beside her, looking at her brother with a smile brighter than the sun, I know that no matter how many mistakes I made in the past, they are my right, and I thank the One with whom I had a poor relationship for a long time — God.

"It's very quiet."

"I'm thanking the one I stole you from."

She reaches out for me to come closer to the edge of the bed.

"God knows our hearts. I truly believe that. So, I have no doubt that He always knew it was to you that I belonged. In the book of life, our paths were already laid out, Lorcan. Perhaps we didn't know the stops we'd make along the way, but in any case, the end of our love story was already written."

"Because if it weren't, I would rewrite the script, Taisiya. It took me too long to find you. I would never give up on making you mine."

One Year Later

Honeymoon

Somewhere in Ireland

"CAN IT STILL BE CALLED a honeymoon even after so much time has passed?" I ask as I watch her casually drop the silk robe to the floor, standing completely naked.

She gives me a sideways smile because I'm sure she knows my mind is far more interested in what we'll be doing than in the name we give this trip.

"I think we can call it whatever we want, husband. Are you really worried about that?"

"No." I stand up and position myself in front of her, grabbing her neck to bring her mouth to mine, sliding my other hand down her flat abdomen towards my paradise. "The only thing filling my thoughts is whether I'm going to suck you while you're still standing or if I'm going to bend you over so I can taste both pussy and ass in one delicious meal."

Taisiya swallows hard, her eyes glazed over, already completely aroused. Our desire ignites too quickly. Sometimes, a word, a touch, a tease is enough to turn a spark into a blaze.

"You're a romantic, Irishman."

Despite the irony, she's already pressing her lips against my chest, licking and nibbling at the flesh.

"I don't know pretty words, my Russian princess, but I am yours. With everything that implies, I belong to you."

The End!

Did you love *Forbidden Flames*? Then you should read *Forbidden Desires* by Amara Holt!

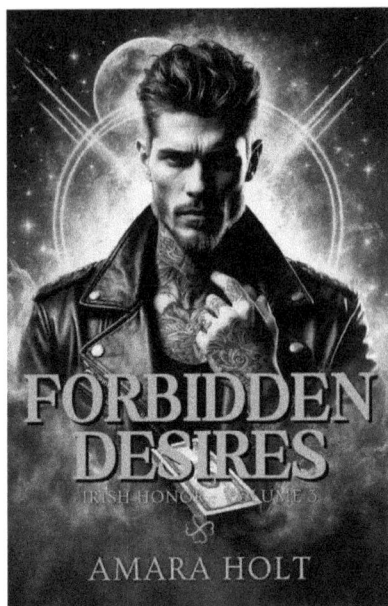

Forbidden Desires

Tulia, a fierce and loyal soldier of the **Russian mafia**, finds herself caught in a deadly game of power and **passion**. After angering the wrong person, she's punished with an assignment she detests—becoming the bodyguard to a novice. But Tulia is determined to see it through, hoping to earn forgiveness and reclaim her place in the dangerous world she knows so well.

Love is the last thing on Tulia's mind, especially after a **painful past** that left her heart hardened. But when two dangerously **handsome** and **dominant** Irish mobsters, Keiron and Rourke, enter her life, everything changes. Keiron, known for his **irresistible charm** and trail of broken hearts, is drawn to the forbidden allure of Tulia. Meanwhile, Rourke, a **widower** haunted by guilt, battles his own desires as he finds himself captivated by the mysterious **Russian woman**.

In a world where **loyalty** is everything and **desire** can be deadly, Tulia must navigate her way through a tangled web of intense attraction, **dangerous secrets**, and unforgiving enemies. As the heat between them rises, so does the danger—threatening not just their hearts, but their lives.

Three hearts collide in a world of **power**, **passion**, and peril. How far will they go when **desire** becomes deadly?

About the Author

Amara Holt is a storyteller whose novels immerse readers in a whirlwind of suspense, action, romance and adventure. With a keen eye for detail and a talent for crafting intricate plots, Amara captivates her audience with every twist and turn. Her compelling characters and atmospheric settings transport readers to thrilling worlds where danger lurks around every corner.

Milton Keynes UK
Ingram Content Group UK Ltd.
UKHW030146051224
452010UK00001B/89

9 798330 596126